THE ACADEMY
OF REALITY

THE ACADEMY OF REALITY

a novel

Steve Putnam

MADVILLE
PUBLISHING

Lake Dallas, Texas

Requests for permission to reprint or reuse material
from this work should be sent to:

Permissions
Madville Publishing
PO Box 358
Lake Dallas, TX 75065

Cover Design: Jacqueline Davis
Author Photo: Cynthia Lydiard Putnam

ISBN: 978-1-956440-99-7 paperback,
978-1-963695-00-7 ebook

Library of Congress Control Number: 2024939445

\

to Cynthia

PART I

The Institute

1

A pigeon lands at the brick-and-mortar entryway and pecks absently as if looking for a stray bug or crumb. The pigeon peers upward to a peaked roof propped by six pillars, creating an old country church façade of civilized innocence. Just behind the peak, a rectangular penthouse raised slightly above supports a square clock tower with a domed belfry. The building's wings splay out on either side, same brick and mortar, same four-story height. What kind of financial asylum did the founders think they were founding? Casino or insurance business? It doesn't matter. I park and head inside.

Everything feels routine. It looks like just another day; the Coordinator's wearing the same business-serious ruby red tie he wears giving evaluations. "Goose your numbers, make a quick upswing," he says. "Attend that new motivational webinar, *Tune-Up for Technology, Elevate Client Perceptions*. It must be good. Everyone's talking about it."

"Now, don't blame me," he continues. "This next one's on HR. You need to coauthor a booklet they're already calling *Fifty Places to Picnic: Employee Benefits for Today and a New Tomorrow*. Your partner's Mia Monroe, that research assistant in behavioral studies. Off the record, she might be your type. Charged with disturbing the peace, she made local front-page news, prime-time TV; you name it. Tried helping a girl who was camping out on a sidewalk grate, she was trying to shelter her kitten. She's nothing but an embarrassment with that *Homeless veteran of the Institute* sign against her knee. This lady Mia told the homeless one she'd help her find shelter.

The girl said she goes where her cat goes. She's still on the street, right in front of our home office."

"I didn't notice a girl with a sign this morning. Anyone who can embarrass the Institute gets my vote. Mia sounds like someone I'd like to know." There I go again. Telling the truth always bites me in the ass.

The Coordinator ignores me. "I'll get you on the fast track for success," he says. "We'll meet monthly to evaluate your performance. I know you do your job. Just watch your numbers."

In a work world where you either fight or walk away from problems, I'm running out of options. I owe money to The Institute's collection department. They just mailed notice that another payment is overdue.

Mia and I both arrive at HR early. Her brown hair's shoulder-length, tossed, carefree, but not careless. Her eyes wide open, lips parted slightly, she has a face that never has to say "cheese" for photos intended to look candid. Her beauty reflects her attitude, turning me on and making my mind race. She's slightly offbeat, not very Institutional. I don't much believe in matches made in heaven, and usually follow the love doctor's radio advice, avoid looking for love in all the wrong places. I find myself more optimistic about a match made at The Institute.

Taking a chance, ignoring etiquette, and trying flirtation, I extend my hand. "Allow me to introduce myself as another resourced human."

Talk about attitude. Instead of talking about picnics, we talk performance improvement. "Institute radar just started tracking my numbers," Mia says. "Research thinks I waste money, feeding black oil sunflower seed to the lab pigeons. Not exactly gourmet; it's really for the birds. Experts think organic can't replace the formulated kind we feed to research pigeons."

"I don't know much about pigeons. Complaints about money wasted on pigeon feed must come down from the Director. How much can someone who never visited a pigeon ranch know?"

"Pigeons know more than we think—and think more than we know. The Director's no expert. Even I can taste the difference between black oil organic and medicated, manufactured. Research people tell me not to get involved with the pigeons. They're sending me to a seminar, *Self-Indulgence, the Cathartic Key to Indifference*. Somehow, humanely treating research pigeons transforms solid science into junk."

"You have a right to be concerned." My careful mix of tact and truth is for Mia's benefit, not to advance knowledge about pigeons.

Even though Mia and I already met in the waiting area, the HR coordinator introduced us again. He explains what we need to do as coauthors, reciting the booklet's complete title, *Fifty Places to Picnic: Employee Benefits for Today, and a New Tomorrow*, as if we don't already know. Nothing fancy, it's just a pay-raise substitute, a low-cost employee perk, a morale booster.

Does hidden talent make Mia more capable of writing outdoor picnic travelogues than caring for pigeons? Do I have the aptitude to assist a research assistant? "Will writing this booklet be enough to make up for weak performance numbers?" I ask.

"Communication is the key to solid relationships," the HR rep says. I'm not sure if he's talking about picnic research or sharing relationship pointers for Mia and me. Either way sounds like funny advice from a burned-out executive coach, promoted or demoted to coordinator; I'm not sure.

The behavioral lab's reception area features an industrious pigeon pecking an illuminated disc. Pigeon's frantic as if confronted with a dreaded Performance Improvement Plan, the last chance for corporate losers. The digital monitor above the pigeon's cage tracks job performance; every peck triggers a counter blip, increasing the total by one.

Lab's a perfect place for talking Institutional picnics. Cubicles lined up in a straight row, as perfectly as the pigeon cages. For every pigeon, there are four researchers. Mia's a senior lab assistant, so she gets a cubicle larger than most keyboard jockeys. Framed PIP hangs over her desk for everyone to see. Beside it, an enlarged newsprint headlined *Cat Lady Arrest at the Institute.*

Picture of a lady with tossed hair, back turned to the camera, has to be Mia. She's leaning over the girl who's sitting against one of the front entrance pillars, huddled under a blanket, holding a swaddled kitten: perfect finishing touches, random specks of pigeon dung splotch the sidewalk.

"You must feel like a celebrity."

"It's really about the girl and kitten. The Institute doesn't care if either one is safe. It's alright if they survive—anywhere but here in front of the building. All the shelters for humans refuse to take in pets. I knew the two were inseparable."

In large numbers, homeless people numb my mind enough to protect me from sorrow. If you can't afford to give a buck to each one, it's easy to avoid giving at all. I've walked by the same girl. Somehow, Mia almost makes me care again.

"PIP's supposed to be a punishment for helping the girl and kitten—instead, it keeps me focused on things I need to do, and rules I need to forget."

Large mail tubs neatly stacked under a *Misguided Output* sign. A poster stapled below warns, "Don't Be Embarrassed. *You Are Not Alone. Anyone Can Get Swindled by Paper Pirates.*" Loneliness is sometimes my friend. The pirates, old-fashioned toner phoners who cold-call Institute offices, never scam me. Pretending to be approved vendors, they sell overpriced office supplies to unsuspecting employees not authorized to be buyers.

In a zone, trying to understand my strange surroundings, I have trouble thinking and speaking at the same time. Afraid my words might sound like the mating call of an out-of-tune ostrich; I try talking nonchalantly, relying on style more than substance. "Don't dance in the sun with butter on your head."

Somehow Mia gets me, "Are you inviting me to lunch," she asks.

"Sure. I just have to stop by the Machine to check it out."

"What kind of Machine?"

"It's one of those stationary robots, a printer that sucks paper in, spits out prints. Scans photos and documents, to store them electronically. Somewhat primitive, InfoTech people have to upgrade the Machine's software continuously. I can always tell. Every time there's an update, a little cartoon man on the monitor swings a sledgehammer, driving a lever that sends a puck skyward toward a bell. He never stops swinging the hammer, never gives up until the puck hits the bell, sounding a weak electronic ding, a wordless shout that new software's loaded."

"That's it?" Mia asks.

"No, there's more. This whole place is a Machine."

"The Institute sells insurance, investments, Sid."

"I'm thinking this place is a machine that hustles life insurance to people afraid of dying, makes money on those afraid of living. There's a rumor corporate wants to eliminate live therapists, only reimburse electronic ones."

"Are we a little paranoid, Sid?"

"That sounds slightly condescending. My fears are real, not imagined."

"So how did you end up here?" Mia asks.

"A hand specialist repairing my index finger referred me, not that that was his intention. He pretended to concentrate on the x-ray of the saw's cut, halfway through the bone. 'I can reconnect that nerve,' he said. 'But I'm not going to. Not on this one. Workers' comp won't pay enough to cover it.' He laughed. 'Maybe you can find a guy who works out of a cellar somewhere. Next time tell your boss to buy insurance at the Institute.'

"I couldn't work while my hand was healing, bill payments were overdue; charge card people called weekly. I'd tell them I was hurt, that I had jack shit. Insurance would settle as soon as I finished physical therapy. I could pay for everything overdue and more. 'Jack shit' almost sounds like someone's name. It's just an expression for a losing hand of cards. Maybe I sometimes choose words that make me look like a loser."

Mia's still listening, so I keep going. "How much can you send right now," the collector asked every week.

I stopped answering the phone. What's the use when people don't know jack.

I remembered the hand specialist's referral to The Institute. A place that supposedly sells the right insurance might be a pretty good place to work. I combed my hair in a wave since I'd read that tall men are more likely to get hired. I shaved to make myself look less bug-eyed. As luck had it, I turned out looking a few years younger than I am. When I went in to apply, I stood tall, hoping to add a couple of imaginary inches to my five feet eight. I'm not proud that I went as far as telling the interviewer, "Teamwork makes everyone a winner." As luck had it, the collection agency was a subsidiary of the Institute. Flipping paychecks over to collections, I would make everyone look good. They sent me to the Technical Academy for advanced training for twelve weeks, in return for my agreement to repay tuition.

We walk down the corridor. My rubber sole shoes squeaking on the marble floor almost distract me from noticing new pictures of pottery, yet to be hung. We catch an elevator to the lowest level, an area that stores pipe for plumbers, wire for electricians, cable rolls for IT, and lumber that carpenters rarely need to repair a brick-and-mortar façade with marble interior. Boxes and boxes of fluorescent light bulbs fill the hallway outside of my office, a purely functional, chain-link cage. Plush executive chair coffee-stained, metal desk rust-specked, strewn with Styrofoam coffee cups, manuals on discs and chips, old paperback manuals full of useless information, two self-help books: *Paradox of a Positive Attitude; Positive Impact of a Negative Self-Image.* A rack loaded with scopes and meters allows me to monitor the Machine remotely. Framed *Systems and Tech Specialist* certificates hang on the chain link outer wall for the Director and coordinators to see.

"Impressive," Mia says. "Real over-achiever, you must be proud."

I'm relieved Mia sounds a bit sarcastic.

Colorful pipes and wire bundles hang overhead. A gray, electrical busway, routes bundled wires and cables to the Machine which resides on the third floor. Small cooling vents make perfect slots for hooking coat hangers. A red decal with black print encourages flirtation with death and dance with life simultaneously: "Danger! High Voltage. 600 Volts."

Now and then, the sewer pipe heading south to the municipal treatment plant gushes with wastewater, creating a pleasant babbling and gurgling ambiance, feng shui of a TV beer ad brook running down a Colorado mountain, a flow of positive energy. But make no mistake. At the Institute, we drink no beer.

Self-diagnostics leave little to do but listen to the musical sounds of the sewer pipe above, make minor adjustments, and monitor the Machine's temperature, voltage pulses, phase shifts, and sine waves. A stressed employee accidentally feeds a staple or paperclip causing a welcome interruption, an easy fix. If nothing's wrong, I make myself visible walking the halls, enough to remind the suits I'm on the job.

Right now, at least, all systems are go. The meter reads one point seven billion. It looks like some witty but bored, after-hours fax correspondent taped a document page into a loop, feeding and refeeding the message long enough to overload the Machine with the same repetitious message: MARTINI MISPRONOUNCED: MARTOONI RHYMES WITH OPPORTUNITY. MARTINI MISPRONOUNCED: MARTOONI RHYMES WITH OP-PORTUNITY. MARTINI MISPRONOUNCED: MARTOONI RHYMES WITH OPPORTUNITY. At the Institute, too much information's better than too little.

Just to show off, I tell Mia, "Watch this." I key in the word THINK on the keyboard. As if it understands my meaningless command, the Machine stops humming. Its drone of cooling fans intensifies. The scope's red sine wave drops to form a hor-izontal line. Rather than crunch information, the hard drive spins, wasting energy doing its calisthenics. Alarms remain silent. It's almost peaceful.

"You should call dispatch. Report the Martooni loop?"

I usually wouldn't bother. For Mia's benefit, I make the call. A ghost voice that's not electric or alive answers; monotone but cheerful, it sounds somewhat stilted, possibly amoral. Everyone refers to it as the "electronic slut." No interest in female deg-radation; they merely condemn cheap, automated, words from misguided electrons. The voice thanked me for calling and put me on hold to save someone's time. Helpless, with nothing to do, my mind spins its wheels. Although this was Mia's idea, she seems impatient. I hang up, saving more time, and making the Institute more efficient at both ends of the phone line.

We step off the elevator, I bump into a mail robot. A random envelope falls from its top tray, a symptom of overload, a sign of another drastic increase in productivity. With mechanical indifference, the robot keeps going. It doesn't resemble a human. Instead, it's a large, box-shaped cart with a designated shelf for each department it services. On wheels, it's more graceful than a walking robot; it carries as much mail as fifteen competent mail humans combined. Robot's sensors track a transparent, invisible map sprayed on carpets and marble floors, indicating its route and the stops it needs to make. Its high-pitched beeps warn hallway pedestrians to move aside. If they don't, it stops, beeping impatiently, until they step out of its invisible path.

We walk past more pictures of pottery, past portraits of successful men who look like they liked having their photos taken. These men are not Institute founders—having found themselves they were only promoted. They're as durable and reliable as pottery, but not rigid enough to guide corporate conscience. Who knows what the pottery did to get photographed?

Lunch hour takes two hours. We eat jumbo shrimp. There's much to discuss, but I'm still at a loss for words. Mia asks, "What do you think about shadows?"

"I have to admit I don't think about them much." I lift my coffee cup for a moment but lower it back to the table, hoping Mia didn't notice a slight tremor from a pinched shoulder nerve. Was it caused by repetitive movement from a hammer, or canoe paddle? Who knows? I'm afraid to find out.

The background noise of a thousand other cafeteria voices diminishes—The Director and suits sitting at a nearby table talk about tree injections. Voices gradually heighten. I should recognize them but don't. Neckties, different shades of red, burgundy, maroon, and crimson, provide subtle clues of importance, making it easier to decide who is who. "Why pull up the pavement?" one asks. "Why inject nitrogen into the soil? You could buy a thousand seedlings for the price of injecting an old tree."

"And dig up more pavement to plant the remaining nine hundred ninety-nine?" another asks. "Fewer parking spaces would force another layoff."

"Make the smaller parking lot sound like a new opportunity." Someone mentions a recent press release that urges the government to get crime back on the streets where it belongs. The conversation goes silent as if they're afraid to say something everyone already knows.

Heading out for some air, away from the suits, mail robots, paper stacks, and electromagnetic fields, we take a shortcut through the new wing, dimly lit, and somewhat eerie. Not yet occupied, it feels abandoned.

Behind the parking lot, located on the Institute's outskirts, the park is convenient. It's too bad; we've already had lunch— the weather's early October fresh, crisp. Primal, peaceful, and remote, it's perfect for a picnic. We walk down a grassy embankment to the river. Mia stumbles. I support her elbow, instinctively reach for her hand but catch myself. A wild pigeon flies directly overhead, in unison with a fighter jet flying miles higher. A two-person team paddles a sleek, carbon-fiber racing canoe that cuts through water swiftly.

Mia sits onshore on an above-ground tree root that bends bench-like. I crouch beside her, watching the water boil, flowing over, under, around, and through trash wood trapped on the riverbed. The current is hypnotic. We are alone. With one movement, she reaches for the bottom of her blouse and pulls it upward. Her flash is an electric spark of life, primal beauty, original creation untouched. It's only a glance, a fleeting vision of Mia flashing topless. Noon sunlight squints between darker spots of soft tree shade, creating lightness of her breasts, and subtle shadows beneath. At least for a few moments, Mia glistens. My mind can't keep abreast of it all. Even in my fog, I know that forgetting about Institutional concerns is a sign of mental health. The Machine can wait. Here we are, living a dream, re-creation of the creation, a near-perfect place for two humans fleeing fluorescence, fleeing visions of the homeless girl huddled on a grate, hugging her swaddled kitten.

Mia hands me a card that doesn't seem to reflect the Institute's mission. I've never seen or heard anything quite like it. For sure, it doesn't have anything to do with picnics.

REFLEXIVE FUSION
FUSE THE MOMENT WITH MOVEMENT

It seems like Mia fits in well at the Institute. Is Reflexive Fusion a new obsession? Up until now, seeing her in the hallway, I thought she was the product of a comfortable childhood, filled with emptiness. In the short time that I've known Mia, she has changed. It's hard to tell if this is good or bad. For sure, she's not clowning. Did the moving water or pigeon that flew overhead inspire her to hand me her card? It doesn't matter. She must have done it because she felt it needed doing. She watches me intently. "It's not exactly alternative medicine. My breast makes a carefree appeal to the child in you, Sid. For a moment, I was your earth mother."

"Who are you now," I ask.

"More important, who are you, Sid?"

Hard question if you want the truth, hard to answer if I try to impress. I take Mia's hand, not that I should, not in the Institutional shadows of unrealized Performance Improvement Plans. We start heading back toward dead air, fluorescent skies, and pale keyboard jockeys boxed in individual cubicles.

"Open space of the river park's the only place to find closure."

"You're joking. That's all you've got? For real, who are you," Mia still wants to know.

How to sync my thoughts and words? "I'm tired of this American dream world of robots beeping in long hallways, endless seas of suits and strange faces, hustling as they come and go. Keyboard jockeys and techs, all frantic, as if looking for love lost and never found. From this fog, a strange focus distorts day-to-day facts but accurately reflects the day-to-day realities."

"That's all? That's it? Who are you?"

"Sid Sidney, same name HR used this morning. Just call me Sid."

Must be, I trust Mia. I have never given anyone my full name all at once unless I have to, ever since Boy Scout camp.

Call it superstition. I was supposed to introduce myself, give a demo, showing fellow campers how to douse a campfire. It was more about public speaking than fire safety. But after I said "Sid," I froze and forgot the rest of my name. Everyone laughed. My takeaway is a logic that took on a life of its own: Knowing who you are must be more important than knowing what you do. At parties—anywhere—I never start a conversation by telling people who I am. I've always reassured myself that my full given name "Sidney Sidney" would have been even more humiliating. The name was my father's idea. It must be my mother liked his sense of humor.

In any event, the Coordinator was right. Mia seems like my type. She's not turned off by my name, at least.

2

Institute's doomsday people can't predict my time of death. Faith in industry averages gives them the courage to place bets on my lifespan. Even optimists agree everyone dies sooner or later. The good news, life insurance profits fund the river park, our refuge, a fantasy island at the edge of the Institute.

After breakfast, before work, Mia and I get together and relax in the so-called communications commons. I'm reading the obituary, an old ritual some won't admit to, some joke about. I read it for reassurance that I'm still alive. If my name doesn't come up, I'm sure this world is nothing other than real.

Mia nudges me. The TV's breaking local news, its picture showing the girl and kitten huddled against the base of a large oak tree. The girl's staring out toward the river park's bridge in the background. "Homeless people stop panhandling when people stop handing them handouts," the dubbed voice advises. "You never know if your dollar buys drugs or food. Instead, hand out business cards that direct the homeless to the nearest shelter."

"Who knows if they moved out back voluntarily or if Institute Security relocated them?" I ask.

"It doesn't look like the news people tampered with the video. The girl and kitten still look hungry."

Life goes on. All we can do is try to forget. The creation can wait, and so can HR. River Park is an ideal location to have our first picnic. But things could get a little awkward if the girl with a kitten refuses Mia's help. Nothing better to do over the weekend, I offer to help paint Mia's one-room condo. Reaching out this way might make me seem more useful working rather than dating.

It's a one-of-a-kind space, somewhat funky, and sparsely furnished. The round table's small enough to seat two. At its center, a vase filled with beads, adorned with feathers: red, black, deep purple. Two ghost-white Mardi Gras masks, one sad, one glad, a vintage pigeon auction poster, animal rights convention flyer, all tacked to the wall. I'm not one to whistle while I work. I listen to the news on a vintage beat-up boom box I found under the kitchen table.

I'm priming the wood trim. Mia returns with more brushes, mixing sticks, and another drop cloth. Unusual getup for painting, she's wearing a black fedora, torn jeans, white shirt partly unbuttoned, flash-ready but modest. The black jacket matches the hat. I want to kiss her, but what if my timing's off? Instead of making a move, we talk about paint, no surprise, considering the circumstances.

"Chemicals! We could die breathing fumes," she says.

If we keep talking and become acclimated to the odor, we'll forget Mia's advice. Tact before truth; style is more important than substance. Risking a spoiled moment, I try mixing both. "Not to worry. Anxiety kills faster than latex paint fumes."

"I worry, Sid. You're the one who always seems wired, slightly anxious."

"Does Reflexive Fusion help? Would that help me?"

"People confuse Reflexive Fusion with alternative medicine. It's much more than chicken soup for the soul. It electrifies the psyche."

"I have to admit; you turned me on in the river park."

"Movement distracts from the moment, creates a new one. Reflexive Fusion is just movement for the moment. Quick brain chemical tweaks bring sensations of well-being. Original and new is better than tried and true."

"Is that a new kind of psychology, some kind of cure?"

"It all depends. My Dad said that I suffered from T.E.S.— Toxic Entitlement Syndrome. Under his breath, he often called me a spoiled brat. Either way, he was a challenge. My mother was more insightful. She claimed I'm an Indigo child who can effortlessly shift from one reality to another."

Still breathing in pleasant latex paint fumes, I'm finishing the baseboard's last coat. Cleaning up, we break out cheap sparkling wine and drink to Mia's newly painted space, toasting *Fifty Places to Picnic*, yet to be in progress. Not that I drink too much, I at least drink enough to loosen up and invite Mia to my funeral, a rare but welcome opportunity for death to bring us closer together. Even though darkness can sometimes brighten things up, my invitation was supposed to be a joke.

Without hesitation, Mia promises to attend. It's no small commitment. Is she just polite? Worse, trying to humor me? Is this a show of professionalism or flirtation? Funeral planning might only make a convenient excuse for drawn-out conversation. But if things are going well, why ask why?

We agree that putting on a proper funeral presents problems. It's no picnic eulogizing someone you love. Oddly enough, it's a painful walk in the park saying goodbye to someone you don't care much about.

"Not to sound obsessed, but Reflexive Fusion brings life to any funeral," Mia says. "A spontaneous, tearful outburst, simple words with dramatic tone can do wonders."

"I know—but easy questions and answers could sound scripted. Not to insult with suggestions, but what if I ask you to ask how such a good man could die? Work with me. I'm having a rare moment, optimistic enough to make me hope for the best."

Mia's smile seems uncertain. "How can you require rather than inspire spontaneity for a sendoff to the afterward," she asks.

"Let's face it. 'Sensible' understates me. 'Brave,' 'courageous,' 'bold,' 'strong' or 'intelligent' might exaggerate."

"They are nice words. Maybe I could wear purple Lycra tights with a black cape," she says. "You know, that old rock star look."

Even if she's not sarcastic, she still might be joking. I try to think before I speak. "Purple attire could help you forget the tragedy of death, help forget that girl and kitten." I put my hand on Mia's shoulder in a way that's more friendly than familiar. "You're beautiful." She laughs and pushes me away. "You shouldn't take on the whole burden of making a funeral fun, Mia. If only we knew the date, it would be easier to pack a picnic in advance. Oddly enough, we'd have our first chapter for *Fifty Places*, an employee funeral with refreshments. Maybe I should be thankful; our timing's off on this one."

"Funeral plans could be troublesome this early in a friendship," Mia says. "A conservative suit like those worn by Institute women might be more appropriate. Skin-tight Lycra might upset the more conventional people."

"I'll admit, you'd be trying to please the hardest to please, an unconscious me. Dilemma's simple. People easily displeased would be conscious; the person to please, dead."

Does my way of thinking spook Mia? She stands, telling me to wait. She returns wearing a black cape and unwraps herself. She pirouettes. "Does this shade of purple work," she asks.

"Yeah, that works! The depth of the purple, it's so true to form."

What a relief. I forget my worries. For once, it's easy to pay attention to detail; easy to say the right thing. Lycra's peaks and valleys follow Mia's curves. Her beauty distracts me from my shallow life and death fog, the laughable responsibility for the Machine. I have a vision of a ghost-faced goddess looking outward, hoping to catch a glimpse of whatever it is that's within. She's standing motionless, statue-like with a pigeon perched on her shoulder.

A friendship with Mia, it's still new enough to allow flirting, almost old enough to make familiarity comfortable without breeding contempt. Mia and I, just two refugees, safe from the ravages of hunger, victimized by truth and denial. We hug, fusing a long moment without much movement.

Live long, die young; everyone wins at the Institute. The Machine burdens robots with more paper that confirms existence; paper that confirms death. Performance indicators and improvement plans presented as well-meaning fuel my rage, and feed Mia's optimism. The Institute is a place to forget everything and cultivate denial, perfect for acting like a sad clown or happy loser.

Is the Machine waiting? Will I know I'm dead after I die? At least my name didn't make the obituary. And I feel well.

Mia interrupts my thinking. "This *Fifty Places* thing—the added work is supposed to teach us a lesson. If we can plan a picnic for a funeral the way we did, we can plan anything. We don't have to make anything up. Report an Institute picnic as is. The Director and coordinators will miss the ready-made humor. Keyboard jockeys will read between the lines."

3

At last! After forty years, the American dream: my first new bathroom scale and vacuum cleaner. No headlights, bells, or buzzers, both reflect pure, functional beauty. The bathroom scale is jet black with red LED readouts; the vacuum cleaner is fire-engine red with jet black wheels. When I arrive home with my new toys, it's raining so hard I'm afraid rain-soaked boxes will make the American dream a wet one, an unsafe circumstance whenever electricity's involved.

Bathroom scale perfect for an underweight, over-exercised, middle-aged male. Vacuum cleaner just the right size for a third-floor, one-room, garret apartment, just right for a retreat from a spouse-less life.

So, here I am with a new life, vacuum cleaner, and bathroom scale. I left with nothing, my bed is a camping mat. In the morning, I kneel in front of my dorm-size refrigerator, microwave, and full-size wastebasket. Home cooking: pour canned soup on a hot potato. Potato warms soup; soup cools potato: no wasted movement, no fusion with reflection. When I finish my meal, the paper bowl goes into the trash.

Our divorce finalized, I asked my lawyer, "What about love?" "What about it," she replied.

How much does my lawyer know about love? Mia wasn't in the picture then; no way for anyone to suspect that someday, I would kiss her. Jumping ahead to a love life imagined, would Mia want kids? If so, what do I say? My former marriage, troubled with the complexities of family planning, inspired me to prop a tablet against an old radio on the refrigerator. The tablet is always turned on; its charger's always plugged in. Except for my browsing for occasional glimpses of couples acting out the art of reproduction, the world population clock runs non-stop. I never take the tablet to work. Why create the impression that I'm obsessed with the idea that overpopulation is a dirty trick on a continuous supply of newborns?

So many metrics, make me feel like a director monitoring numbers. Digits blip in unison, announcing in-the-moment population increase and loss—birth count, deaths, consumption metrics, health costs, cars produced, bicycles, computers, and new book titles. Suicides, deaths by cigarette—the cost of ready-made happiness is currently eighty-four billion for illegal drugs.

We are heading to another meeting. In early morning fog, there's not much to talk about, except the fog. All I can do is complain, "What a waste of time. This meeting has nothing to do with picnics."

"Too many meetings about teamwork," Mia says. "People want to focus on things that don't matter. They keep saying, 'We need to change along with change. Adapt. If you can't delegate, you'll overextend yourself.' Technicians have no one to delegate to.

"The Director and his suits miss the point. If a crew doubles the speed of a conveyor that loads mail on the robots, they get bonus money. In the meantime, a robot tech gets a bonus for scheduling downtime for maintenance. Mail and tech unions unite to protest their differences. Coordinators take the issue into advisement. The opportunitators recommend more teamwork."

"You're cynical. Most of the time, it seems like everyone's pulling together."

"Should I be the one to tell them incentives interfere with mail production and conveyor movement? These days, better to keep quiet. Besides, the situation sounds isometric. Two departments moving at equal speeds in opposite directions nurture illusions of teamwork and corporate well-being."

"Why worry?" Mia asks. "The Director's happy. The

Institute broke another record for storing the most paper policies ever. Celebrating fires up salespeople to take it to the next level.

"Celebration inspires keyboard jockeys to go paperless. A focus on teamwork makes workers forget the mission. Remember, he likes to say 'Profit's not a four-letter word?' Forget teamwork and profit. Take more field trips to the river park. It's an Eden with canoes silently gliding, and pigeons flying overhead. Maybe we'll find a few tomato plants growing. It's a perfect place for a picnic."

The Opportunitator will be commemorating our latest Institutional success, breaking another record, an oversized likeness of a vintage record, a vinyl disc that stored canned music for the masses and almost rendered live bands obsolete. The few popular groups that remain keep music on chips, hard drives, and the cloud. The sky's the limit. Underemployed here at the Institute, so many gifted musicians play quiet, mono-tone, monorhythmic, overextended riffs on desktop keyboards, converting information into digital beauty as best as they can.

Alone, I like to sit in the back, furthest away from the spotlight. Mia thinks proximity to the action creates more excitement. Today, we sit in the front row. Either way, front and rear theatre seats are just as comfortable. Mia thinks the best ones are closest to the action. I like to please Mia, but I'm not sure the word "action" belongs in the same room, or on the same page as some penny stock motivator. Where to draw the line? When does an opportunitator accomplish anything be-yond speaking? Is the opportunitator entertaining? You might as well ask, what makes a picnic? Does an indoor outing with popcorn and soda make this a good fit for *Fifty Places*?

A huge stainless-steel disc hangs from a tripod like a gong in the old *Gong Show*, a TV contest for amateur performers. If boredom or poor taste inspires, you might find online reruns that either slipped through or stood the test of time. If an au-dience disliked a performance, they booed their disapproval. A demonic muscle man struck a massive gong with an oversized padded drumstick. The performer retreated from the stage, his sick act a primitive revelation for whom the gong tolls.

The Opportunitator is too sophisticated to copy a TV show. To memorialize the new Institute record, he will destroy a steel disc, a crude likeness of a record that's not vinyl. He dons welders' goggles. A rookie tech lights up an oxyacetylene cutting torch, the gas ax of the working people. He twists a valve slightly and adds more oxygen to the mix. The flame turns from yellow to a dark blue; the severe hissing sound intensifies as if to intimidate. Room lights dim. He directs the intense blue flame at the platter's topside. Steel turns cherry red, burns through, and showers yellow sparks on Institute officers, keyboard jockeys, and techs alike. The torch melts downward, slicing through stainless steel. Flying sparks sting, but don't burn those of us in front. A golf ball-sized molten chunk breaks away and drops on the Opportunitator's foot as if to suggest it's not best to put your best foot forward. Smiling a forced smile, he hands the torch to the rookie tech, removes his goggles, limps a few steps, stops, and turns to face the audience. Without a gong, emptiness floats in a silent vacuum, momentarily but long enough to draw half-hearted claps and cheers from a well-meaning audience, but not from me. It's hard to tell what they liked, or if they liked it at all. In defiance of corporate etiquette, someone snaps a picture. From his expression, the Opportunitator seems pleased.

Were the fireworks spectacular? The Statue of Liberty's gentle flame is nothing compared to the power of acetylene. Take my words as bias or sarcasm: Let there be meetings.

Mia and I attend the reception that follows. "What do you think," she asks.

"About the dog and pony show?"

"No—I was wondering about the stuffed mushrooms."

The suits ignore us; at least the wine is free. We refill our glasses and leave to walk the Institute halls. Tonight, my shoes don't squeak on marble floors; I don't know why. Whenever we take walks together, I'm too energetic to stop and look at pictures of pottery. We keep moving until we reach the main level of the rotunda and stop in front of one of the marble columns that reach up to support the dome. I glance behind us to make sure we're alone. I ask Mia, "Hug me—a hug for a vintage, romantic picture? We can call it 'Sid and Mia at the Rotunda.'"

We embrace momentarily, but her concern breaks my little league magic. "There is no camera."

"No problem," I reply. "There's no film."

On our ascent to the second level, we're so quiet you could hear a pin drop or shoe squeak. With so many steps, our climb seems to take forever. We hold hands like a young couple on their second date, taking their first walk in an anxious search for a moment of truth, a passionate source of any young lover's dreams.

Standing at the balcony's circular brass railing, we look down at the lower level. Pillars frame the reception area, temple-like. I still can't explain why the Institute displays so much pottery. I doubt that Egyptian pottery lends credence to the Institute. Do these artifacts bring value-added sophistication? Is the Director a would-be historian, still inspired by a freshman Art Appreciation course? It doesn't matter. Oversized clay jugs add authenticity to the scene—great pharaohs used to smash beautiful pottery to celebrate broken records of the non-vinyl kind. Times certainly change. No pharaohs, no slaves, only survivors—directors, keyboard jockeys, every underling in between. This pottery remains intact. If you want broken pottery, try an archeological dig. If you like beautiful pottery, visit the Institute. To move your spirit, find a place somewhere in between.

I'm getting anxious. I hope I don't spill my wine.

No security guards in sight, Mia and I are alone, standing at the balcony's highly polished brass rail. A stray pigeon does a fly-by—maybe it's one of the wild ones whose feathers and dung clog rooftop air conditioners. I put my arm around Mia, hold her tightly, and say, "Someday, this will all be yours."

"The railing?" she asks.

I shake my head. "All of it." She doesn't question my credibility or ask what I mean. From her expression, I'm guessing she doesn't want that much to do with the Institute. Does it matter that I'm only a tech? Do I place too much emphasis on success? Does it matter that I've achieved nothing?

No camera, no music, I whisper, "Somewhere, someone is playing our song."

Mia says nothing. I'm thankful she didn't ask for the title. Don't try this at home. Save romantic, playful words for picnics. Pretend to be a comedian; rejection hurts no more than death or denial.

The worst kind of picnic, our funeral gig, was planned but not carried out. Our second one unplanned ended up being a real party. Mia's words:

"An indoor outing too good to be true, an opportunitator brings us fire, an arousing mix of oxygen and acetylene. The Institute provides popcorn and seltzer. Afterward, we walk the halls drinking free wine and posing for fake pictures.

"The rotunda's a perfect place to explore our fantasies. Sid says it will all be mine someday. As generous as he is, his naiveté touches me. The odds are just as good that it might be yours someday. Work hard. Increase your credit line dramatically. For now, take a picnic basket, enjoy."

4

The most recent edition of *Financial Products News* reports recent antics at the Institute. Its headline makes the front cover: "Industry Blow Torch on the Cutting Edge." Mia sips coffee and reads aloud:

"Some welders enjoy standing around, telling stories. A few corporate types like to suspend thought, light torches, and burn metal instead. Not to be outdone, a competitor's opportunitator cut a giant, surplus flywheel, new and unused but obsolete, intended for a World War II army tank. This one wears goggles designed for acetylene torches, not for electric arc welders. His arc cuts the flywheel with difficulty and drama, blinds half the audience, mostly low-level techs and bosses."

Mia pauses and sips coffee, giving me a chance to speak. "Intense light doesn't discriminate." Even if my comment's a bit obvious, Mia can at least see that I'm bright enough to perceive reality dancing in the coordinator's flame.

Beyond my interruption, Mia doesn't miss a beat. She keeps reading aloud:

"Blindness is only temporary, eye damage is permanent. Thanks to workers comp, half-blinded workers receive free bifocals."

"You know already, Mia: staff infections take many forms. In the future, corporations should hire street people to perform destructive shows of success. With so many jobless people more experienced and competent than the suits, applicant pools should deepen."

Mia goes on; she can't resist. Even though we're still on

our first cup of coffee, she shows me a black-and-white picture of the Institute's rooftop, its quiet herd of shiny ventilation ducts glistening in the sun. "Facilities department is screening air intakes, supposedly to prevent future pigeon damage," she says. "They claim they're taking back the rooftop, one duct at a time. They're more worried about air conditioners than pigeons."

I reach across the table, lightly brush Mia's hand, wink, and leave the cafeteria for a meeting. As usual, I take the elevator. Whenever I think and ride at the same time, I succumb to elevator lag, a rare condition that's rarely talked about. At its worst, I feel at home while working; it feels like I'm at work when homing. Feeling lost sometimes, I can't decide where to go next. On a bad day, I've gotten off on the wrong floor, amusing fellow elevator travelers. I know the rules. If you know you're wrong, get right back on; pretend you have something more important to do on another floor. If you don't realize you're lost right away, act like you know where you're going. No one laughs that way. If you look like you know what you're doing when you don't, you'll supposedly make a great director.

The boss is pleasant, even when things are bad. He's a funny guy I met before I started work here. Hustling life insurance, he tried selling me a policy. If I remember, his dark suit created an almost disrespectful distance. He pitched whole-life policies that supposedly help you profit, no matter if you live long or die young. He pushed a quick deal, balancing cold probabilities and possibilities with warm references to otherworld supremacy. I'll never forget his pitch. "If something should happen, God forbid," he said, his words, precise with a measured touch of holiness.

Calling on a user-friendly spirit to forbid hypothetical death, just to soft sell a numerical American dream, didn't sound like a sound policy. "Who pursues the creation after I die?" My question was purely diplomatic, a refusal to buy in.

Face deadpan, he kept talking about beneficiaries as if he was talking turkey. I spaced out; he lost a well-deserved sale. Of course, a carpenter young like I was, living on cigarette smoke and occasional doses of sawdust, made it easy to flaunt death, easy to say no to insurance, good deal or bad. Even if insurance offers a lifetime guarantee, a salesman can't guarantee how long I'll live. He shakes my hand, and walks away, muttering under his breath, "Crazy." Must have been God-fearing, afflicted with self-doubt whenever he failed to close a deal. It turns out, he has what it takes. He's now my boss. I've never figured out if he remembers me not buying the Institute life policy I couldn't afford.

His face lights up with a cautious smile as if I were the one who scheduled the meeting. He chats about feral pigeons populating the Institute. "Increasing numbers nest in the brick-and-mortar ledges. Facilities people are getting more concerned. They're posting 'Don't feed the pigeons' signs. I hate to say pigeons are populating the planet almost as fast as people. Eradication's probably the only answer."

Nothing new, I've heard it all before, the ecological threat of pigeons competing with people for food and space. It's the sound of the word "eradication" that darkens my mood, tunnels my vision, and heightens my fears. What's his point? What part of our conversation is real, and what's not? In our last meeting, he told me I should be more positive. Just in case he's going to be a pain in the ass, I say, "There's always hope. Overcrowded pigeons might evolve from feral to virtual."

The Coordinator's smile goes south. His forehead wrinkles. as if he doesn't get my humor. "I heard one of the opportunitators describe you as somewhat subversive," he says. "Now I know why." He hands me a new PIP, designed for underachievers. "Let's drill down into the metrics."

I scan the document if you can call it that. Reading it gets me ahead of the Coordinator's words: "Key Performance Indicators, KPIs, are still below expectation," it says. Under comments: "Machine jams paper too often on Mondays."

"I've heard there's more erratic jamming," he says. "Machine's down again, down enough to drop your numbers two points. Director's going to notice, sooner or later."

If I keep reading ahead, I'll still end up having to listen. "Clients aren't complaining," the Coordinator says. "It's just that your numbers affect my ratings. If they fire me first, they'll just hire another someone to fire you."

Coordinator continues. "Clear jams. Don't lie about your stats. Canceling calls should massage your numbers enough to swing them back to positive. Working the numbers gives corporate people like me a vote."

The Coordinator doesn't understand. The Machine's routine malfunctions are no problem to fix. It's the non-existent, imaginary problems, intermittent unexplainable ones, that get me in trouble. I look downward, focusing on the table's oak veneer, muttering under my breath, "Jesus Christ."

I look up. "I should have known there'd be trouble. Yesterday, a group of keyboard jockeys standing around the Machine were having a Star Trek theme day, giving the Institute a Halloween feel. People who think they belong in Star Trek's engineering department wear red uniforms. Scientist wannabes wear blue, would-be commanders, gold. Costumes aren't exactly business casual. Tights are too tight and mini skirts are too short to comply with HR standards. The would-be Trekkies are passing an open bottle around, its contents supposedly a fragrance called, 'Because Tomorrow Will Never Come.' They claim the scent allows them to go about Institute business boldly."

"Captain Quirk wore a gold turtleneck, making it hard to tell if he's a keyboard jockey or coordinator." More sarcastic than intelligent, he gets all rhetorical, speaking in a voice too loud for a small room. 'You, again,' he asked. 'We should get you a desk. Better yet, a cot.' Desk or cot, the joke's too old to be funny. But the keyboard jockeys seem to get a laugh over a crisis that endangers no one."

"Is the captain's name Quirk or Kirk," the Coordinator wants to know.

"It doesn't matter much. The captain's name must have been Kirk, but he did act a little quirky. Anyway, there was also a cute blonde in a miniskirt and tunic who kept rubbing fragrance on her neck."

"We're professionals. Act accordingly."

"I tried testing to verify the problem. The Machine passed

paper, making everyone laugh again. Keyboard jockeys knew I'd already swapped forty-eight rollers and five circuit boards. They're happy. They think if I can't fix it, the Institute will replace it."

I have my boss's attention for once; I continue. "When I departed, Captain Quirk gave me specific orders: 'Live long and prosper.' He sounded more serious than usual as if his imaginary role as commander of the starship Enterprise has a higher priority than Institute responsibility."

The Coordinator ignores me. "The Machine's becoming a crisis," he says. "Your numbers are still pulling down my numbers. Understand my concern." He pauses as if he's searching for better words.

I can feel blood rushing to my head. "If it's a crisis, why hold a meeting? What are you going to do? Be realistic and work on the problem? Or live in your metric wonderland, talking numbers?"

It's better to be sarcastic than suggest the Coordinator's attitude has gone bad. After all, he can't explain to the Director how a jammed piece of paper relieves the planet, at least temporarily. Running, the Machine passes a hundred fifty-plus sheets a minute. In training, techs more sarcastic than I am called it "The Deforester," as if there's something wrong with that. Fewer forests used to mean more pasture. Today, where do we get paper pulp with fewer trees? A new-age consumer, the Machine competes with wildlife forced to migrate from disappearing forest land into suburbia. Back when farmers completed the circle of life, leaving young trees to grow, harvesting mature ones. Was that a crime? Is it flip to say a tree a day keeps the ecologist away? Now that the Machine's down, the ecology movement might endorse its existence.

As usual, the Coordinator reminds me that canceling calls will improve my stats in situations where I can't solve a problem. He dismisses me.

I forget about farms and forests and trees that keep the ecologists away. The immediate problem creates a dilemma. Choose among unlikely fixes or hope the jamming problem disappears by itself. With trial and error, trials are certain, errors are unpredictable. Doing nothing, I've succeeded more than once.

The Machine passes paper now. I didn't understand at first, but the blonde lady who inputs positive indicators explains how she fixed it. Still dressed in sexy starship black slacks and a gold top, she looks like Tasha Yar, Chief of Security on the Enterprise. After coming back down to earth, she noticed that the Machine stops every afternoon, at around 3 o'clock or so. Sunlight shining directly through windows from the west, she shuts the curtain. The Machine works. She opens the curtain and the Machine jams. Blessed with a 'can-do' attitude, a critical element of the American Dream, she tapes a pigeon feather to the paper exit. Blocking the afternoon sun prevented its beam from tricking the photo sensor into thinking there was a jam. Problem solved, a relief.

5

The Machine is alive and well, up and running for now at least, it gives us a break for our first real picnic. Mia has already prepared a box lunch in a wicker basket. I hate to admit we have trouble thinking of a place unique enough to mention in *Fifty Places to Picnic*. It's dark outside. A guard's always guarding the rotunda. The lounge is unlocked, but I can't find the light switch. My office space is an obvious choice; its technical ambiance feels dark, even with the soothing hum of flickering fluorescent lights.

We decide on taking the elevator, the safest way to travel unless you happen to be an elevator technician. I hit the "close door" button, knowing the door won't close any faster. Mia keys in an unauthorized password, allowing us to ascend and descend repeatedly, without stopping and opening its doors. She spreads a blanket and breaks out wine, bread, and cheese. "We have it all," she says, "everything but Musik, that non-fattening, thoughtlessly bland ear candy."

"Algorithmic mood music, computer-generated by lazy composers for elevator people too lazy to take stairs."

"It's not all bad. Believe it or not, stress and anxiety from obnoxious music helps some people with weight control."

A small monitor by the doorway shows a tiny robot playing keyboard, a bland sample of three repetitious quarter notes alternating with four, original three plus one more. Without adding or subtracting an offbeat, it says "Press to select."

I touch Mia's forehead. "Unless you want to dance, let's skip the music. We have each other."

Cynics might think an elevator's too cramped for a picnic. This one's just right. Imperceptible much of the time, I don't know why an elevator's motion mesmerizes. Whenever we change directions, movement between the outskirts and center reverses. Every time we reach the upper or lower level, wine gently ripples in our glasses. The elevator drops downward, the wine rises to high tide. When it's going upward, the wine drops to low tide. No matter which direction, I can feel some tension rising. It's not long before we become practiced elevator drinkers. Mia raises her glass and says, "Cheers." At a loss for words, I raise my glass and smile a satisfied smile. My mind slows down to a speed slower than the Machine passing paper. I could ride with Mia forever. For once, I'm not thinking beyond the moment.

It feels like Mia's elevator password is taking us on a magical trip through the ups and downs; no need for the bland sweetness of elevator music to help us forget the fear of falling. We descend to the outskirts of creation, a place devoid of sterile information, a place filled with contentment, picture-perfect lovers on a river shore, holding hands, watching wild pigeons fly overhead.

I reach out to Mia, too late. Time's up. The onboard computer cancels our code. The elevator shudders violently at first, then more slowly and gently. As luck has it, the doors slide open at the rotunda. We're decent, still fully dressed, but Mia's not wearing her shoes. Security makes me insecure; the guard looks at us suspiciously. What to say or do, I don't know. We find ourselves elevator speechless.

Security people write us up for joyriding on the elevator. "Even if your feet were only exposed, you're guilty of indecent exposure," the guard tells Mia. "Save your caged pigeon show for the lab. Performing a lewd act almost in public doesn't reflect well on the Institute."

The other guard is apologetic. "I would let both of you go. But the video camera had already captured Mia's exposed toes, and you, Sid, wide-eyed. You both looked like deer caught in a hunter's jacklight, startled, frozen, staring at the source of your blindness. It's a dilemma. I wasn't sure if my responsibilities were professional or artistic."

Rules force Security to recommend that the legal department put Mia and me on a one-week probation. They notify HR to adjust our key performance indicators downward. Off the record, Security people think we're funny. One was kind enough to share the irony of it all. "Alone and intimate, you embraced, fully clothed as if picnicking in public, in a park or on a beach. The sanction is not supposed to encourage lewd behavior. Rather it should encourage you to take advantage of opportunities should they arise. If you act like this in your personal lives, what are you like at the Institute? Would you know a good deal if you see one?"

I'm surprised that I feel a little defensive. "Growth of a healthy relationship takes a different trajectory than picnic research or study of the creation."

Security only manages a blank stare. "Creation?"

"Creation might be close to the outskirts of human development, a place where Institutional rules can be forgotten or broken, a space where my mind centers and stops racing. If you don't understand the center, I don't dare describe the outskirts."

"Are you real?" he asks.

Rumor has it that a few coordinators acquired copies of Security's video. Maybe they play it at parties to liven things up. I can imagine a host or hostess telling guests, "You should see this video of two elevator people at the rotunda."

Jaded by porn, greed, violence, and life at the Institute, guests would watch in wonder, admiration. Even so, they will probably focus on the elevator, and miss the peace bouncing back and forth between the creation's center and outskirts.

Mia's words for *Fifty Places*:

"No one describes the Institute's elevators as sensuous; I find riding with Sid exciting. Don't forget the obvious. Load your picnic with affordable wine and cheese. If you prefer the doors to remain closed, remember that advanced programming is required.

"If you're ever trapped in an open elevator and ambushed by a security camera, kick off your shoes. Wiggle your toes in an erotic dance of sorts; if you're facing punishment while following rules, you might as well make the most of the moment."

Is this a plug for Reflexive Fusion? I'm not sure. It seems inappropriate to ask. An intimate moment with Mia is romantic enough to treasure rather than question.

The video chip sounds more exciting than I first gave it credit for. We'll never get access unless we find a bootleg copy on the street.

6

There's always been a rumor that the Tech Coordinator's eyes light up whenever someone says "metric." I've seen for myself; that his performance evaluations prove that it's true. At meetings, he makes the word metric sound poetic, even when his numbers imply falsehood stranger than fiction. Metrics and numerical truths make reality easy to describe in thoughtful transformational ways. Metrics make productive employees worthless, reveal imaginary shareholder profits, and inspire Research to try new experiments.

We're watching one of Mia's research pigeons working. The pigeon's too busy to watch back. Above its small experimental chamber, a digital counter counts the pigeon's key pecks. "Metrics are opiate-like for the Coordinator. Watching the same numbers makes me feel as bad as someone on withdrawal."

"I know what you're talking about," Mia says. "This pigeon works day and night, oblivious to the numbers. Big deal, his hunger proves food pellets are motivators. Research Coordinator's like a St. Peter wannabe who counts good deeds but forgets to promise any kind of heaven in return. From the numbers, he thinks he can tell how much work the pigeon does. The counter counts key pecks, not wing flaps or one-legged leg stands. The funniest part is the pigeon gets rewarded, no matter if it pecks the disc or not."

Mia knows what's happening. There's more. "Even suspicious pigeons become superstitious when rewarded for doing whatever they happen to be doing. This pigeon's not pecking enough to meet expectations or meet an imaginary quota.

Supposedly it didn't do much pecking at all. It turns out the pigeon lifts its right leg, wiggles its claws, and pecks the outskirts of the disc, furthest from its center. The outer edge of the disc is too insensitive to trigger the micro-switch and too blind to measure consistent work. If the output is only as good as the input that feeds it, the counter can't reflect the pigeon's reality. No credit for pecking. No trophy for dramatic leg and claw movement. No picture on the cover of *Scientific American*. Bad data from bad research must make Research superstitious."

Another way to look at it, pecking the edge of the disc suggests that life is less measured on the creation's outskirts. Either I'm not making sense, or Mia doesn't get it.

The pigeon's name is Penguin Four. There's something warm about the vibe of "Penguin" and something efficient about the tone of "Four." A barcoded wing band clipped to his wing looks flashy under fluorescent light.

Mia knows Penguin Four's history, a possible inspiration for her devotion to the animal rights cause. An excerpt from *Legacy of a Pigeon*:

His great-great-grandfather, many grandfathers ago, served in the United States Army Air Force during World War II. It was a time when inventing better ways to deliver bombs was a higher priority than building better mousetraps. Japanese, one-man suicide subs were supposed to blow up enemy ships. German Shepherds, man's best friends, were trained to deliver backpack bombs to kill the enemy, man's worst friends. Not to be outdone, Americans designed a guided missile to be driven by three pigeons. Talk about teamwork. The pigeons were supposed to peck the target as seen through a lens, unwittingly guiding the missile toward its mark. Unlike the bomber dog or suicide sub's navigator, each pigeon took a break now and then. The remaining two continued driving. No one called the pigeons heroic. In on the deal for a consistent payment of formulated food pellets, they did what they had to do.

After intensive pigeon training, the Armed Forces director concluded that the guided-missile inventor was a crackpot and decided not to use the pigeons. Penguin Four's ancestral grandfather of many generations received an honorable discharge and survived wartime stateside. Who knows how many if any fellow pigeons cooed a sincere thank you for his service? Energized by his survival and genetic programming, he served female pigeons, discharging friendly, generous contributions of sperm where the need was or wasn't needed. Penguin Four comes from this gene pool's friendly skies.

7

Symbolic or just coincidence, the Machine is located on the third of five floors, in the middle of things, next to the rotunda. It remains a central figure in the Institute, the source of my economic survival. I try to keep my spirit pure in the rural outskirts, a more peaceful place than the center. Caught between the two, it's a relief to daydream about Mia, I'm not sure if I should mention lust. I try to read *Zen and Robot Maintenance—Why Shut it Down if it Runs?* My mind keeps racing. As usual, it can't concentrate. Thinking is painful. Not thinking is worse.

Research remains a priority. Since we can't find a bootlegged video of *Elevator People at the Rotunda,* we ask Security for a copy. To protect the Institute from ridicule, and to discourage the impression that work is a picnic, they refuse. "Our work is serious," Mia says. "It's an official assignment from HR. After all, I wasn't acting when my toes danced their little erotic dance. And neither was Sid when the video caught him doing nothing."

"No need to worry about technicalities," the guard says. "Law department can't find release forms."

Not to be a wise ass, but just to prove that work is as essential as a picnic, I ask for the video of the Machine's original half-ton primal inverter, pinning me in the elevator. The inverter was large enough to protect most of me from the camera eye, but my hands and forearms remained in view, jerking in spasms as if that would help me escape serious injury. As a safety video, it could provide a more realistic view of work here. People who think work is a picnic might apply for employment elsewhere.

Again, Security refuses to provide the video. To replace it, I could reenact my life-and-death battle with the inverter, but that would damage the Institute's solid reputation as much as my artistic credibility. I tell Security that my attorney calls once a month, hoping to generate new business. It sounds crazy, but this is more a fact than fiction.

My mind races, my headaches, and I have things to do. I call Human Resources to get them to call Legal. Electronic Slut answers. As usual, her monotone voice thanks me for calling and transfers me to another extension. The same voice thanks me again for my call and puts me on hold to wait for another Institutional message. Pennies saved; pennies earned.

Daylight savings are well-spent until spring. Early darkness and cooler October air make beach picnics impractical. Mia and I plan an evening trip here at the Institute, not only for rest and relaxation but to mix in more research for *Fifty Places*.

To reach tonight's destination, we hike the depths of the Institute, through the tunnel to the east. A ventilation duct blows a steady but boring Chicago-like breeze at our faces. Though a pleasant fluorescent evening, it seems like an endless walk. Rubber soles muffle my footsteps and don't squeak on painted concrete. Mia's high heels make staccato echoes pleasantly percussive. Vast expanses of functional beauty, concrete walls painted off-white, tinged with the warm color of wheat, floors painted dark brown, pipes color-coded red, blue, brown, and white. One way or the other, they create a colorful sense of direction. We pass paint, metal, carpentry, and maintenance shops, doors closed and locked. Gradually, the endless concrete floor and walls create more open space. Chain link encloses generators, turbines, and giant electrical transformers, all painted fire-engine red and jet black, colors of the American Dream. The sounds of humming machines blend, creating harmonics, not altogether unpleasant.

Even with the balmy Chicago breeze, it's so warm I wish we could wear swimsuits. But we're concerned people might ask questions. I have a question for Mia right now. But I'll wait until we take pictures. After our experience with Security, we'll have to do the photography ourselves this time.

We take a branch off the main tunnel and enter a room, an abandoned, obsolete generator, its mechanic was a guy named Jonson who graduated from my alma mater, the Technical Academy. I tell Mia about the consequence of his layoff from the Institute.

Jonson found a night job at Sky Pilot, a nearby sports bar. After hours, a police officer caught him with a cute, middle-aged waitress at the bar, both fully clothed and wearing shoes. The officer cites him for Drinking While Cleaning after hours. In return for a lenient reprimand from the Liquor Commission, the bar's owners fire him and scold the cute waitress for wasting time, counting tips. The last I heard, he was disillusioned and jobless.

Though out of use, the generator is spotless and shiny, still bright red. The spot is secluded, well-ventilated, and warm under fluorescent skies. It's almost romantic. We spread a blanket and set up the tripod for an old-fashioned selfie. There's no photographer, but this time we have film and a camera with an electronic shutter that can take random pictures when we least expect it. We want to be candid.

We remove our business casual attire—not that I'm sure you can call Mia's purple gown casual, but I trust her judgment. In swimsuits, we can better enjoy the beach-like atmosphere. Mia opens her picnic basket containing wine, bread, and cheese. "Since you like surprises, I brought the same spread as last time," she says. "After all, you'd never expect the same menu."

We lie under a sunlamp that someone left behind, probably Jonson, who must have been in a hurry to escape an American Dream poisoned by the Institute. Now and then, the camera shutter clicks.

We hold hands, my fingers rubbing Mia's palm. I look in her eyes. "Would you go to the prom with me?"

Her eyes take on a glassy, dreamy look, "I thought you'd never ask." She pulls the blanket over us and hugs me. "Which prom are you thinking? And when?"

Reluctant to admit I'm somewhat shy, I remind myself, this is only a test. "I'm just checking," I reply. "I've never been to a prom, not even a semi-formal." She doesn't blink. It doesn't seem like she's turned off by a pimple on my chin. I should have proposed marriage.

The shutter click interrupts my daydream of what I should have said and regrets about what I did not do.

A pigeon glides overhead and lands on a blue, freshwater pipe. For a moment, it feels like we're basking in the warm fluorescence of a Walmart picnic supply aisle.

8

Prom plans are still in the works. Searching online and looking through vintage yellow-page phone directories makes finding an October prom for adults hopeless.

"No prom," Mia asks. "No fall shindig, no autumn wing-ding?"

Mia's playful words sound too retro and more cynical than I'd expect.

Our beach picnic created a reality I can believe in. It's not a creation that belongs to another universe. It's a creation so close that its blur makes reality hard to see. Technically the generator still belongs to the Institute. But we left the rules behind, took it all back, and gave something of ourselves. I like our candid photography. Kudos should go out to technology for the tripod and camera's random, electronic shutter release. Two pictures show Mia and me embracing under the beach blanket as if hiding our somewhat adolescent, romantic hug. An attempt to be modest would have been self-defeating. The photo creates the illusion of a climax that captures the moment's reality. I can say that Mia and I weren't faking. While keeping ourselves decent for the camera's eye, we should at least get credit for doing things we didn't do.

The floor almost looks sandy but lacks a normal grainy texture. A wide-open lens blurs the blanket, makes it look as if it's flowing, creates a surrealistic sense of movement underneath, and keeps us in better focus. We are lying on our sides, hugging, looking into each other's eyes in a static pose. You'd never know I had just invited Mia to a prom that likely won't happen. Directly behind us, an original Harley Davidson shop manual sits on a ledge, waiting for Jonson's unlikely return, or waiting for me to return it to Jonson, I'm not sure.

HR likes Mia's generator take, another brief chapter for *Fifty Places to Picnic*:

"Bask in sunny florescence, a desert-like atmosphere of barren concrete and abandoned generator. It's glorious, like Bermuda, not too hot or humid. The gentle, ducted sea breeze sounds are a bit too steady for my liking. That loose pigeon flying the halls lends a touch of class to the Institute. No seagulls here, thank you. Think of low travel costs. Think of savings that buy good wine and cheese."

We plan our own Halloween party at the rotunda's second level. Even though we have official clearance, it's best to pretend we don't get preferential treatment. Anyone who picnics here will be on his or her own. We find a spot that keeps us out of sight of the guard and his security camera. The risk of the hidden and forbidden heightens our experience and promises excitement to those who follow in our footsteps.

We pour wine into a small pottery jug and pull two jars of artichoke hearts from our wicker basket. We remove our business casual attire, bulky from wearing togas underneath. We roll out mats side by side and lie down, rest our heads on our elbows, sip wine, and drink in the ambiance of comfort and luxury. On this level, I have to admit we miss the random appearance of an occasional pigeon.

"When in Rome, do as the Romans do. At the Institute, do as the Institutions do," Mia says. She loosens her toga and draws a knee up to her chin, revealing her deep-purple tights, but keeping her thighs covered. Even if her attire is ideal in October, it's inappropriate at the Institute. Will she get fired? Is this Halloween, or is this the end?

It can't be the end. Not counting pictures, *Fifty Places* is only three pages right now.

9

"Not that it matters," I tell Mia, "Supposedly, some humans dream in black and white."

"Life goes on in living color here at the Institute."

So far, so good; at least no one crashed our Halloween party at the Rotunda. Those who read *Fifty Places* will be happy to know Mia and I didn't get fired for choosing an out-of-place place to picnic. Mia's critique of our Halloween party deserves a look.

"Ah, Rome! Not exactly the Vatican, the rotunda is luxurious and opulent, not to mention the beautiful pottery. During a brief stay on the balcony, I felt like a beautiful nymph, introducing a play. Wear something surprising. Beware: the surgeon general warns some visuals can cause mild arousal. If you don't believe it, ask Sid."

Someone downloaded Security's video and photos of Mia and me. The collection commonly called *Elevator People* now resides on the Machine's primal inverter. No surprise, Mia was fully clothed, except her bare feet, of course. No one knows who downloaded these pictures. Security won't admit the breach. After all, nothing appears stolen. Off the record, they think the hacker's a fun-loving troublemaker, a corporate rotten apple. Some suspect it might be the phantom vandal Johnny, the guy who tosses apple seeds in Institute flower gardens. As far as we're concerned, it's an exciting development. Now that Mia has the video, she can submit it to as many film festivals as she wants. We still worry.

"Are people printing out the pictures and taking them home?" Mia wonders.

I answer Mia with another question. "Can the Machine broadcast them all over the world, without our knowing?"

It's quite a picture. The camera lens focuses on Mia's feet as they point upward, arched as far as feet can arch, toes straight, toes curled. Hard to believe, pictures from one of Security's ceiling-mounted cameras make Mia's ankles even more attractive than they are in real life. Keyboard jockeys print photos out and staple them on cubicle walls. I hope this attention doesn't increase the Machine's workload.

10

On rainy days, the Coordinator never says, "Nice day for ducks." He greets me with his usual, "Bad day for pigeons."

The Machine's meter reads three point one billion. My numbers move downward to three-point-four this time, nothing to celebrate. "Keyboard jockeys wish for a new Machine even though the old one still runs," the Tech Coordinator says. "Your performance numbers seem to be circling the drain on that downward spiral. The Machine could burp or fart anytime, start jamming paper again, and trigger another crisis. Regardless, you get a bonus for fixing it for Captain Quirk—or Kirk—whoever it is."

I didn't bother telling the Coordinator that the woman who looked like Tasha Yar, the one who inputs positive indicators, solved the problem. No matter if her genius was accidental or not, she used one of her treasured pigeon feathers to shade a photo sensor from daylight, fixing the problem, and boosting my numbers. The Coordinator, who likes to pretend he's an opportunitator, approves a two-percent pay raise.

Not to be a wise guy, I need to ask, "What about the metrics? How did you arrive at two percent? If random events are meaningful, is meaning random?"

Do the Institute's great visionaries think in black and white? Do they think in ones and twos, threes or fours, maybes or maybe nots? It doesn't matter; rumors abound. Workers worry about their jobs; the Machine still belches and farts out paper misfeeds now and then. With their corporate survival in question, coordinators can't depend on their reasoning to evaluate the Machine's self-diagnostic appraisal. Its printout, *Not to Be*, explains how an upgrade would enable it to upload, download, unload, offload, and read its own mail.

An upgrade can replace fifteen hundred employees. If its electrons move randomly enough, it can reduce labor expenses even more by ignoring mail. While the new model might make the few workers who remain feel somewhat diminished, the upgrade will empower the Director and coordinators more than ever. It can automatically mail token checks to soup kitchens, small tributes to those who worked here until layoff. Its new electronic alarms replace vintage buzzers and bells that have too many inconvenient, moving mechanical parts. It sings "Orange Oscillators of Oxford" in Old English. No waste of hot air on a lone bugle, sundown triggers an electronic rendition of Taps, a musical piece to honor the military dead. How could this upgrade ever become obsolete?

Running on old software, the Machine lacks a sophisticated instinct for self-preservation, and its circuits are too primitive to plan a logical demise. Its best guess suggests enshrinement in the lower rotunda, making it a monument to planned obsolescence. Like an Institute accountant, it's neither self-serving nor sarcastic when it considers the labor hours needed to disassemble itself: three seconds to pull the plug, five hours to dismantle and remove. If scrap values and costs of electronic toxin removal remain stable, salvaged parts could bring in $430. The Machine can't compute one crucial detail: if replaced with a new model, I'd have to go to Japan for training. *Fifty Places* might end up with only twenty. How can we measure that kind of loss in terms of employee benefits?

As the Machine's technician, I'm expected to attend a meeting to discuss its future. Who knows why my Coordinator advised me not to participate?

The first coordinator, a white-haired man with a mustache, looks too old to do much work, too young to retire. He pulls a cigar from his suit jacket and looks at it for a moment. He's a caricature of the wealthy owner of Boardwalk, real estate located on the familiar Monopoly game board, designed during the 1930s Depression. Cigar smoke facilitated big business deals. Reoccurring dreams of imaginary abundance visited many of those impoverished. Today, Institute rules and state laws don't allow indoor tobacco smoke, forcing keyboard jockeys and superiors to pursue poor health in new ways. The wise, old white-haired one returns the cigar to his pocket and speaks with authority as if the world depends on him. "If my colleagues agree to install heavy-duty axles on mail robots to prevent the so-called information overload and burned-out wheel bearings, I'll vote for an overhaul."

"Even if a new machine replaces fifteen hundred workers, even if two new machines do the work of three thousand, replacement is out of the question," says the second coordinator, a young, rugged outdoorsman. A civic-minded man, he often goes golfing to balance stress and relaxation. "Rebuild allows tax write-offs. The more overpriced a part, the more money saved. Only forty starving infants or twenty freezing seniors would suffer from an insignificant loss in tax revenue."

"What a small price for repaving a few miles of the information highway. And what about that homeless lady with her kitten," I ask. The Coordinators' smiles disappear. It must have been apparent I wasn't joking.

Rugged outdoorsman replies. "Cat Lady's probably tweaking on meth. She's probably too strung out for shelter, too strung out to find a restroom when she needs one."

I've heard that the righteous, rugged Coordinator probably goes hunting on Saturdays to shoot feral pigeons and piss on trees.

The third coordinator is cute. At first glance, her serious expression appears too severe to create the spontaneous, in-the-moment-movement she might need if she ever wants to do Reflexive Fusion. She asks, "You're a sharp man. Are you up to speed—quick enough to work on the Machine while it runs?"

Few people call me sharp; I appreciate the recognition. Her easy question is hard to answer. "Working on a Machine while it's running? That's possible but risky. The mechanical movement could be much too intense to fuse with the moment. During operation, rotating rollers and gears can pull a tech into harm's way, a dangerous path less traveled. Replacing a logic chip with invisible electrons dancing in its head can cause informational flashbacks, scramble its memory, triggering instant techno amnesia."

"Is that all?" she asks.

"Not that this is about me, but I have concerns. Constant interruptions from keyboard jockeys, who need the Machine most when I'm working on it, would slow things down, and push my numbers downward. Shutting down, stopping paper flow long enough to install a new Machine would allow them to catch up on their work, improve their stats."

In response to my misgivings about an overhaul, the three coordinators apply advanced motivational theory, its sophistication well known throughout the corporate world. "I'm sure you can find a way to solve your problem," says the white-haired one, a coordinator who could become an opportunitator if he wasn't so close to retirement.

"You call yourself a technician?" asks the golfer.

The cute coordinator looks less severe. She taps her index finger, possibly a reflex that helps her reflect. A vague finger shadow brushes the table slowly; she raises an eyebrow and smiles. "You need to bring in consultants."

The white-haired one acts as if the Director forced him to mortgage his favorite hotel on Boardwalk. Maybe he just needs to get in the last word. "What about timing?" he asks. "Does it make sense to overhaul the Machine before next year's global rollout?"

Corporate speak hints at false promise in "rollout," a word that glamorizes mundane ideas and creates drama from nothingness. Everyone nods. Are there pleasant surprises in the Institute's future? More likely, are they hiding something? I remember the new wing still vacant, and mysterious, with hints of new furniture or equipment hidden under huge, black plastic sheets.

The three suits maintain an uncomfortable silence until the golfer whispers, "Rollout, my ass. Maybe we're setting the stage for our demise."

11

The meter reads more than four billion; my performance numbers are still three-point-four. We're running out of fair weather for picnics outside. Mia and I need to get out before the elements turn bitter. We meet at the Institute bank, three hundred and four marble slabs away and two stories down from the rotunda. We stand at the counter, eat donuts, and drink black coffee. Before I know it, Mia backs away a few feet and snaps my picture. I hope the camera doesn't catch crumbs on my chin, or coffee stains on my shirt.

We're waiting for a group of coordinators we invited to join us for a picnic near the Institute's back wall. Believe it or not, this outing's inspired by the girl with the swaddled kitten, huddling on an outdoor grate, fighting cold weather. Even after we explain how the picnic is heated, coordinators are reluctant to accept. Thanks to Mia, who offers to bring a hot apple pie and cider spiked with cinnamon, they finally agree.

The wind chill makes it feel colder than the reported thirty-five degrees. I'm not a meteorologist or even an ornithologist for that matter, but it feels almost too cold for pigeons. Heat escapes through the grate, and mixes with bursts of cold air. When the wind dies, the rising heat feels toasty like fireplace warmth. We need a picture. I step back and lean against the giant oak tree, the one saved by nitrogen injections. I should have a video camera. When the wind picks up, the coordinators shuffle around as if they're playing a grotesque form of musical chairs without the music or chairs we usually expect. Shivering, they continue their shuffle, heads bowed as if reality has morphed into a never-ending dance. Everyone wants the warmth of the center; no one wants the outskirts. It's almost dark. Shivering, I try to steady the camera. Its lens is wide open at dusk, and movement blurs detail, especially in the outskirts. No surprise, individuals become lost in the group trying to find the center. A lone pigeon perched in a maple tree, its head tucked under its left wing, looks to be in perfect focus. Beneath, the homeless girl waits patiently for the coordinators' departure to reclaim her place on the grid.

"Can we help," Mia asks, even though she's asked before.

The girl shrinks, leaning backward. "What about my kitten?"

"Does it have a name?"

"Toasty. They won't let him in at the soup kitchen. 'Code violation,' they always say. Animal shelters take kittens; soup kitchens take humans."

Mia adds another blurb to *Fifty Places*. Sometimes it's hard to believe that truth can be stranger than fiction.

"You might think of us as characters, real pieces of work. We invite people of diverse backgrounds to a ludicrous picnic on a heated, in-ground grate that's almost as pleasing as a campfire. Everyone enjoys apple pie and hot cider. We play a good game of musical chairs, a real-life example of Reflexive Fusion. It's much more than in-the-moment movement—it's life. According to Sid, it might be part of the creation.

"Thank Security, thank the coordinators who, afterward, allowed the phantom homeless lady and swaddled kitten to return to their rightful place, that space heated grate."

12

Penguin Four's disc pecking does not meet expectations. The pigeon loses his job as a disc pecker. The Research Coordinator wants Mia to teach the pigeon ping pong to show how leisure time affects the unemployed. I ask the Research Coordinator, Mia's boss, "What happens to the pigeon at the end of the experiment?"

"Who cares," he replies.

The pigeon, Penguin Four, gasps for air, waiting. The ball rolls into his court, he nudges it back. Drinks of water reward good ping pong, but if he drinks too much, he misses the ball and misses out on the water. No one's looking. I take Mia's hand and whisper, "Welcome to the real world, Penguin Four. Be thankful you have a job, especially one that involves leisure. Be thankful your life beats flying in the sky, dodging BBs."

"Stop," Mia whispers back. She squeezes my hand, a gentle reminder that truth can sound sarcastic, that sarcasm can be mistaken for belief. Worst case scenario, an unsuspecting coordinator gives me a glowing review for expressing an unintended truth.

During better times when life was simple, people asked which came first, the pigeon or the egg. Now they want to know what's next. Feast or famine; is new-age abundance imagined or real? Trivial questions don't bother Penguin Four. It's the constant pecking from too many ping pong tournaments that's a pain in his neck. A vet diagnoses his condition as severe tendonitis. A layoff might cure him, but joblessness might be depressing. If he's lucky enough to find a mate while unemployed, domestic life could make him restless. Who knows? Penguin Four might make a good park pigeon, the kind you throw bread to, not out of compassion but for entertainment.

13

Wearing her purple Lycra a few weeks ago, Mia made me so absent-minded I became forgetful. She leaves a voicemail, asking if I want a brush that I left in her bedroom. Yes, I do. Just a coincidence, it's one of my favorites, a two-inch sash brush with one hundred percent china bristles. It's like an old friend. Mia and I get together and drink flavorless seltzer water known for its sparkling nothingness. I describe the paint brush's merits, its soft tapered bristles, and handle with a comfortable grip. I want to make up for ditched prom plans but can't dream up a way to segue into "Ten Ways to Repurpose a Paint Brush for Bedtime," a new game I've recently invented but not yet tested. Instead, Mia wants to talk about dream interpretation. She describes a dream that she asked a coordinator to interpret. He laughed and said, "We are not children. We don't do dreams."

"Why didn't you ask me?"

"It was about a death that involved you. I didn't want you upset."

I don't do dreams, but even if Mia's vision is upsetting, she needs my help. I should pay attention. Mia and I were camping on the rotunda's second level while she was dreaming the dream that needed interpretation. She wasn't dreaming about lust as I'd hoped. Instead, she died before me. The odds of that are fifty-fifty, even in dreams. My not showing up at her funeral was the strange part. In my defense, time with Mia makes me so hopeful that I forget to read the obituaries.

Of course, how would Mia know? Since she's alive and

well, it makes sense that I didn't get an invitation. Anything can happen when we sleep together. But I'm upset that she could camp with me and dream of death at the same time. This one is hard to interpret. What matters when death is but a dream?

Mia looks sad. She's silent for a few moments, looks up, and asks, "How could I feel lonely at my own funeral? You only need friends when you're alive."

Her question makes sense. Not to be flip, but I remind her: "If you die young, more friends attend than would show up if you die old. The odds are seventy-thirty. As long as I'm alive, I'll be there if you need me."

Mia smiles for the first time today. "Would you wear Lycra? And say 'You can't die, Mia. Not now, not this way. You're too young, too beautiful.'"

Real men don't wear Lycra to funerals. But Mia is young— and beautiful too. I should remember there is a question of equality. "What would you have done had you not found my brush?" I ask.

"What would you have done had you not known about my dream?" she replies.

That's a hard-to-answer question. I can't tell if we are in the moment or a previous dream. Either way, we're at a loss, sitting together, trying to create an afterlife prematurely. Our silence is a relief. We return to the Institute to check on Penguin Four.

The pigeon's taking a break from ping pong, lying on his back, his claws half-curled. He's not as conditioned as he was a few weeks ago. How do we know if the experiment is a success?

The Machine's counter reads four-point-eight billion. How will that move my numbers?

14

Mia is not here. I'm alone, almost lost in space, that place where loneliness and freedom coexist, the tension so intense it almost crowds out love. To avoid eating alone, I grab a quick sandwich, and join Institute workers who lounge in the communication commons, watching lunch-hour soap operas, the comic tragedies that sadden the lonely and amuse the spiritual. As good entertainment requires, the audience suspends disbelief. TV men and women in love need space. People lost in space looking for love need less space. No matter what they're looking for, it takes them forever to find it. It seems like everyone's searching for the creation.

Soaps make cynics laugh, even though nothing funny is going on. I should know. Things that happen on TV have happened to me. My demons are much like those of everyman. Our stories could feed soap opera scripts forever. If you're ever curious, watch a few. After all, if you ask what happened to me, I'll tell a dramatic story about dogs and ponies, horses dying, cows going lame.

For better or worse, TV soap advertising encourages the cleansing of the body as if it's a temple. Soap-sponsored romance sends a convoluted message that somehow implies spiritual cleansing. Watching a good soap makes it easier for oppressors and the oppressed to live with a clear conscience. Portraying love's villains and victims, actors and actresses show real-world players that they're not alone, bearing the pain of love-makes and heartbreaks. Married souls lost in love triangles condemn soap characters caught in pentangles. Real-life cheaters get to watch soap cheaters cheat on cheaters, situations that create a confusing cluster of mating patterns. I'm getting too vague.

I need to get to a meeting, but before I do, I should describe today's scene: Dillon, a local cop, and Natalie, a stay-at-home mom without children, find themselves burning in passion's lustful heat. Adding fuel to the fire, they lose themselves in an embrace. Natalie's shoulder straps are falling. Dillon is so close to her that he can't see her cleavage as well as we can at the Institute. Natalie's fancy McMansion happens to be within cell tower range. Dillon's old cell phone, a folding one with racing stripes, happens to ring whenever there's a routine, irritating, or urgent call. The phone alerts him to emergencies; it also serves as a primitive but effective birth control device. Today, it rings at the awkward psychological moment of a passionate kiss. Dillon pulls the phone from his jacket pocket, flips it open, and says, "Dillon here." His answer is not only existential, it's professional and honest enough to reflect well on the local police department.

This call must be urgent. Dillon folds his phone. "Damn, woman. You know I love you. There's been an accident with multiple casualties. They need me." He embraces Natalie. They kiss a long kiss that's a little too long when there's an emergency if anyone asks me.

After the passionate moment that seems like forever if you're watching, Dillon rushes to a car accident a convenient half-mile away. Alone, half-reclined on the couch panting, Natalie says in a surly voice, "Oh, God, help us." Her beautiful face morphs into one of disgust, then gradually, it fades out.

Where's the frustration coming from? Was it the emergency dispatcher breaking a magic moment's spell? Was it Dillon's sense of responsibility that drove him to take ownership of something that didn't belong to him? After all, he could have ignored his cell phone. He could always tell his boss he was out of range, or say he shut his phone off during lunch hour.

A beautiful woman smiling in a shower appears, her head soaking wet, shoulders sprinkled with enticing water droplets. She shampoos her black hair with SeaKelp, natural, and fresh from the ocean. A doctor in scrubs, wearing a stethoscope, explains how kelp fights dandruff and dryness naturally, without chemicals man- or woman-made. Is it the kelp, I wonder? Or is it the millions of gallons of jet fuel aircraft carriers used to dump into the sea, a wasteful way to save time while heading for the shipyard? At the time, petroleum dumping seemed quite natural to most humans. Supposedly the good Lord provided seawater to dilute jet fuel and grow kelp to soak it up. A natural shampoo, sea kelp continues its circle of life, finding its way back to the earth, rinsing, running down the woman's body, and finding its way down the shower drain.

An accident scene appears on the monitor. Victims must be in shock. Their injuries are severe enough to make onlookers feel sorry, but the victims are well enough to crawl into woods away from the road. A woman sits beside me, and asks "What's happening?"

She seems worried. It's better not to upset her with the truth. So I whisper, "Daphne lost her glasses, Dwayne's helping her look—Seems like Dwayne's always the one to help out."

The woman sitting next to me scowls. "Daphne never wore glasses."

"Maybe Dwayne's unaware that Daphne wears contacts. Could be she lost her sunglasses. Maybe I'm wrong. Could Daphne and Dwayne be looking for a valuable show pigeon?"

The woman stands up. I'm not sure, but I think I hear her mutter "asshole" under her breath. I hope her word choice is only a product of my imagination. Back when, if a mother caught her child saying a swear, she would wash the child's mouth with soap, often a brand advertised on TV.

The woman, who seems disgusted, finds a seat far from me, closer to the TV monitor, just in time for Dillon to arrive at the scene. If I didn't like her company, why do I feel abandoned?

In today's episode, a beautiful dream becomes a nightmare. Dwayne's heart palpitations, primarily in the left aorta, are beginning to spread to the right ventricle. Small-town selectmen diverted ambulance funds to pay for a rained-out firemen's festival. Triple-A can't start the old ambulance. EMTs hijack a double-decker livestock truck, built to carry pigs, but under the circumstances, a perfect vehicle to rush today's victims to the hospital. How much does Dwayne know beyond the intense beating of his sick but not yet broken heart? He should be careful. His wife is a nurse who happens to be working the day shift in the heart palpitation wing at Dwayne's destination, Highland Hospital. What a small world, she's the one who cut his hydraulic brake hose. Depending on the scriptwriters, Dwayne might develop a severe castration complex when he finds out. Who knows what happens next? Even those of us who keep up with the latest pigeon research can't predict how humans react in tough situations. The script must have been a challenge to write.

Dillon returns to Natalie's mansion, takes his cell phone out of his jacket pocket, and says, "Damn thing. Technology's birth control can't stop me." He throws the phone over the balcony and pushes Natalie onto the bed, his tough-love rough to prove he's a man, gentle enough to prove he's a lover.

The soap we're watching maintains strict standards of cleanliness and assurance that Dillon and Natalie will catch nothing more deadly than heartbreak in bed. Somehow, I feel cleansed, my mind wanders. Could I earn a living, standing beneath the rotunda's balcony, waiting for passionate moments to corrupt the Institute's sterile atmosphere? How often do lovers who are falling out of love throw engagement rings, shredded credit cards, a paintbrush, or an occasional sex toy? You could hope to catch the latest and greatest cell phone. But be aware. . .

Mia returns tomorrow. We'll go for a walk, miss the next episode. I'll never find out what happens next, probably. I wander over to the rotunda and stroll the inner outskirts, keeping the center at arm's length, the outskirts within reach. I sneak glances upward. The guard eyes me suspiciously. I pretend to look at pottery. Without my glasses, colorful designs blur. An olive, most likely from the cafeteria, comes from above and hits my nose. A coordinator walks away briskly. Is he mad that nature's sunlight has the power to trick a photo sensor? Does he resent that my lunch hour allows a little time to relax, and forget problems? How much do I know? He could be a careless slob who means no harm. At its least, it makes a teachable moment: Not all good comes from heaven.

One thing is for sure, as authors of *Fifty Places to Picnic*, Mia and I need to include consent forms, applications for goggles, glasses, and safety classes. Even the Director would admit harm's way attracts those who follow safe paths, a silly concept for an insurance company that relies on risk management. The Institute could be liable if harm trips and falls over someone who wanders its way.

A picnic without Mia is like turning on the Machine without paper. I think the word I want is "empty." Without Mia's zany touch, the creation seems lacking. Mia's sensuousness is not purely in the way she acts. It's her being that surrounds it.

Hurry back, Mia. Please?

15

Except for the adage, "No brain, no pain," we don't know much about bird-brained birds. Sometimes, it just takes a little common sense to do what we have to do. Mia and I load a ping pong ball with three BBs and sneak it into Penguin Four's experimental chamber, the ping pong court, the pigeon's last resort. Does the ignorant pigeon find words that curse us for increasing its workload? If he could talk, he'd be smart to say thank you. It might be hard to keep the ball rolling now, but Penguin Four can drink water more leisurely than before. Work hard, drink hard.

In less than a week, Penguin Four's tendonitis begins to subside. Things are looking up, especially when he takes a break, lies on his back, and wiggles his claw nails to relax. Mia stands over the small chamber, recording the pigeon's behavior on her clipboard. She marvels at the shadows of the pigeon's claws on one of the chamber's walls. She makes a note, and tips the clipboard for me to read: "Reflexive Fusion, nature's consequence unintended, serves the scientists right."

"Who knows," she says out loud. "Do pigeons prefer shade to fluorescent skies?"

"Mia, maybe Penguin Four's training you to hold the clipboard over him, like a canopy. Sounds crazy, but I think Penguin Four winked as if he had it made in the shade. Or maybe he caught a speck of grain dust in his eye, scientific proof that nutritious formulation's no protection against ocular irritation?"

"You never know. Maybe Penguin Four likes people watching."

16

Yesterday, Monday—I wasn't awake or excited enough to remember the Tech Coordinator was holding a meeting. He had planned to announce the master plan for the Machine's rebuild. Since I'm a key player, he postponed the meeting a day. Rumor has it he achieves whatever he believes. "Do you think he planned for me to be a day late," I ask Mia.

"I'd be afraid to ask. Always show up on schedule. If your boss planned on your being late, he'd invite you to come a day early."

Even though I'm late the following day, the Coordinator acts as if I'm on time. "How can a team of factory-trained techs resurrect the Machine without a master plan," he asks.

I try to respond in a tone that's as humble as it is professional. "No need for a master plan. Instead of employing a basic main circuit infusion, we bypass the primal inverter. Turn on the juice and trigger an electrical transfusion to the logic circuits. The Machine continues running. We replace its five hundred forty-two feed rollers and clutches that drive them."

I'm afraid to say this, but I do anyway. "A team of four can accomplish our goal—as long as the suits meet elsewhere, preferably at a location, remote, far away enough to prevent interruptions while we work."

"We have a lot at stake. Believe it or not, there is no elsewhere," says the Coordinator whose voice hints at anger. "I'm not going to miss this. The Director requires Institute officers to attend. Besides that, we're entitled. Remember: that paycheck that arrives on your desktop comes from The Institute."

"Bypassing the primal inverter sounds easy. Keep in mind the Machine keeps running during this process. The slightest hesitation while hooking a jumper wire for the electronic trans-fusion could morph million-dollar policies into penny stocks."

My hands shake almost uncontrollably, just thinking about all this. Humans are primitive beings; they cost a lot to main-tain. The primal inverter is a component much more sophisti-cated than its name implies. It can flip five thousand sheets of paper faster than a hundred humans can flip five hundred. Its simple inversions twist logic and rearrange truth more quickly than even the best industry directors.

The Director is well aware that a one-nanosecond voltage spike through the primal inverter could lobotomize the main auxiliary logic circuits. He'll keep his distance. If something goes wrong, there's less pain and responsibility that way. My mind keeps racing. In my mechanical way, I can almost identify with the Machine's scrambling electron cluster. I'm nervous about another missed meeting scheduled for Wednesday, a day when I can't use Monday as an excuse.

17

Fifty Places to Picnic progresses: Mia and I meet for lunch in the archives. We kiss a well-timed kiss that's appropriate for the Institute. Sitting directly across from each other, as far away as possible from sunlit windows, we kick off our shoes, relax, and read antiquated, hand-typed forms used fifty years before the Machine's existence. Snacking on gourmet food for thought produced from useless information grown right here makes transport from the West unnecessary.

I sneak a glance beneath the table. Mia reaches out, extending her left foot toward mine; my heart beats at a marathon pace. I can tell she's not joking. My mind slows down, the tranquility a rare but welcome break. My toes stretch and curl. Still wearing socks, I look to make sure there are no concealed cameras, until I ask myself, why look for something that's hidden? Mia's picnic riff:

"If you're on a strict diet but like picnics, the archives make sense. If food for thought sustains hunger for knowledge, repetitious nothingness of blank, obsolete insurance forms make a great soundless mantra. Pleasant dreams!"

Mia's artistic pursuits continue. Thousands of feet ride the Institute's elevator daily. To our knowledge, few ever kick off their shoes to watch their toes dance. For just a few moments,

Mia's feet are the creation—not for being what they are, but for being what they do. What if she starts a movement?

Mia enters Security's video chip, *Elevator People,* in the Reflexive Fusion Movement's film festival, avant-garde contests, and online magazines. Her hopes are humble compared to mine. My blurred, out-of-focus shoes could become famous for framing her feet. I always knew I had it in me. Mia complains about postage costs for contest submissions. "Just the price to mail a video chip or glossy toe photo costs more than you'd think." Multiply that by ten or more contest mailings at a time.

"Why not send your shadowy work on its way online?"

"Maybe I don't trust internet highways and byways as much as I should."

"You're right. Electrons go random sometimes."

Mia remains calm and goes postal.

18

Penguin Five, Penguin Four's half-brother, has trouble nudging the ping pong ball back to Penguin Four. It weighs over eight grams and usually takes two nudges to move it from one side of the imaginary net to the other. Penguin Four has little time to catch a drink, and can only relax a second or two before returning a serve, an arduous but rewarding task. No tendonitis now, his neck feathers bulge from muscular development beneath. I wonder what happens if we replace the heavyweight ping-pong ball with one that's the standard regulation, lightweight.

19

In preparation for the overhaul, I order parts, no easy deal when you consider the consequence of a mistake—getting the wrong part at the right time, the right one at the wrong time, anything can happen. Part numbers are sacred, a reality that makes matters worse. Experts discontinue old numbers, supersede new ones, create charts of superseded cross-references, and ultimately refer readers to recent bulletins, soon to become obsolete. A thirteen-digit number can evolve so often that it becomes the same part number that it was in the first place.

I feel sorry for part number specialists. Imagine holding an inverter infuser in your hand and asking, "Should I change the three to a five? Make it a seven? Seven sounds too arbitrary—what about two?" Sometimes, it costs more to create a new number than it does to redesign and remanufacture a part.

We need fifteen hundred and forty-seven mechanical parts and fourteen rebuilt circuit boards. The Machine orders its own as I key them in. Things go well if I read the diagrams right, don't blink my eyes, read the bulletins, and check stock levels. In the warehouse, barcode readers can't blink when reading pick slip numbers of parts pulled from the shelf. The forklift guy needs to pick up the right pallet and load it onto the right truck.

Like conscientious coordinators, Mia and I plan a Friday night outing. Not only do we need to check out another picnic site, but we also need numerical relief from the nothingness of numbers. "The lower rotunda," Mia says. "It's more contemporary without the pillars and pottery you see on the main level."

"It's circular. Those five halls head in and out, depending on whether you're coming or going. Only forty feet in diameter, it creates a wide-open feeling."

It's hard to describe a round carpet in a circular room as wall-to-wall. Is center to outskirts more appropriate? A white star weaved into the carpet's center; there's no furniture, but the room is otherwise tasteful. A built-in showcase displays a large plaque that commemorates something I can't remember. To be candid, I'd rather see an aquarium with fish looking outward.

Mia pictures a diorama of shadows.

All said and done, it's just a circular room that happens to be barren. Mia insists we try it, no matter how challenging. We've done the elevator, generator room, and warm grate outside in the cold. Tonight, it's on a Persian rug in a round room. I shouldn't argue, even with complicated logistics. Mia's so excited she writes a biblical-sounding blurb for *Fifty Places*.

"The lower rotunda, nothing but an inhospitable circle of darkness. Bring a round Persian rug forty feet in diameter. Color should complement tan walls. We also recommend a carpet pad. Not counting the photographer, count on five or six athletic, ambitious guests to carry carpet, ice bucket, wine, and hors d'oeuvres."

Believe it or not, we don't have five or six friends. We can't figure out who brings the Persian rug or takes it away. We pack the same old beach blanket, picnic basket, wine, and of course, our trusty camera and tripod that we always borrow from the Institute. Automatic shutter release does its work taking pictures until ten, leaving the rest of the evening for just the two of us. If my sense of identity is still intact, this plan includes me.

20

Cold, blustery winds must make tough flying for pigeons crazy enough to brave the elements. The winds are harsh enough to make me wish we were meeting our support techs at the bus station. It's too bad publicity for the mission began when they boarded a D.C. helicopter to fly into the Institute together, a show of force as a team. I hate being part of this minor-league spectacle, but I'm the resident tech. Like it or not, this gig is on me. Here we are, Mia and I, awaiting the techs' arrival in front of the hanger. Talk about teamwork!

We're waiting, shivering; what a time for conversation. Mia mentions that she met with a coordinator, not to discuss a dream, but to talk about something real that happened. Mia's beautiful, sometimes too idealistic. I hate to say she expects too much, hate to make her aware she's somewhat naïve. No worry. She must see through my somehow transparent façade. "If they don't deal with dreams or talk about reality, what do they do?"

"Make money," I reply.

I know that's not what Mia needs to know. She wanted to talk about her cousin who recently died and happened to carry a life policy, purchased from the Institute. Unfortunately, the coordinator can only discuss the probable deaths of people who are still alive. Mia should think things over before she talks about living. Talk gets to be expensive if you end up buying a policy. As far as she's concerned, death can wait.

Contrary to Institute rules, the three techs get off the helicopter as its rotor blades continue to spin. Strong gusts combine with rotor wind to create sporadic, chilling bursts, nature's celebration of the Director and his coordinators' strength combined.

What are the odds? Three consultants, surnamed Smith, Jones, and Jonson, fly in on the same helicopter at the same time, their names defying Institutional diversity. I've reviewed documents and photos to become efficiently acquainted.

The first technician Smith, 0849312548, hunches over as if to become less conspicuous. Probably just cold, he has nothing to hide. He looks like a good soldier, dedicated to a rigid command chain. He's loyal, commanding, a man who makes things right. Tech of the year four times, employee of the month forty-three times, and the largest quarterly bonus earner of all time, Smith lives in a modest mobile home on the southern side of the Potomac.

"Congratulations," he says. "A game well played. You'll forgive me for rooting for the opposition." He must be referring to our home team's recent Super Bowl win which was somewhat controversial. Thankfully he doesn't refer to our team with their new street name, the "Deflatriots." Aside from idle small talk about inconsequential victory and loss, Smith looks like a real winner in the game of life.

The next tech is the only woman on the team. She's New York beautiful and New York tough, not fragile. Jones, 8765841996, has earned the coveted Master Tech award three years in a row and has twice won runner-up. She and her husband live in a beautiful, one-room luxury efficiency condo located on the wrong side of the Potomac. She reaches out, saying, "You must be Sid? And you're Mia?"

"Welcome aboard, Jones." It might be my imagination, but even in unison, our voices sound somewhat hollow.

The third tech makes the most memorable first impression. Despite the wind chill, Jonson, 0273904078, saunters off the helicopter as if the weather's mild enough for a picnic. He looks pleasantly paradoxical, a happy-go-lucky sophisticate who never looks inward. His list of master tech awards and qualifications for incentives keeps his resume short. My impression: he seems like a loser in the real sense of the word. Beware. The mind's a workshop, not a storehouse cluttered with confusion. There could be a genius hiding behind his ignorant façade. If the genetic crapshoot awarded him with an overdose of common sense, is he a winner or a loser? At this point, we don't know where he lives. Leave it to Jonson. His first words are "Call me Jonson."

On the way to the cafeteria, we pass the idea room. As usual, it's vacant. I'm embarrassed that our guests might feel an aura of emptiness.

We sit around a round table, eating lunch. Although none of us attended the Technical Academy at the same time, we somehow manage to reminisce. Jonson is quiet; he seems bored, but we've opened a hot topic for Smith and Jones. Even though Mia is tapping her foot, there's no hint in her expression that she might remove her shoes. To create the impression that my hands won't shake when I perform the inverter bypass, I try to appear calm. Mia is writing notes:

"If you don't cook for large numbers, the cafeteria's perfect—it's open at breakfast, lunch, and supper. To avoid long lines, be punctual. A large selection of prepared foods serves heart attack-prone and health-conscious alike. No one needs reservations. Tell them Sid and Mia sent you."

The Tech Coordinator joins us to welcome our consultants. "What a coincidence," he says, "a Smith, Jones, and Jonson on the same mission. Human Resources should be thankful you're not all Smiths." He pauses. "You're among our nation's most sophisticated techs. Remember why you're here. The Machine's resurrection is a formidable challenge. Its success will enhance paper production and proliferate information. You'll inspire Institute employees to strive for success." He hands out business cards and contact information out of date, a result of a recent paradigm shift that designates higher phone numbers to coordinators. He encourages the three consultants to call or text, should they need anything. He shakes hands with each tech, and departs to attend a lunch meeting to discuss *Opportunitation: Get What You Want, Without Looking Like an Opportunitator.*

I can only speak for myself, but there's an awkward silence as if we're all embarrassed that we weren't impressed. Before I can mention that "resurrection" is code for "restoration," Jonson asks, "Who the hell was he?"

If he wants to know who the hell he was, his name on the business card is still correct. But I'm glad Jonson asked. It turns out he is the same Jonson who maintained the Institute's generator. He must be guest-starring in his own nightmare, trying to figure out who looks familiar, who's old, who's new, who is blue, and most importantly, who approved his prior layoff.

21

The Institute's warehouse is a vast information storage facility loaded with boxes and boxes of paper on rows and rows of shelves that reach the steel-trussed roof. InfoTech center stacked with servers and computers, ceiling-high, side by side, back-to-back, aisles, and aisles. Acres and acres of storage space make it surprising there's no place open enough to spread out schematics, the Machine's circuit diagrams, its electronic roadmaps. We move from the warehouse to the lower rotunda, its forty-foot expanse, the only area large enough to spread out large electrical schematics. Spreading out the foldouts on the ground floor should only divert low-level foot traffic, mostly keyboard jockeys.

Smith says, "Perfect," a perfect way to express approval.

Jones lives in a wonderland of amazement. She pirouettes. "This room, so round, contemporary, and bright, makes me feel appreciated."

Jonson, the most outspoken of the three techs, often seems irritated with strategic thinking, small talk, or ritual, which accomplishes little or nothing. Standing in the center, he pivots slowly, taking it all in, making every word count. "A circular room's worthless for storage. Good enough for watching people come and go, but barely adequate for tracing electrical circuits."

"Jonson must be holding some grudge. Does he need some serious therapy?" Mia whispers.

I can only defend him. "Maybe he's a genius who sees reality through a misty fog. Maybe he's a subversive at war with the suits."

The Machine resides in a room large enough for three techs to work at a time. Plate glass windows in the hall allow front office coordinators to stop by and watch us, the same way we go to the lab to check out Penguin Four working in his cozy test chamber. Jonson circles the Machine, sizing it up. He removes the primal inverter's rear cover, and peers into a maze of wire bundles and hardware, his nose an inch away from the main drive gear. I hope he knows what he's doing.

Rarely needed for overhauls these days, meters and oscilloscopes face the outer perimeter, their monitors displaying electronic oceans of pulses and waves. Jonson insists the displays need to have a dramatic impact on the Director. "If we look good, we get a bonus. If we don't, they PIP us with another Professional Improvement Plan."

I add two random wave generators and an antique meter with a round dial face. Given Jonson's appraisal, a visual barrage should earn enough extra cash and recognition to last a week.

We've eaten lunch with our new technical friends, two days in a row. Getting to know each other isn't easy. No surprise that Smith says he likes watching pro football on TV. Mrs. Jones shops at the mall to avoid watching college football with her husband, Mr. Jones. Jonson plays touch football on Thanksgiving, only if there's snow on the ground. Says he'll keep it up until his knees give out. Mia explains how Reflexive Fusion allows the creation of in-the-moment shadow art of her moving toes. Smith and Jonson might as well think she's talking about a new primal inverter attachment. As if to avoid looking clueless, they drop the subject.

Now that I'm less shy, I converse more comfortably and naturally. I'd like to talk about canoes. Instead, I bring up pigeon farming, a neutral but exciting topic that should offend no one. Mia seems interested, not so much in the subject but in my interest. Smith and Jones talk about the mortality rate of World War I carrier pigeons. To pay his way through the Technical Academy, Jonson says he cared for a flock of pigeon ranch pigeons. It sounds like something you can't make up.

"What a small world," Mia says. "Speaking of pigeons, Penguin Five got hurt badly, playing one of those lab-sponsored ping pong tournaments with Penguin Four. Poor thing, you should see him. The right side of his head's swollen, his eye almost shut, and his beak's distorted. I made sure no one was watching before checking the ball. Someone replaced the weighted ball with a regulation one."

"That's all it would take. Penguin Four must have given the usual strong nudge needed to move that heavier ball, inadvertently launching an airborne missile."

"Must be," Mia says. "Penguin Five refuses to play now."

"Poor sport, or bird that makes poor choices, motives don't matter. Avoiding mandatory playtime is not the best option for a lab pigeon that has no clue about consequences for Institutional pigeons who can't, won't, or don't play well with others."

Memories of pigeon ranching must influence Jonson's thinking. For once, he seems more engaged when he speaks. "I can't over stress the importance of food, water, sanitation, and of course, adequate ventilation," he says. "And you should never forget safety."

Mia and I couldn't be more articulate when writing *Fifty Places*. For humans as well as lab pigeons, something else might be missing, but I'm not sure what that something is. As usual, the creation has to wait, even though it deserves higher priority.

22

Smith complains so much he makes you feel like a boss if you're crazy enough to listen. "I can't afford to seal my mobile home roof," he says. "There aren't enough pans to catch rainwater that drips into my living room, bedroom, and kitchen."

It's hard to tell if the problem solver Jonson is practical or sarcastic. He suggests, "Drill drain holes in the floor, directly below each roof leak. Fabricate pottery jugs instead of buying more pans. Better yet, put solar panels on your roof. Cash in on the electricity savings; collect the water for irrigation and plant a garden."

"Too much work," Smith says. It looks like he would rather complain than listen and consider new ideas.

Unlike Smith, Jones has an attitude more positive. "My husband and I pool our earnings. We make enough to cover our condo fee and let the association worry about roof leaks. We're living proof. Award-winning winners can sample the fruits of success, without risking addiction, vegetation, or sloth."

Leave it to the funny one, Jonson. "Earn more, spend more. I built a tiny house on wheels, less than a hundred-fifty square feet, less than the size of my garden. Whenever I get bored, I hitch my car up to my half-wide, post-prefab house. I can drive away to find a new home for my old home. The only disadvantage, every time I move, I end up leaving my tomato plants behind. If there's enough time left in the growing season, I can start a new garden. I'm still looking for the ideal human self-storage device. I think prefab capsules suspended from warehouse ceilings might outdo a tiny half-wide post-fab."

Our expense account doesn't allow us to wine and dine with our three consultants. There's no time for long, ambitious excursions, in or outdoors. As things are, Mia and I are missing deadlines for *Fifty Places*. A compromise with reality, we plan a short getaway, down the south tunnel, further than the generators and steam plants, to search for pottery in the Institute's depths. Without having to dig, we'll uncover and rediscover pottery discarded by past directors who replaced old with new. A morale builder, our picnic should promote the spirit of teamwork, challenge, and adventure. I'm excited already.

It remains to be seen whether the Institute buys the recognition dinner Jonson recently predicted. That doesn't stop us from using our expense account to buy raisins, dates, apricots, and pomegranates. Since our picnic involves team building, we also buy five sets of khaki shorts, tan shirts, and safari hats at the outdoor adventure store, located indoors at the only local mall not yet virtual.

It looks like we're going on a real safari. Everyone wants to help. Jones wears an Egyptian ankle bracelet. Barefoot, Mia sports bells on her toes, attractive though somewhat annoying apparel. It could be hard to keep our whereabouts secret. Smith brings a moisture analyzer to see if the pottery was kiln-dried. Jones carries a new, used copy of *Pottery, Now and Then*, a hardcover acquired at a library going-out-of-business sale. Jonson plays the song of a hip nomad *Ahab the Arab* on the oboe he found at a thrift shop that donates proceeds to the homeless. The song's lyrics might sound insensitive these days; it must have been far more harmless and laughable back when. No matter what, the oboe creates an exotic ambiance as we walk southward. Mia's toe bells jingle with the music. Jones almost dances on her toes as she walks. We've escaped the pressures of the Institute, taking the tunnel less traveled. Why did we not think of this sooner?

Some pottery is neatly stacked, most piled carelessly, and a few pieces are broken. Next time, we'll have to bring glue. I take a jug from the pile and hand it to Smith who takes a moisture reading. He passes to Jones who classifies it, referring to her *Pottery, Now and Then* book. She hands it over to Jonson, who organizes the jugs in an empty corner, more carefully than I'd expect. Once in a while, I pull the wrong jug from the pile. Sometimes pottery tumbles and crashes. It's up to me to provide a little reassurance. "We're not here to have fun. We're here to perform a public service. If the suits don't like it, they can do it themselves."

Mia stubs her toe on a blanket and stumbles into more pottery. Another jug falls and shatters; bird bones scatter outward on the concrete floor. Jonson thinks they're pigeon bones. I don't know enough to agree or disagree. Assuming the bones are the remains of pigeons from the lab, previous coordinators must have consigned them to pottery jugs, either out of respect or necessity to conceal the truth. For sure, they wouldn't have used the pottery for pet carriers.

Did they worship carrier pigeons? Sit in the penthouse, shoot squabs for sport? Are these the remains of pigeons victimized by research? No one else seems concerned, not even Mia, who looks to be in denial. She pulls an apricot from the picnic basket and lies down on the blanket again. She stretches her toes, basks in the fluorescence, ignoring us, handwriting notes for *Fifty Places,* dancing her toes to their own bell music.

Inspired, Mia outlines comments on our recent dig:

"Pray for pigeons alive no longer; hold a life celebration; take a camera. Go out and picnic. If you can't afford raisins, grapes, apricots, and pomegranates, find a sponsor. To be prudent is prudish and sometimes sublime."

23

During the Machine's resurrection, our schedule won't allow rest, relaxation, picnics, or time to dream about the creation. We plan staggered shifts, always three of us working at a time. Parts arrive, only two hundred and twenty-three of them were recently superseded by new numbers. Not that it's Mia's responsibility to keep us from throwing a monkey wrench into the works; she gives me a checklist to make sure we leave nothing behind. Everyone knows that a stray tool can strip a gear, blind a photo sensor, short-circuit intelligence, or spark electronic revolt.

The overhaul should be routine for techs of our caliber. Running in bypass mode slows the Machine noticeably. But it's the only way to reroute paper paths long enough to replace five hundred forty-two new rollers and clutches. After testing, we'll bring the Machine up to full speed so that we can devote attention to the primal inverter.

I need to admit, that any job that seems endless gets monotonous, especially when I'm in my office monitoring the Machine. When I get tired of sitting, I take a break and visit the three techs. Jones and Jonson must be coping with boredom by playing an impractical joke on Smith—it's a surprise they think Smith has never heard of it. Jones confides in Jonson, her whisper loud enough for all of us to hear. "I have another migraine," she says, "just a reaction to a metal plate in my head. It goes back to a car accident with my former boyfriend Jones, now my wonderful husband. When we met, my name was already Jones. Believe it or not, we're not cousins."

Jonson continues working as if he's unconcerned. Joke or not, it's no surprise that embedded metal should and would cause a headache occasionally.

Smith stops working, and stares upward at the ceiling, as if afraid to look at Jones eye to eye as if searching for words sincere. "You'd never know—you seem so normal in an above-average way."

I don't interrupt Smith to explain that "normal" is a word out of fashion. Instead, he should use "typical." To discuss above-average normality, he should try using "typicality."

Later, when she thinks no one's looking, Jones glues a magnet to her forehead. She scowls, complains about chills and cold flashes, touches the magnet as if she's just noticed it, and blames Jonson for attaching it.

Smith turns away, hiding a grin as if he sees the humor and he's too embarrassed to enjoy a cruel joke. Jonson laughs hysterically, thinking Smith's fooled. Smith starts laughing, not at Jones and her magnet, but at Jonson, who can't stop laughing like an idiot.

Before the glue dries completely, Jones removes the magnet from her forehead and assures Smith, "Don't worry, I'm OK. On better days, you probably notice my magnetic personality. During lovemaking, my husband, Mr. Jones, moves the magnet closer to my ear. The move arouses and intensifies my climactic intensity."

Jonson is still laughing uncontrollably. Smith regains his composure and congratulates Jones for facing her problems head-on.

The trick is too tricky for me. Did Jones's glue hold a joke together? Or did it hide a legitimate disability? If the plate's real, the trick is on Jonson. If the plate's fictitious, it's on Smith. Fair question, is Smith pretending the joke's on him to protect Jonson from looking like a fool? Are Jones and Jonson making fun of making fun? It doesn't matter. I'm not even sure if stainless steel or titanium plates are magnetic. Maybe the joke's on me.

Without a stool pigeon, there's no monkey. Ethical issues require that I report Jones's antics. Good judgment requires that I don't; if the consultants confuse me, they might confuse

Security. If there's no metal plate, another joke is on me for reporting. And what happens to the Machine if our three consultants lose their jobs, a threat that could undermine our mission? Without laughter, there's no joke. Without laughter, there's nothing left but paranoia's teachable moments. If this is a cruel joke, the victim is hard to identify.

Jonson confesses. "The joke was unintended, it just happened. At least we forced the stuffy sterility out of this place, made reality more real."

Jones takes her first break. I resume monitoring all systems while Smith and Jonson begin the resurrection. The Machine's meter reads almost eight and a half billion. Despite record-breaking document production, the tasteless fruit of our hard labor, my performance number drops to two-point-eight. Tough luck means tough it out. I settle back in my chair and put on a black Stetson discarded by a former director now a bankrupt pigeon rancher. I munch on dried beef and sip dark muddy coffee. Whenever Smith's or Jonson's hands or tools interrupt photo-electric paths, sensor signals blip on the monitor.

To investigate a rumor that the Institute sacrifices a pigeon every Thanksgiving, I'm reading a somewhat obscure but credible book that I lifted from the archives. *The Great Pigeon Sacrifice* describes an ancient rite: to nudge the gods, members of royalty sacrificed a pigeon in return for power, wealth, and sexual prowess. At first glance, offering up a pigeon to gain a few of life's benefits looks like a fair trade. Taking a pigeon's point of view, I wonder why front office suits think they're so civilized.

A strobe flashes. I look up; Mia's holding a camera. Must be she thinks she just captured another picture to go with the next chapter of *Fifty Places:*

"A picnic's an attitude, not a place. Find an obscure spot, and put on a cowboy hat. Eat dried beef. If life hands you lemons make lemonade. If life hands you mud, make cowboy coffee and sing 'Home on the Range."

24

During my first eight-hour break from the resurrection, I found out that coordinators scheduled two concurrent meetings on the virtual calendar, one on prioritizing, and one on procrastination. I had planned to attend the first half of one and the second half of the other. To avoid hard feelings, I didn't go to either one.

While skipping meetings, I continue reading *The Great Pigeon Sacrifice*, the only book that provides answers to questions only evident at the Institute. Why name a pigeon, "Penguin Four?" It turns out the name's no joke. The book's anonymous author used the word "penguin" as if it were an old English word synonymous with "pigeon." Traveling by ship was risky. Luxury cruises to the Antarctic were out of the question. The place was not yet on the map; no one had ever seen or heard of penguins. No one needed two different words to describe one northern hemisphere bird. Who knows if Old English favored "penguin" over "pigeon." It doesn't matter. Calling a "pigeon" "penguin" might make Institute bird life confusing but stop and think: history's choice of bird words makes as much sense as the names of our three consultants, "Smith," "Jones," and "Jonson."

Why sacrifice pigeons? Why not? In the days of old, rich kings needed quick communication when knights were bold. Homing pigeons that could carry notes faster than the fastest runner or racehorse were the best options available. Imagine an economy that's booming. You're royalty, as powerful as a director, but you're not keeping abreast of the times. You want to buy into the Crusades. Timing's always perfect when prices are right. But you have no quick and easy way to let the king who lives down the road know you're ready to buy in. You're not keeping pigeons that belong to the king down the road. He does not keep any of yours since you don't have any. No airmail this month. You're stuck with the Pony Express unless you deliver the mail yourself.

A more optimistic scenario: You're a medieval king or queen who keeps up with ornithological technology. You and the neighboring king send pigeons back and forth. Your riches multiply, not that that always makes life better. Even members of royalty have a bad week now and then. If your favorite horse dies, you'd better choose the perfect gift for the gods, a nudge to get them to lighten up. You've already lost your best horse. The second-best horse might insult the omnipotent. Torching a stone castle makes a sorry excuse for a sacrificial fire. Even with the best intentions, spousal sacrifice causes separation anxiety, sadness, imprisonment, and possibly death.

A good king or queen never gives up, especially when the solution's obvious. A pigeon makes a beautiful gift. Thoughtful and inexpensive, it doesn't put the gods on the spot, obligating them to do the right thing, no matter what the right thing happens to be. If you sacrifice a pigeon, you have two choices. Kill one of your own that you keep at your castle to teach it where home is. Or sacrifice one that belongs to the king down the road but lives at your place, waiting to fly a message home where its heart is.

I'm still sitting in my office, by the way, watching Smith monitor the Machine. Jonson and Jones are adjusting the thirty-six primary clutches in the primal inverter's backup unit. I don't much like using my cell phone. If we were together in the same room, I'd say, "Keep up the good work!"

The ceremony leading up to the pigeon sacrifice is beautiful. Imagine you're sitting at an oak slab table, eating spareribs of venison and wild grapes, not the wimpy seedless kind. A beautiful woman, with long brown hair, wears pre-Lycra tights and plays exotic music on a wooden flute for the Penguin Dance, a ritual that usually lasts for hours, but takes days on occasion. How tiring would that gig have been for a non-union flute player? A well-trained pigeon balances on one leg while lifting and curling the claw of the other; it pirouettes, flapping its wings slowly to maintain equilibrium. In the time it takes a smart pigeon to dance a perfect dance that ends with a smooth pirouette, the average king can eat a bunch of grapes, spit the seeds, and devour two ribs of venison.

Dogs stay close by because they're loyal dogs with a realistic expectation that someone will throw a bone, usually a meatless rib. If the dogs are patient, they might get to share a sacrificed pigeon. Sooner or later, the pigeon gets dizzy from too many pirouettes and falls from the table onto the stone floor. Dogs transfer it to the afterward and eat the remains, thinking it's a new brand of venison. Scattered feathers are the only evidence of the pigeon's struggle in a trial more critical than existential. Light, almost imperceptible drafts drift feathers slowly into stone castle crevices and corners. Occasionally, a few random feathers escape through an open window.

Inept pigeons that couldn't do a simple spin lived longer. Visionary pigeons that sensed their impending demise didn't spin and lived longer. In time, tinkers developed more efficient ways to make pigeons dizzy. The sacrificial pigeon danced on a rotating pottery wheel, powered by a foot pedal, powered by the flute player. Fewer flute players, fewer chefs to cook the venison, smaller vineyards to grow the grapes—all made possible by a pottery wheel wisely adapted to alter the pigeon's state of consciousness, making it dizzy enough for a quicker demise. The only unintended consequence of efficiency: quicker sacrifices meant fewer job opportunities, and more dog pounds. Out of necessity, more pigeons came in from the cold and became lab pigeons, unwitting participants in leisure time studies.

I've never seen Penguin Four pirouette. In the Institute's lab, trained muscles must favor ping pong over dance. Thank God or whoever's responsible. Thank Research if you must. From now on, I'll get nervous if Penguin Four stands on one leg, even if he's just showing off.

25

To prevent too many people from congregating in one place, guests can only attend the Machine's resurrection by special invitation. It's not a problem for keyboard jockeys. Most believe going for it is more important than arriving. No surprise, Institute coordinators think arrival is more important than the journey. We still wish the suits would hold a daylong meeting elsewhere. Instead, they stand at observation windows, waiting and watching to watch me. Smart ones, better said, aggressive ones, arrived hours early for windows that allow direct views of the inverter. To record my hands remaining steady during today's crucial bypass, Mia and I mount our camera on the tripod and set the automatic shutter release.

The resurrection is more complicated than most realize. Bear with me as I try to explain. Primal inverters have always printed text on a page's flip side before printing side one. Technology's advance makes these moves more poetic than practical. Marketing people encourage engineers to add new features and integrate electronic functions with mechanical. Today, the name "inverter" inadvertently serves another purpose. Have you ever discovered something you said isn't so? Did you lie, or did reality reverse itself? Such is the need for new-age inverters. If the Director misspeaks, inverter logic distorts or substantiates truth, the Machine prints out new documents to prove that which was not, now is. It's a logic that can't always tell misspeaking from wishful thinking.

Two inverters can't boost the Machine's power, but here's the magic. A double flip flop creates output that's identical to input—much like a car with two transmissions. If a driver selects reverse on each gearbox, reverse reverses, making it move forward. With only one inverter, we can't make a routine detour. During the bypass, we need to block the inversion process and save information to reroute later.

If this is confusing, stay with me. We need to trigger a negative inversion in the second primary feedback circuit—a thirty-millisecond reverse bias voltage doubles. Generated positive inflection triggers electronic infusion. Such a complicated process goes beyond the scope of my humble account of professional life at the Institute.

The Research Coordinator arrives, nervous, impatient as if he won't get the attention that he wants but doesn't deserve. Though the room is chilly, his forehead beads with sweat, and he sniffles like he can't tell a lie without dripping postnasal drip. He steps up to the keyboard to key in a last-minute inversion. I don't know what my problem is, but I can't help but hope the bypass scrambles his request into the afterward.

I'm too busy to see the result of the Coordinator's inversion. Smith, Jones, Jonson, and I need to make a last-minute decision. "Why not draw straws to see who performs the actual bypass," Smith asks. "It's only fair."

"Why not let me be the first woman to perform the bypass in public," Jones wants to know. To her credit, she's not pushy.

Jonson is solemn today as if he's trying to act professionally. "Choose a favorite, choose by gender," he says. "The luck of the draw pulling straws. Fair play involves choosing someone who's not a winner. What about me?"

All said and done, the standard convention reserves this honor for the resident tech. The Institute depends on me. Priest-like, I prep my hands with rubbing alcohol to make my skin electrolytically correct. Even if this belief is superstitious, the prep puts on a good show for spectators. I don't ask for assistance.

Nevertheless, Jones wipes my hands with sterile disposable towels, even though alcohol evaporates without intervention. I step up to the Machine. Despite rubbing alcohol's coolness, my palms sweat; my mind keeps moving in a five-four time signature, spinning its wheels in the mire of nervous energy.

My ears seem more sensitive than usual. An out-of-tune oscillator signals it's time for the bypass. The whir of feed tires pulling paper into the paper pusher sounds amplified. Jones and Jonson stand behind me, backups should I become incapacitated or incompetent. I hope that's not what they're expecting. Everyone's watching. My reputation is on the line. Too late for Jones, Smith, or Jonson to take over, I wish I'd chosen a faster shutter speed that could hide the high-frequency tremors in my hands. Monitoring the Machine's monitor, Jones shifts the inverter to full phase. At least the sour sounds of the oscillator alarm keep me on my toes—the camera strobe flashes.

I probe connector Five B, take a meter read, and flip a switch to create a thirty-millisecond bias. I connect a jumper wire to connector Four D; with the other end, probe the main connector. As casually as possible, I pull the jumper wire, accidentally loosening connector Four D, an in-the-moment lapse of judgment, a mistake, Reflexive Fusion at its worst. The camera strobe flashes. I push the main connector, making sure it's tight, hoping a slow arc or sudden spark doesn't scramble the Machine's questionable logic or destroy a circuit board. I turn to face the applause of the suits. Lucky for me, Smith, Jones, and Jonson applaud too. If they didn't clap, the coordinators might think I made a mistake—the oscillator alarm's gone silent. The Machine's humming motors and oscillating buzzers and bells provide reassuring comfort. The camera strobe flashes once again.

Despite rules that prohibit intimate contact, Mia hugs me.

In my mind, today was no picnic. But reading Mia's notes, I find a new perspective.

"What a day! What a heroic performance! Here at the Institute, we're proud. And rightfully so! Imagine a world, where one director and forty-two coordinators eat donuts, drink coffee, watching Sid perform a bypass. Be advised. When Sid's on the job, there's standing room only."

26

An archaic policy prohibits the Institute from paying for raisins and apples purchased for our recent pottery search. Exotic fruits—dates and pomegranates—are covered. We're still waiting for a decision on apricots. At least the Tech Department holds a banquet in the private dining hall, honoring our three consultants. Jonson was right; the Institute pays for the meal. I'm encouraged. In this economy, you can't be too careful. Instead of expensive steak or cheap peanut butter, we get tuna fish sandwiched in wheat bread, without enough mayonnaise. Mia's not surprised or disappointed—she's been here at the Institute for years. I hope Smith, Jones, and Jonson are pleased.

Each tech gets a beautifully veneered birchbark plaque, engraved with each name spelled correctly. I warn Smith and Jones not to hang these priceless fire hazards over a campfire or fireplace, should they ever have the chance. No need to inform Jonson. As soon as he's out of the Coordinator's sight, he drops his in the nearest trash can. Inscribed on each plaque including the one trashed:

"A Salute from the Institute. To Smith, Jones, and Jonson. Team Players, Achievers of Technological Excellence"

Inscriptions are so tasteful without tech numbers. I wonder who thought of eliminating them. I get a birch-framed, black-and-white glossy photo taken with our camera. I'm grasping the main harness. Blurred images of the coordinators appear in the background, clueless but pleased as if things are going as planned. Smith, Jones, and Jonson are the only ones who know that I fumbled, pulling the wrong connector. They also know Jonson's idea about living human storage devices has inspired me to save for a capsule, small enough to fit in my garret apartment. No one wants me to lose my job. The three techs follow the team's unwritten code, the elementary rule of street crime graduates, school kids, and corporate players alike. If anyone asks, don't tell. I've reconciled my mistake with the idea that an unconscious but powerful drive drives me: admire the power and glory. My fingers were moments away from lobotomizing the Machine, yet light years away from doing anything so foolish, a conflicting truth that evades logical explanation. What's done is done. Maybe I'll learn from my mistake. In my funny way, I fused the moment with movement.

A high school color guard stands on the helipad at attention, saluting the guest techs' departure. Jonson's not leaving empty-handed. Clutching his Harley Davidson manual, he glances at the color guard and mutters under his breath, "Horse pucky!"

Even though they're not in uniform, Smith and Jones return the salute, their display of etiquette a down payment for their next technical award.

The Machine runs for two days, with only five isolated instances of phantom documents, data from nowhere—output without input. I've said it already; there's nothing wrong with too much information. You can sift through excess but can't sift through a deficit.

Research Coordinator discovers a document that appears random, something that almost resembles a true or false question: "RUDDERLESS DANISH CRUISE SHIPS DRIFT THE SHORES OF DENMARK."

"Call it a throwaway," I tell him. If I admit the Machine lost or found new data during the inversion, I could lose the picture of my steady hands framed in birch bark. The Director demands an explanation. I use an old meter to trace the Machine's circuitry, not so much to solve the problem but

87

to buy time to dream up a better answer. After all, I've heard the Coordinator claim that failure creates opportunity.

Mia sifts through the phantom output, separating intelligence, true from false. She pigeonholes useless information, those tireless documents that fall into the middle, the maybes and maybe nots. Mia can't understand why Penguin Four's pedigree arrived in the same batch. At least it proves that the name "Penguin" runs in the family. The pigeon comes from a proud tradition of Penguins without any apparent identity crisis. As much as we'd like to withhold these developments, it violates ethical guidelines to do so. Mia hands them over to Research.

The stress of business as usual, along with all the surprises, takes its toll. We'd rather go on a retreat than picnic instead. But *Fifty Places* needs another outdoor picnic. Global warming, act of God, meteorological reflection with fusion, there's a break in the weather. We escape to the sunny esplanade, the cobblestone park between the Institute and the river. It's my turn to bring food. Mia insists I shouldn't surprise her. After our tuna fish lunch at the ceremony, I feel like going all out. I buy hot dogs (eighty percent beef), beer (five percent alcohol), and birdseed (fourteen percent sunflower). We sit on a park bench, eat hot dogs, drink beer, and feed pigeons, impinging on their freedom with the temptation of birdseed.

By the way, Mia thinks that I think too much, a rather profound thought in itself when you think about it.

We attract over fifty pigeons, an unusually messy flock that makes indiscriminate deposits of whitish droppings on cobblestones. Mia doesn't notice. She removes a shoe, holds birdseed between her toes, and extends her leg straight out.

A pigeon approaches.

Sensing beauty in the fusion of human nature and ornithology, I snap a picture.

A guard, a former airport security officer, orders us to move on and threatens to make us pay for stone cleaning.

"We're not criminals," Mia says. "I'm a Reflexive Fusion Artist. At the very least, you can let me put my shoe back on. Would you want the Director to look out his window and see me limping back to the Institute? Respect my dignity."

"Your dignity looks hard to maintain already," the guard says.

He has a point. We retreat, our bag of birdseed leaking. At least a hundred pigeons gather along a trail of seed that follows the long sidewalk, from the esplanade to the Institute. As the pigeons clean the birdseed, they drop more whitish deposits on cobblestones.

The guard must have seen enough. He pulls out a cell phone and turns his back. Hard to tell who he's calling.

What an afternoon. What a joy it is teasing wild park pigeons with birdseed. I wonder if our kindness enables them to continue overpopulating the planet—I keep my thoughts from Mia.

27

Penguin Four's cage is more cramped than a pigeon's ping pong court. Though resting comfortably, the pigeon looks bored as if he's asking himself, what's next? If birds could understand English, he wouldn't believe it if I told him. No matter how certain the scheduled pigeon sacrifice is, certainty creates more questions. No dogs among us, who performs the actual sacrifice? Does Penguin Four need to be rescued?

Even if you know everything about work and leisure, how do you dispose of a burned-out lab pigeon that made this knowledge possible? One coordinator wants the pigeon set free in a nearby park after his mission is accomplished. Another nominates Penguin Four to become the main ingredient for a homeless family's Thanksgiving stew, a gift that might seem too humble. A more logical point of view: if the impoverished make poor choices and bring hunger upon themselves, they deserve it. The coordinators' pleasant sense of superiority seems drug-induced and possibly addictive. There are few side effects otherwise, the only noticeable one, is a crippling philosophy that prevents them from wondering, who paved the way for Penguin Four's plight?

Coordinators agree the homeless deserve free potatoes; no one deserves pigeon meat unless they shoot their own. "Give them a pigeon; they eat for a day. Teach them to shoot BBs; they eat for a lifetime." While solving the dietary requirements of the homeless, they unwittingly spin out a commentary that vindicates Penguin Four's sacrifice. "He's not a burned-out lab pigeon, ready for cost-effective retirement. He's the best, our favorite, most deserving to be sacrificed."

When Mia hears the news, she mutters "Scumbags" as if the Institute employs people who belong on *America's Most Wanted*, a TV show that showcases the lives of criminals, too desperate and unworthy of joining respected gangs, too disorganized to find a niche in organized crime.

Random, mythical, imagined, or real, the Machine continues to produce phantom documents, profound but conflicting: AN UNEXAMINED LIFE'S NOT WORTH LIVING. AN UNLIVED LIFE'S NOT WORTH EXAMINING. If no information has been lost, there's no need to question intelligence posing as wisdom. Forget about the Machine's textbook triteness. Instead, focus on the mission, the pigeon sacrifice.

At least the Tech Coordinator makes time to schedule my performance review, two weeks overdue. "I have to apologize," he says. "You're commended on your execution, performing the Machine's resurrection. Jamming seems to have disappeared completely. But we're perplexed by the Machine's random output of excess information. An unexamined life, rudderless Danish ships? What's that all about? And I have to ask; how do you think you're doing?"

"Not to brag, but I work well independently and read part numbers well."

My stellar performance convinced him I should take on a new confidential project. I welcome added responsibility but wonder if an increased workload is an honor or a burden. My suspicion's well-founded; this new assignment requires that I convert a pottery wheel into a turntable, and mount it on a pedestal. While describing the project, he slips and calls it a "Lazy Penguin."

"Does it have anything to do with Penguin Four's departure," I ask.

"What do you mean by 'departure'?"

"Sacrifice."

Eyebrows raised, the Tech Coordinator looks surprised as if my question supports his ongoing suspicion that I know too much. "You know I can't reveal sensitive material without consulting the Director," he says.

I remind him, "I work well independently and read part

numbers well. My long list of technical achievements should make me worthy of your trust."

Satisfied, he explains. "The Institute adapted the pigeon sacrifice to suit its purposes. Don't ask me what they're thinking. If we profit on payouts committed to survivors of the dead, there might be ways to profit on policyholders as long as they survive."

At the risk of sounding like a know-it-all, I try to explain. "The Institute sacrifices only one pigeon, but kills two or three birds with one stone, so to speak. It honors a burned-out lab pigeon most worthy of sacrifice, reveals its financial commitment to survivors of the dead, and its willingness to exploit the prospect of death among the living. It promises a fair tradeoff between insurance payouts, peace, and contentment. News of the sacrifice is not only entertaining; it hypes things to come."

The Coordinator stares a blank stare, a gesture used by charm school graduates to project disbelief. What more can I say?

"How does the pigeon get transferred to the afterward?" I ask.

At first, the Coordinator thought that I said "afterworld" instead of "afterward." He speaks in a condescending voice, a poor strategy when talking to a technician. "We are not monsters. Here at the Institute, retired lab pigeons die, sacrificial ones don't. A sacrificial pigeon rides the turntable, gets dizzy, loses its balance, and falls on a padded micro-switch to document its end on the Machine: 'Authorization of Death,' 'Release to the Afterward,' 'Paradoxical Certificate of Non-existence.' Later, hopefully, much later, the pigeon dies of natural causes."

"Is going for death more important than arriving? Is that what your sacrifice is all about?" I ask.

"I can't think about those questions. I have a family to support."

Mia rescues me from my discontent and suggests we take corporate's advice to boost our morale with another HR-sponsored picnic. We find a quiet remote office, empty for renovation, walls off-white, plush carpet dark red, painter's portable spotlight black, all colors of the American Dream. We lie on the floor, trying to devise a plan for saving Penguin Four from the legal nightmare of an imaginary death. As if we're living in a life-sized shadowbox, Mia wiggles her toes in front of the spotlight. Larger-than-life toe reflections appear on the opposite wall.

Mesmerized, I can barely speak. "The things you see when you don't have a camera, and you're living the dream. I feel contentment for once."

Mia turns toward me and smiles. "In a life-size shadow box, possibilities are endless—as long as you have light and toes to interrupt it. Sometimes I worry when my efforts don't get recorded. So far, there's nothing in the shadows worth a picture."

I admire her patience as she looks for the perfect picture that reflects Reflexive Fusion as it should be reflected. I forget that we forgot to bring food.

28

Does building a Lazy Penguin fall within the realm of my expertise and job description? Is it humane to spin a pigeon on a turntable to make it dizzy? Does such efficiency divert attention from the ceremony's solemn but obscure meaning? Beyond these difficult questions, the task sounds simple, even if Institute specs seem strict. Searching back issues of *National Geographic*, I'm surprised that journalists have never covered the evolution of medieval pottery wheel design. In the Institute archives, I only find a disappointing lab video starring Penguin Four. No surprise, it's a classic pigeon show, lifting a foot, wiggling his claw, pecking the outskirts of the illuminated disc, proof that sensors don't always sense that a lab pigeon lives on the edge, over and under the scientific radar. The theory's nothing new; pigeons are supposed to peck the center. Penguin Four finds joy, poking around the edge of the outskirts. If it doesn't look like a mating dance, how do you explain an extra movement that brings no apparent reward?

The Lazy Penguin needs to spin thirty-three and a third revolutions a minute, the same speed you'd get from an old army surplus phonograph's turntable. Pure coincidence, the square root of thirty-three and a third equals a pigeon's standard IQ. If a pigeon's uncluttered mind spins at the same rate as its IQ squared, it gets dizzy and falls off the spinning platter. Centrifugal force drives the pigeon outward, toward the Lazy Penguin's outskirts; he gets dizzy faster than what was possible in medieval times. Overconfidence is a free ticket for a freefall into harm's way, foot braces keep him from slipping.

I should feel sorry for putting Penguin Four through test trials. If he could talk, he might thank me. After repeated spins and frequent falls off the turntable, you'd expect him to resist going for another ride. Just as documents cushion the impact of imaginary death, well-padded ergonomic foam protects him from harm by micro-switch. The soft mat surrounding the pedestal symbolizes the circle of life as well as the circle of the afterward. Twenty-four inches in diameter and three inches thick, it complies with animal rights guidelines, fire code, and Institute safety specs. By the looks, it has to be fun. Every time Penguin Four falls, he jumps up and scrambles back onto the Lazy Penguin.

Consider how the new, improved pigeon sacrifice might influence the gene pool, and increase the life spans of pigeons. Those that can't pirouette, fall, live long, and procreate. Those that can pirouette fall onto the same soft, foam padding, live long, and procreate. It sounds like a good deal, almost democratic. Sacrifice won't eliminate prolific and ambitious pigeons, or those who can't, won't, or don't meet expectations. The best news for humans, a willingness to offer up a pigeon is more important than conducting a real sacrifice. To rescue a pigeon from its fall is more important than its salvation.

The Institute revises forms and documents and creates updated versions that continue to mock reality. There's talk of an imaginary death policy, a futuristic product that competes with the state lottery and local casinos. As time goes on, I'm having more trouble telling the difference between real and imaginary. As time goes on, I'm more reluctant to criticize the pigeon sacrifice.

Mia's newest picnic vision is a stroke of genius. We picnic at the Center for Phone Training, located on the edge of the Institute's campus; the abandoned space allows intimacy and distance at the same time. We're alone and together simultaneously, in full view of each other, a few feet apart, separated by copper wires that carry sound from one phone to the other. Today, wireless technology violates air space with gifts to the gifted: text, voice, pictures, silent cries for space in outer space, all blessings, and reminders that sending is more important than receiving.

I accept Mia's offer: peppermint candy and a small bottle of seltzer. She pushes the number keys on an old touch-tone phone. My phone rings. Her voice is soft. "Hello. I'd like to take a few moments of your time to ask survey questions about the Reflexive Fusion Movement. Would you consider untying your shoes?"

29

Resurrected but easy to neglect, the Machine still makes phantom documents and produces blank sheets of paper, extra copies, nonsense syllables, mathematical formulae, and meaningless policies. The Institute's reverence for information pays off. One ghost printout, some electronic artifact, or vague reference to the American Dream: "SEE THE USA IN YOUR CHEVROLET." No one complains about something old if it looks like something new. A few make favorable comments. The Machine burps and farts an occasional paper misfeed, but not often enough to anger keyboard jockeys or *Star Trek* wannabe, Captain Kirk. Since the resurrection, it hasn't recorded any jams or misfeeds. That must explain the stability of my numbers; with few up or downticks, they're too inconsequential to catch the Director's or coordinators' attention.

At my most recent evaluation, the Tech Coordinator admitted he doesn't know what to do. Everyone knows—everyone's afraid to mention that keyboard jockeys are directing increasing numbers of phantom documents to Misguided Output, the only department to add new employees this month.

The speed at which information travels is more important than its value. A vote to buy another mail robot is unanimous. The Tech Coordinator deserves to be an opportunitator. A natural, he tells me to ignore Security's order to reduce excess data. Instead, I should locate the source of its origin. You never know when you'll need more information should it ever become scarce. In the meantime, the mail must go through.

Mia and I meet with Security and Maintenance to discuss the birdseed spill on the esplanade. Though rich in nitrogen and other plant nutrients, they hosed away the white deposits left behind. Maintenance tells us we need to foot the bill.

No surprise, Mia responds as if Maintenance is treating us like lab pigeons. "Not to be blunt," she says. "We're not stupid. If your people had patiently waited for rainwater to clean the cobblestone, they would have saved wear and tear on the garden hose, not to mention a lower water bill."

To make matters better, Mia shares a more complex truth. "You're not complaining about the wash water that floated some of the nutrients to the parking lot's giant oak tree. If you want, we can continue feeding birdseed to the same wild pigeons that are dropping droppings on the esplanade. Call it what you want, pigeon poop or fertilizer."

"You've offered a generous concession," Maintenance says. "But that doesn't solve our problem. Your offer makes things worse. More birdseed creates an overabundance of bird droppings, no matter what you call them."

"Here we go again," Security says. "I can see it now, another slip and fall, another lawsuit, another negative performance review, directly from the Director."

Mia and I try to discuss the pros and cons of subsidized brick cleaning. Instead, both coordinators want to make small talk smaller, a strategy that turns out better than we expect. Their wives belong to the same church, a favorable circumstance that inspires problem-solving, an activity often enjoyed by people in power. One wife belongs to the Audubon Society, an organization that's for the birds they tell me. Audubon members want pigeons to get the same recognition and respect that eagles get. The Institute takes the popular position that modern pigeons are not penguins. Both organizations value teamwork so much, that they forget the cleanup costs of dropping-splattered cobblestone. Without asking what we think, they agree to drop the matter as if it's nothing more than another drop in a proverbial dropping-splattered bucket.

Shorter days make cooler weather. Fewer canoeists get out for river training. With the increased risk of frostbite on her bare feet, Mia spends more indoor time looking at pictures and reviewing video footage. She records toe movement shadowed on the wall, most with my shoes lurking in the background. I work hard, keeping my feet motionless while we conspire to prevent Penguin Four's transfer to the afterward. How do we save him from a nightmare life, conflicted by the freedom to leave and the instinct to stay at the Institute, home where his heart is?

Mia interrupts my daydream, with a dream of her own: "If my work isn't recognized, I should create a contest, preferably one that's not contested by other contestants."

At midnight when most electronic clocks strike weakly and silently for the twenty-fourth time in a day, Mia's phone squeaks out a feeble alarm, as if begging for help to help itself, as if it doesn't care if we're awake or not. We go back to the Institute, take the elevator to the fourth floor, and check out the hallway's barren, off-white walls, perfect for displaying Mia's shadow work. We hang seventy eight-by-ten black-and-white glossy prints. The work makes me almost too tired to critique them. Nevertheless, Mia pours champagne; we stroll back and forth, each holding a glass in one hand and holding hands with the other.

Subtle, diffused light brings out the beauty one expects in shadows. An occasional bright spotlight reveals the ghost in all of us. Natural fluorescence in another life-size shadow box brings out the best. Shadows stretch movement from center to outskirts, drawing our attention to surreal contortions and distortions, a reality most apparent when hidden. We forget we're at the Institute.

The echo of footsteps sounds steady and deliberate, it's probably a night guard making routine rounds. Too late to change our minds, there's no time to take everything down to avoid another negative evaluation. No way to explain this one, we close our eyes and hug.

30

The guard looks at Mia's pictures, curious but possibly embarrassed that he can't tell the difference between medical claims and art samples. Mia's still holding her wine glass of champagne, a subtle hint that we're on another picnic. "Where did this stuff come from," he wonders aloud. "Where are they going with this?"

To be cautious, I ask, "Are you wondering about the origin of the champagne or the destination of the shadow art?" We try acting as embarrassed as the guard seems to be. We offer to help find the perpetrator, most likely some shady artist in search of recognition. Now that the guard's presence makes us fully awake, it feels hotter and more humid than it was in the bright fluorescence a few minutes ago. Beads of sweat drip over Mia's brow. Her eyes water. Security could confiscate her photos. She could lose her job. I can't wait to escape the Institute's confining ambiance, go out to walk the esplanade, and breathe night-fresh coolness.

Insider or outsider, the guard seems to care more about keeping his job than about Security. He does seem intrigued by an art display that breaks rules and regulations with no harm done. Instead of sounding the alarm, he stares at a photographed shadow of Mia's large toe magnified by distance. Coincidence or not, his calm expression looks more appreciative than you'd expect. Maybe we're all on the same team, living a pretense of Institutionalization, quietly rebelling against it.

We depart. A robot passes. The constant squeal from one of its wheel bearings drowns out its warning beeps. To maintain the appearance that our night visit is routine, we check out the Machine. A document, random or intended, drops onto an exit tray. Blank on both sides, its stark expressions of nothingness make it easy to identify. Paper wasted, at least there's no sign of excess.

Mia wakes up, wondering how or why shadow art challenges Institute rules. We buy energy bars and soda, so we can picnic in public, and conduct clandestine surveillance out in the open, in the shadows of her shadow art. Employees gather to enjoy the exhibition or watch us; we're not sure what draws their attention; after all, both attractions were unannounced. For the daytime guard's benefit, we act surprised. "What a collection," Mia says with some conviction.

"This collection looks like a work of genius. How long is it on display?" I ask no one in particular.

A man and woman act as if they think of themselves as art aficionados. The woman says, "Genius, sure, but be honest. Attending to irrelevant detail doesn't make one gifted."

"No, it's orthopedic shadow art revealed," the man replies. "It's a critique on medical documentation, something you'd only see here at the Institute."

Man and woman walk away. A ghostly silence forces me to assert myself. "We've been waiting for years! How could they keep this from us? When will there be more?"

Keyboard jockeys nod in appreciation. It's nice helping people see the light at the end, without having to look through the tunnel's darkness. The masses seem grateful. I need to admit that acting like a coordinator feels good. Besides, the exposure we get having a public picnic accounts for our time, and lets HR know we're on the job.

31

Mia's art disappears, a loss imaginary for us, real for employees. Many become hysterical. Not that they enjoy bare feet reflecting shadows, it's just that they hate thinking the art is stolen. Some seem upset enough to join a cult if they only knew who they should follow. Since the Institute didn't sanction the exhibit, Security can't investigate. The truth is we're the ones who removed the entire collection, leaving tack holes in the Institute walls that we hope Security won't take valuable time to investigate. Mia's not sure if our actions were reflexive or intended. The art theft, if you can call it that, was an art in itself.

Believe it or not, we gathered things up after work hours, and walked away in broad fluorescent nightlight, Mia carrying a portfolio filled with the photos as we headed for the elevator. We pass the night guard we met the night before. He keeps walking as if we've never met, as if Mia and I are bystanders, innocent champagne drinkers, trapped in the Institute.

Even though Security won't investigate the theft of something that doesn't belong to the Institute, we thought it better to hide the portfolio than take it off campus. We grab our picnic basket, a ready-made survival kit with candles, matches, a camera, pretzels, and wine. Seeking refuge in the Institute's depths, we crawl into the heating duct that directs warm breezes to the generator. The warmth is refreshing and being so close to each other, exciting. The sheet metal path splits two ways. Unable to determine which road is less traveled, we choose the route with a calmer breeze, making it easier to keep our candles lit while on the move. Dragging Mia's portfolio along on the sheet metal,

I hope Security won't think they smell rotten fish in Denmark or think they hear entitled rats, pitter-pattering through the ventilator duct.

We reach another junction, a spacious rectangular space that reroutes the steady Chicago breeze from one duct to many. Like coordinators meeting in a meeting, it redirects hot air in many directions. With so many choices and no destination, it's hard to keep our bearing. We light another candle, pour wine, and relax. Mia attaches the camera to the tripod, reclines, and removes her shoes. She keeps her bare feet immobile while I move the candle. The camera captures shadows flickering like campfire shadows of long-ago cave people. Holding the candle makes it hard to enjoy our surroundings the way we do on a typical picnic—at least there's no worry about finding pottery here. But we're startled to see Mia's newest foot shadow superimposed on a pigeon that appears recently sketched on what might be the north wall. How do we explain this in *Fifty Places?*

Mia's newest picnic blurb, actually two takes; one from the heights of Fourth Floor South, the other in the depths of the ventilator duct:

"Pictures at an exhibition make the science of shadows shadowy. Sid thinks he sees the light at the end of the tunnel. I'm thinking focused beacon wrapped in darkness.

"Crawling on our bellies like sensuous reptiles, Sid and I creep through ducted darkness. Sid holds a candle to our candle's flickering shadows, shadows shaded by light, lightness reflected in an artificial night. Camera flash clears the air, flashing itself out of existence."

32

Few employees bother to visit the Institute on holidays. The rotunda has to remain open; its four levels are all booked for Thanksgiving this year. A formality, the Director invites us to attend the rehearsal as well as the official sacrifice. Mia is the carrier of the pigeon, and I'm the operator of the Lazy Penguin, so we can't decline. We're each allowed to bring a guest. Bringing each other brings substantial savings to The Institute.

Mia insists on including Penguin Four.

Research Coordinator scowls. "I know there's a lot at stake. But if a pigeon is supposed to just act like a pigeon, how can it botch things up?"

"Historians, ornithologists, psychologists all agree nervous pigeons don't sacrifice well," Mia replies. "Penguin Four needs to take it from the top by acclimating to the strange people who, oddly enough, frequent the rotunda."

Mia wears jeans for the rehearsal, making me more comfortable than I would have been had she worn Lycra. My mind races enough as it is.

Director, coordinators, and opportunitators rehearse *Penguin on a Pedestal,* a poetic chant that I'm not authorized to reveal. Annoyed, Penguin Four ruffles his neck and back feathers, making them extend straight upward and outward, a useless attempt to look like an intimidating, giant pigeon. Mia places him on the turntable, and gently positions his claws in my not-yet-patented foot braces. Penguin Four stares at Mia, who, as I've already mentioned, didn't dress for the sacrifice. No matter, she's beautiful as usual, serene, solemn, and goddess-like. You can tell she handles herself well in sacrificial situations, a sign that she'll do well at my funeral. I turn on the turntable. In turn, it turns me on with confidence that the rehearsal will prove my design successful. Penguin Four spins slowly at first; gradually, the turntable picks up speed. It might be my imagination, but Penguin Four appears fixated on Mia. If he is, it could take longer to fall from the rotating pedestal.

Mia stands proudly, unaware that her presence might prolong the pigeon's ride. But as a perfect sacrifice requires, Penguin Four's feet slip out of the foot braces, he lands on the foam pad. As I said, I'm no ornithologist, but I discern a satisfied grin on his beak. Mia picks him up gently and puts him in his gilded cage. Penguin Four shakes his head. Dizziness subsides as he comes back to a more static reality.

33

The Machine continues to run. Somehow, keyboard jockeys still accept the rare spasmodic paper jamming. No one seems to notice the gradual increase of documents, most containing information, credible but useless. Low numbers concern me less now, at least for the holidays. Thankfully, we can celebrate Thanksgiving without fearing the ravages of surplus. Mia's take:

"Wind-powered Mayflowers crossed
the Atlantic. Fossil fuel powers modern would-be
pilgrims over rivers and through
woods to traffic jams going nowhere fast."

Sarcastic or not, the Institute is full of pilgrims, most in a rush to depart its almost-hallowed halls. Even though it's Thanksgiving, the Machine continues creating random output, new logic that only a machine could understand. I stay late, listen to old new-age, and watch the monitor, searching for clues that might explain the phantom information's origin. Still a mystery, did my shaking hands break a connection momentarily, create an arc that scrambled memory, brainwashed artificial intelligence? Truth, denial, or self-serving rationalization, I'm the one who triggered another spark of life, jump-starting a new creation.

It's the end of the day. On the way out, Mia and I stop by the lab and check on Penguin Four. It doesn't matter that an official demise and rebirth will delete his name from one file and add it to another. He's resting comfortably, head under his wing, no apparent objections to his impending sacrifice. If he's snoring, we don't hear any noise. To avoid junk candy and soda machines, I pop a pigeon pellet into my mouth. It seems high in fiber, a quality that nine out of ten doctors recommend. But it's rather bland; it might go better with a glass of Chardonnay. I reach out to Mia, another pigeon pellet in hand. "Would you like to try one?"

"Sorry," she says. "I'm not in the mood. I can't get this impending sacrifice out of my head."

34

If the Institute sacrifices Penguin Four, they need to take care of him in a bureaucratic way. Having died an official death that's imaginary, he supposedly gets eliminated from the research pool of pigeons. A nonexistent pigeon's behavior can't be recorded or reported.

Cold air freezes the river's edges, nature's renewable excuse that it's too cold to paddle your own canoe—the weather's less than ideal for spoiled lab pigeons to fly the great outdoors. Indoors, everyone is excited about the sacrifice. Mia's becoming popular. Research provides her with a map, a ceremonial route highlighted for the sacrificial pigeon's quick return to its cage. "Custodial rights belong to Research," the Coordinator says. "It's a tremendous responsibility, Mia. You're the right person for the job. The Institute depends on you."

Not to be outdone or undone, Animal Rights has already sent an email, instructing her to release the pigeon at the main entrance of the rotunda. "Freedom, not politics," it advised. "Penguin Four's already paid his fair dues for freedom. Set him free to fly the skies, streets, buildings, woods."

Mia is kind-hearted. She's committed to Reflexive Fusion; I'm just a tech who makes things happen. But we wonder how Institute suits can sacrifice a pigeon if they disagree on what it takes to make the afterward ideal. Continuous neglect and inattention to Institutional detail force us to plan a beginning for Penguin Four's end.

Sacrifice is a spectacle to behold. Mia, the carrier of the pigeon, embodies the American Dream. Fire engine red shoes expose her ankles in clear view; even with my vivid imagination, I can't see her toes. She wears the purple Lycra tights with the black cape she had set aside for my funeral. As usual, I'm wearing faded business casual. Mia groomed Penguin Four, polishing his beak with an extract of linseed, glossed his feathers with oil of sunflower, and shined his toenails with the best organic vegetable oil money can buy.

Is the atmospheric mix of festive air and business sobriety balanced well enough to be suitable for the occasion? Are conditions grave enough to make guests proud, severe enough to make them professional? Everyone seems uneasy. Would it be good for them to know that the fire and safety code allows the portable fireplace to burn artificial wood with make-believe flames?

HR would be proud. Even though it's midday, the electronic flutist playing medieval tunes wears evening attire, a floor-length, off-white, peasant costume, fitting for a medieval flute player. She should remember that a full-length dress poses a risk of tripping, should she try climbing the corporate ladder. Not dark, glitzy, or glamorous, it could complement intelligent conversation if it were not for the flute playing. Her neckline plunges modestly, enough to tease respect, yet allow fleeting glances and stolen stares. A well-placed spotlight accentuates cleavage shadows, slowly waltzing on her breasts as she breathes. Fusing femininity and allure, she draws in breaths of fresh air to sustain herself, and slowly blows across the mouthpiece to keep the sound of music alive. In her unique way, her fusion is just as reflexive as Mia's.

Penguin Four sits in his gilded cage, watching us eat. If anyone prefers turkey, no one admits it. As always, sophisticated taste requires good judgment. If you host a pigeon sacrifice, make sure you serve venison and potato.

As if they think no one will notice, a few coordinators continue making furtive glances toward Mia. What is it about her? Does her beauty make her special? Or is it her official capacity as an animal rights advocate, the official carrier of the pigeon, Reflexive Fusion Artist? Why ask what or why? At the risk of worship, she is everything to me.

The congregants begin to chant. I feel bound by oath and a signed contract not to repeat their words. I don't think I'm stretching rules if I reveal the chorus:
Dove of Peace. Pigeon, Penguin. Penguin, Pigeon. Pigeon on a Pedestal.
The refrain doesn't take long to memorize. At first, the chant itself seems meaningless. At the rehearsal, an opportunitator claimed that if you repeat the chorus over and over, and listen to yourself long enough, the beautiful rhythm, rich symbolism, and profound but obscure meaning add more to this ritual than most can imagine.

The chanting stops abruptly. In silence, Mia awkwardly fumbles, trying to open the tiny door latch. She removes Penguin Four from his gilded cage and clutches the pigeon against her breast, to calm him and reassure herself as well. She places him on the turntable; I flip the switch. As if a pigeon pageant provides the only excuse to break Institute rules, we stand by, side by side, holding hands, childlike, waiting to witness the pigeon's fall. Guests watch with much anticipation, having heard rumors of pageantry and spiritually uplifting.

The turntable rotates with Penguin Four standing in the foot braces. As if he knows a trick to keep from getting dizzy, he focuses on Mia. I'm not sure if a pigeon could learn this in a lab, or figure things out in a single rehearsal. The pigeon spins and spins some more. How would we know he'd be so obsessed? I watch the big and little hands on my old vintage watch, wondering how long it will take for his mind to start spinning this time. Almost twelve minutes, it turns out.

Penguin Four lifts his right claw from the foot brace, stretches his neck, leaps off, and flies upward with the poise of a champion figure skater, the intelligence of a lab pigeon spooked by a hidden micro-switch. He flies the first level, in a circle, moving upward toward the dome in a gradual spiral, dropping a whitish deposit onto the turntable, centered in the center of the rotunda. The centrifugal force sends the splattered dropping outward. Thankfully or not, it misses the congregants. As I've said more than once, I'm no ornithologist. But I think diarrhea is a possible side effect of sacrificial stress, even when a sacrifice is imaginary. Relieved and well-wasted, Penguin Four swoops down and lands on Mia's shoulder.

Mia flicks a Bic butane cigarette lighter attached to the end of a birch stick, a makeshift victory torch of diversion. Empty cage in one hand, she raises the torch with the other. Penguin Four remains perched on her shoulder, his claws curled with a tightened grip. Like a rock star, Mia circles the room twice and takes the stairs rising to the balcony, mostly occupied by low-level coordinators. Mia circles and ascends to the next level, following the flight pattern of a typical, above-average pigeon. Penguin Four casts a blurred, ghost-like shadow that ascends the spiral with them. The pigeon's not circling the drain. He's alive, very much alive, riding upward without having to challenge the gravity of the situation.

Spectators clap. Everyone stands for a quiet procession to the frozen lawn for pictures. I reach for another rib of venison.

35

Fighting off holiday heartburn from cold potato and venison is bad enough; I can't stop my marathon mind from racing. Mia says juggling a pigeon is much harder than sacrificing one. After making a dramatic exit from the rotunda, she disappeared from the Institute's radar. Penguin Four's cage remains empty. Though Animal Rights and Research both assume Mia turned the pigeon loose, they join forces to search for clues. If he's free, Animal Rights people should be satisfied. To prolong a sense of team spirit and fair play, everyone looks for traces—whitish pigeon deposits, burned-out Bic lighter on a birch bark stick carelessly discarded, purple tunic—anything that might rescue them from cluelessness. They find nothing.

Without trying or intending, Mia and Penguin Four discover a perfect cure for the holiday blues. Alive and well in the abandoned penthouse, she and the pigeon spend quality time drinking seltzer water and eating birdseed, respectively. Penguin Four needs to learn home is no longer where his heart is. His heart's not in the penthouse above; it's still caged in the lab. Conditions are otherwise perfect. The new living quarters are warmer than the streets, more substantial than the lab, its altitude favorable for flying. The only thing missing is a hard-to-find, unaffordable pigeon portrait of his great, ancestral grandfather many generations back, the distinguished, but unknown missile test pilot from World War II, the war to end all wars.

I join Mia for a penthouse picnic, but things aren't the same. Maybe it's the fresh pigeon droppings on the floor and furniture that discourage me. Or two chairs that support a broom handle, a make-do roost for Penguin Four. During the day, he rests comfortably, remaining on his perch, peeking through the small window overlooking the parapet and city. Even Mia's notes about the sacrifice seem bleak.

"Blessed by sacrificial chant, Penguin Four flies the rotunda, high in an indoor sky, living a short afterward only imagined. If we set him free, will he soar with eagles or fly with ostriches? Survive an almost barren world without black oil sunflower seed? Or thrive on GORP trail mix, Good Old Raisins and Peanuts?"

Mia lies on a futon mattress, curls her toes, then straightens them for relaxation. Alone on a loveseat, I try to focus on the Persian rug's design. I have things to do; another fresh pigeon dropping distracts me. I want to kiss Mia goodbye, but I'm feeling somewhat shy. Interrupting her relaxation would be stressful for both of us. I wave in a way that allows me to do what I have to do, in a way that Mia barely notices.

I go down to the lower level to think in the comfort of florescence. Without apparent reason, the night guard who works overtime days happens to visit. He's talkative, an unusual circumstance, since there are lots of keyboard jockeys available for casual conversation, especially on a weekday. He lowers his voice as if the two of us are involved in a conspiracy. Is he crazy, paranoid, or justifiably afraid that Security might be recording us? He raises his voice as if he wants a hidden microphone to capture his departing words. "Reflexive Fusion Artists are troublemakers. If Security can't arrest your lady friend for art theft, they should arrest her for pigeon rustling."

"I hate to say it," I tell the guard. "Lock the lady up and throw away the key." Not that I mean it. I didn't betray Mia with a wish that needs a miraculous reversal. It's just that an attitude of tough love makes a perfect smokescreen. The important thing is that I didn't confirm that we hijacked Penguin Four. I only assured the guard that we're all on the same team, we don't have to take sides on the pigeon matter.

I return to the penthouse with a leftover rib of venison and a cold baked potato. Penguin Four rests comfortably, asleep on his perch, head tucked under his wing as usual. Mia sleeps soundly, fully reclined on a beach blanket. A spotlight shines from one end of the room to the other, making fluid shadows of her feet whenever they move. A tripod-mounted video camera captures shadowed movement, saves it on a laptop, and converts it for projection on the opposite wall. Reflexive Fusion doesn't reflect her intentions. It reflects what she does. If Mia dreams that I tickle her feet, she gets a more animated video than she does if she dreams in peace.

Cold, the rib of venison is still tasty. I don't recommend the potato.

Following the Director's example, officers ignore mail worker complaints about the surplus phantom paper. Costs increase. The facilities department acquires two more robots, orders more paper, expands the warehouse, and spends more on overtime. Efficient keyboard jockeys scan documents, and send more information to the Machine; forklift drivers deliver more paper to the keyboard jockeys; robots carry cases of fresh information to the warehouse. Somehow, paper usage and mail flow assure the Director his ambitious plans are working. If things continue going so well, I might get fired or demoted. I even overhear a coordinator who admits he's afraid of working his way down the corporate ladder, to the bottom where keyboard jockeys share broken promises of opportunity. To save themselves, coordinators mark a meeting on the virtual calendar, to discuss plans to replace the department that reviews random output, and decide what to keep and what to shred.

Since Thanksgiving, the Machine's produced two hundred thousand phantoms, full of nonsense, gibberish, and nothingness. I set up an oscilloscope and meter at an observation window to show the suits I'm on the job to assure them the Machine's a work in progress. My mind still racing, I'm afraid I might sound like a broken record, scratched compact disc, or electronic echo chamber. But I'm not so insecure that I call Security.

36

Pigeons of Science magazine gave Mia the go-ahead to submit the lab video of Penguin Four, standing on one leg, pecking the disc's outer edge. "Should I send it out," she asks. "It's already under consideration for release at a local film festival."

"Jury's still out. We can be optimistic. What are the odds of two judges not liking it? Maybe the fusion's reflexive enough to please everyone."

"What if we collect royalties on the video? What if it's intellectual property that belongs to the Institute?"

"Everyone knows the Institute doesn't own much of anything that reflects intelligence. To be honest, I can't remember if we produced the video during a workday or after hours. Who knows who owns what?"

Before the pretrial conference, Animal Rights and Research coordinators sign forms overlooked during Thanksgiving Day's excitement. Instead of falling on the micro-switch that was supposed to signal the Machine to print documents confirming the sacrifice, Penguin Four leaped upward for his quick trip up the spiral without any of the necessary paperwork—Authorization of Sacrifice, Certificate of Non-existence, and Release to the Afterward. Issues remain. If Animal Rights wins custody of Penguin Four, they release him. If Research proves the pigeon is fully Institutionalized, he remains at the Institute forever, until death he does part. In the meantime, the pigeon lives a perfect life in the penthouse. He's free to stay with Mia, and free to fly in the sky.

Institute and Animal Rights lawyers, coordinators, Mia,

and I leave the court. Outside, we gather in a circle of distrust. The Research Coordinator asks why Mia and Penguin Four disappeared after the sacrifice. He wonders why I testify on Mia's behalf. To calm him, I mention the creation. His face deadpans into a stone-faced, professional facade. Mia suggests that everyone remove their shoes. Pouring wine to facilitate her proven relaxation technique, she leads them from reluctance to nirvana. "Wiggle your toes. Reflect on your value to the Institute." She turns toward me. "Next time you look into a mirror, remind yourself that you work well independently and read part numbers well. Tell yourself the Machine can't run without you." Conversing with myself could sound a little crazy, but most of what Mia says is true. The Machine's increased output testifies as much.

Mia closes her eyes, and whispers to herself, loud enough for me to hear. "Penguin Four needs the Institute for food, water, ventilation, and sanitation. He needs Animal Rights to protect his freedom. I light up lives with shadows. How does Reflexive Fusion fit in if Penguin Four flies upwards into the creation's spiral?"

Lawyers and coordinators seem occupied with relaxation's strange sensations. Four ask for more wine. If Mia times things right, they might agree to a picnic.

37

We walk the halls of the Institute, Penguin Four riding Mia's shoulder. Passing through the rotunda to catch the penthouse elevator, Security recognizes her and checks her identity anyway. Mia acts too innocent for worthwhile interrogation. Penguin Four remains perched on her shoulder, parrot-like but speechless. Fortunately, her Animal Rights badge proves the pigeon is not a penguin. Institute ID verifies Mia's freedom to wander almost anywhere. "Interruptions such as yours make it hard to teach the pigeon new tricks," she tells the guard. "Perhaps you're unaware that the penthouse, his new home away from home, might become his newest center of the universe."

"Your point's well taken." The guard's well-chosen words sound sarcastic.

On Tuesday, we return to court. The judge is suspicious. "How can the live pigeon Penguin Four perch on the same family tree limb as dead Penguins One, Two, and Three?" he asks. "We have a problem that needs investigation."

Animal Rights claims that broken pigeon bones stored in pottery suggest that One, Two, and Three died violent deaths. After all, skeletal remains otherwise suggest they were well-fed and well-wasted.

Research believes that if Penguin Four is set free, he will die by natural causes, most likely unintended. It wouldn't take a pigeon scientist to know that freedom's victims often freeze in a cruel, winter wonderland's sub-zero sky, possibly in the shadows of the Institute.

We offer a letter to the editor that deems hypothermia

violent but natural, a suggestion that creation and Institutional forces conspire to create the perfect winter storm, nature without nurture.

This kind of publicity should make parties think twice before taking a polarized position.

I don't expect any credit where credit's due. But my testimony describes our team-building efforts dedicated to the Institute, how the three consultants assisted Mia and me in conducting pottery research, carefully cataloging, and storing the best examples in the archives. Everything was going well until Mia spilled the bones, tripping over the jug.

"Did the skeletal remains shatter on impact," the judge asks.

"I can't say for sure. The jug smashing right before we found the bones is proof that there's a downside to storing pigeon bones in pottery jugs."

The judge is silent, making me afraid he thinks I've avoided his question. I decide to tell it all. "Creation's full of mystery. The truth lies somewhere between the center and the outskirts. Look at it this way. When thrown outward by centrifugal force, a dizzy pigeon floats in fear until its spinning mind and body synchronize, setting the stage for a peaceful fall into the afterward. Do the outskirts attract those less Institutionalized, those who live life on the edge, in an off-kilter world?"

The judge and two attorneys have fallen asleep as if they've heard it all before.

After a brief, three-hour recess, Mia testifies. As the carrier of the pigeon, she represented Animal Rights at the annual pigeon pageant and worked for the Institute at the yearly pigeon sacrifice. To avoid confusing the judge, she doesn't divulge that both events happened at the same time and place, both featuring the almost famous pigeon, Penguin Four.

"Institute forms and documents discount life's meaning," she says. "I had to oppose orders for the pigeon's release and orders to cage it. As the carrier of the Pigeon, I'm responsible for those I take it from and those I carry it to. It's in the pigeon's best interests. That's all I can do."

Mia had agonized, struggling to dream up ways to accomplish her mission. It turned out that the pigeon's success—conquering dizziness and taking the leap upward—had been her inspiration. No one knew she trained Penguin Four to keep a level head, focus, straighten up, and fly right like an eagle. With the pigeon perched on her shoulder, she carried the torch around the first, second, third, and fourth levels in an upward spiral, following the predictable path of any wild pigeon. Penguin Four's life in the penthouse satisfied the Institute's need for control and the pigeon's need for freedom, without depriving him of food, water, sanitation, and adequate ventilation.

The court seems more interested in Mia's account than mine. Looking back, I should have mentioned I'm the one who gets stuck buying the exotic birdseed these days.

Mia says, "Reflection without fusion reflects desperation." I think she's right:

"Truth, justice, American way: purgatories impartial. A witch's brew of trueness, falseness, righteousness, and wrongness hijacked in an otherworld of direction."

38

Too busy working to follow news flashes or check out pictures of pottery, keyboard jockeys somehow learn of Mia's good fortune. She returns from the Reflexive Fusion Festival, revitalized, recognized, and rewarded with a three-foot trophy, too tall to fit in her condo's only bookshelf, too wide to fit in an office cubicle, it's perfect for the penthouse. *Elevator People*, the video segment of her toes dancing in front of my out-of-focus shoe, gets well-deserved airtime on national TV. Critics see the most promise in her shadow work. Sometimes, you can please everyone.

Corporations have asked Mia to endorse toeless high heels, pedicures, and toenail paints and polishes, every color of the American dream, along with the addition of deep purple. She pretends to consider each offer carefully before declining. It's always a matter of principle. Mia wants to be part of the creation rather than part of the problem.

I welcome Mia with open arms, so to speak. After all the excitement, it's hard coming back down to earth at the Institute. Many still consider her artistic work an embarrassment. "They don't understand," she says. "My toes aren't just toes—they're toes that make shadows. Even though I wear shoes at the Institute, people can't help looking downward at my feet. If I catch people glancing, their eyes abruptly turn upward toward the heavens. What the hell? Are people searching for God or looking for shadows?"

Now that Mia has endured knowing stares of people on the streets; wearing shoes must be a relief. Seclusion in her cubicle protects her from constant scrutiny that distracts her from Institute work. The Machine pigeonholed much of the phantom output for her attention.

Off-hours, Mia still spends time in the penthouse where Penguin Four prepares his heart for its new home. As expected, we have minor setbacks with housebreaking. We violate the fire code by covering the floors with newspaper, but check to make sure this complies with municipal sanitation guidelines.

Institute and Animal Rights investigators continue to argue over pigeon custody, each side presenting its case as if defending truth, beauty, justice, and the American Way. While sorting pottery, they break eight more vases and jugs. Thankfully, they don't find any more bones.

39

With all the legal excitement, I almost forget to investigate the excess information invasion. I arrange a weekend teleconference with Smith, Jones, and Jonson.

As bad luck has it, no one's home is large enough to spread electrical schematics. Smith can't use his floor because it's raining, and his mobile home's roof still leaks. Jones must have forgotten that we scheduled the conference. Sounding surprised, and slightly out of breath, she seems to have trouble concentrating. Someone else, possibly her husband, is breathing hard as if he's climaxing, a psychological moment out of synch with my phone call. Where's her tech-of-the-month plaque now? Jonson's voice echoes as he tells us about his new capsule recently purchased.

Common sense continues to serve Jonson, even in cramped quarters. He reads his schematic the way Moses read scrolls, unrolling one end, and rolling up the other. I hear clanging pots and pans as Smith rearranges his necessary clutter to make room for his phone. Jones's heavy breathing heightens, almost sounding asthmatic.

Jonson interrupts these random noises with a logical suggestion. The sounds of banging pots and pans subside. Heavy breathing and moans from the Joneses are hardly audible. It's so quiet you could almost hear a pigeon feather drop. Someday, I should apologize to Mr. and Mrs. Jones for arranging this inconvenient teleconference, even though it's not my fault. But how can I know if it's Mr. Jones in the background? I'm not sure if I should ask.

As if cell phone electrons randomly bounce around in space, Jonson's words echo and ricochet around the curved walls of his capsule. "Logic's overloading the primal inverter. The Machine's doing more than it needs to do, spinning its wheels on an electronic highway to hell. That voltage interruption must have spiked the primal inverter with misguided intelligence. You need to lobotomize the main auxiliary logic circuit. Zap it with one-twenty volts directly from the wall. Transistors morphed into industrial waste reduce output more than you can imagine."

Jonson's solution makes Reflexive Fusion or pigeon sacrifice look like child's play. I follow corporate protocol, inviting all three techs to help modify the Machine's software with a counterintuitive zap, an electrical power surge routed to a single transistor. Jonson accepts right away and then apologizes. "I need to hang up, get outside," he says. "I have to shade the tomatoes before they fry in this Kansas midday heat."

It sounds like Smith is relocating his pots and pans again, getting them ready for the next rainstorm. No longer involved in the conversation, the two Joneses remain on the phone. Mr. Jones—someone—is filling a phone with heavy breathing again. Mrs. Jones pleads in a whisper, "Move my magnet," as if she needs to be polarized to reply.

40

Mia and I need another picnic to get away from the Institute's hustle and bustle and create some distance from the Machine. This time, our destination is a remote mezzanine that overlooks the warehouse. I bring a llama hair blanket, jogger's mix, and wild cherry seltzer, the best choice for higher altitudes. After taking the stairs to make the forty-five second ascent, we spread our blanket on the concrete deck, close to the mezzanine edge. We slip out of our jeans. In Lycra, we stand at the railing, drinking seltzer, looking down and out over the vast expanse. At a distance, dwarfed workers look like giant ants, stacking cases of paper onto forklifts. A forklift just misses a carbon fiber canoe, carelessly stored by the Institute's new, two-person canoe team. An overhead door opens for an empty trailer truck's departure, framing a full moon in the upper left. Two pigeons soar majestically through a steel-trussed horizon.

A cold breeze brings a sudden chill, forcing us to wrap ourselves and snuggle in the blanket's warmth. I confide in Mia. "Your toes are out of sight. And out of mind for once. I'm still excited, too wound up to snack on jogger's mix. I think I might be in love with you."

41

Call people crazy for using quaint, diagnostic labels like *bats in the belfry*, a euphemistic pre-textbook way to label insanity. Sometimes I'm afraid employees will think I'm talking about the Director if I happen to mention there are rats in the building's dome. Mia and I checked it out briefly, thinking it's perfect for an indoor outing. I like the dome, but we don't stay long. Rats act as entitled to Institute life as any employee or pigeon, especially Penguin Four. Vicious when cornered, the rats scare us enough to picnic elsewhere.

An early Saturday blizzard carpets the grounds with two feet of snow, a perfect storm for an ideal winter picnic. Our only problem, snow obscures lines painted on acres of asphalt, lines that separate parked cars of coordinators from cars of keyboard jockeys. It's hard to choose a suitable spot to build an igloo. A relief that we can't make an intelligent choice, we opt for the parking lot's center. Late afternoon sunlight from the west will allow Mia to create long, ambitious shadows. We built an igloo, eight feet in diameter; if it were square, it would be as big as a freight elevator, smaller and cozier than the rotunda. We twist phantom documents into artificial campfire logs. An igloo in a frigid parking lot seems less extreme than a rat-infested dome, but we still need to be careful. To watch reflections on the igloo's circular wall, Mia removes her snow boots, risking frostbite and campfire burn. I rub her left foot to keep it warm and apply salve on her right to cool it off.

Life in a parking lot turns out too good to be true. A

guard knocks on the doorless doorway's snowy edge. Instead of a knock, we hear nothing but the muffled sounds of the igloo's snowpack crumbling. The door opening increases. Without an apology for intruding or damaging our doorless door, the guard explains how his global positioning device pinpoints our igloo in a coordinator's parking spot. This annoying detail forces us to abandon the frozen fruit of our hard labor.

We begin a disheartened search for a site more suitable, one that might only offend a keyboard jockey. To our surprise, there are ten other igloos under construction. The guard assures us these newer igloos occupy parking spaces of underlings who recently became unemployed. Either we've inspired homeless people to help themselves, or we've convinced the Institute's middle class that igloo camping is not only fashionable—it's the right thing to do. A surprise given the weather, the homeless girl with a cat built a tiny igloo. Hiding under the girl's coat, the kitten peers outward beneath her chin. "Can't stay here too long," the girl tells Mia. "Panhandling at the Institute's not enough to feed the kitten and me. I only got a couple of dollar bills today. Igloo builders must be poor too. Or maybe they feel less sorry, now that my igloo makes me look less homeless. At night, I go to that women's shelter off Main; Toasty sneaks in hiding under my coat."

Under the guard's direction, a facilities specialist plows our igloo into a snow pile at the parking lot's edge. He spares the girl's igloo. Either he has a heart, or her igloo must be in the parking space of someone unemployed.

Even with our igloo destroyed, Mia seems content with today's accomplishments. She removes her gloves, and adds notes for *Fifty Places*:

"In a winter wonderland without pigeons, archetypical Eskimo Nanooka of the North meets Institute Employee Sidney of the South. Heat burn and frostbite in a globally positioned igloo, are perfect hardships to test the boundaries of abandonment, love, and heartburn. Homeless girl and kitten push parking lot's snow-covered borderland outward. Not much to say about the damn snowplow."

42

I haven't bothered to tell my coordinator that Jonson is on his way. Should I give notice or let it be a surprise? It doesn't matter to me. I just want to avoid a performance evaluation that reads, "Sid reads part numbers well but can't fix the Machine."

On Friday, the Coordinator calls a surprise meeting. Even though the previous rebuild was successful, coordinators have heard the Machine needs more work. In my defense, I mention the birch bark plaques of the three consultants, along with my birch-framed photo prove our success. I was honored when you accepted that picture of me grasping the connector harness.

My favorable view of my work somehow makes the Coordinator's outlook more negative. "By the way," he says, "You haven't displayed that birch-framed photo you like to brag about. We need to remind other departments of our achievements."

"As soon as I find a coat hanger, I'll hang it from that high-voltage busway in my office. High voltage will make it more theft-proof than it would be hanging on the chain-link enclosure. I've always been afraid someone might steal it."

The Tech Coordinator yawns. "Too much success too soon keeps a machine from performing at full potential. Excess information overloads the Institute. Face the facts. This efficiency presents a rare case where it creates more jobs. Until we get the problem fixed, we need a press release, not a cover-up."

"No problem," I reply. "We'll contain the primal inverter's logic. With Jonson's assistance, setup takes a day. Reducing a transistor to industrial waste takes a nanosecond, two at most."

The Tech Coordinator ignores me, making it hard to tell if he thinks I'm somewhat cynical. "The Institute needs to make more sacrifices," he says. "Mail workers will work fewer hours, and involuntarily give up overtime pay. We'll have to fire or retire six robots." He looks up. "No one takes saving money lightly. The truth has to remain secret. The Director's going to think a second resurrection suggests the first was a failure. Instead of 'resurrection,' we should call this one a 'lobotomy.'"

43

"The feud over Penguin Four never ends," Mia says. "Animal Rights is selling raffle tickets. The winner gets a free pass to go on an African safari that allows the transfer of big game animals to the afterward. Proceeds pay for Penguin Four's plane flight to Florida where it's much warmer than winter at the Institute."

"Except for the alligators, it's safer than Africa."

"It's ironic. If Penguin Four thought his heart was home in Florida, he could fly there himself. All those wasted funds, not to mention the wasted giraffes, zebras, and lions."

The city pigeon pound destroyed forty homeless homing pigeons yesterday. Today they announced the deaths of twenty more. No one Institutionalizes wild pigeons to save them. Isn't that the way? We donate ten pounds of pigeon seed to the pigeon pound. Since we already feed the many outdoor pigeons that reside around the Institute, it's the most we can do.

44

What a day. I head out to the helipad to meet Jonson when he lands. After a two-hour wait, an old Chevy pickup, spot primed with rust-color paint, drops him off in the parking lot. He's proud of himself, pocketing travel money saved when he hitchhikes. Savings pay for his next capsule, his so-called rental unit of the future. I disapprove but don't comment on his ride. Not that I object to old Chevy trucks, my concern is more about job security. Arrival by helicopter projects hard-earned professionalism. Arrival by rusty truck suggests Jonson might not meet Institute expectations. Instead, it's a hint that the lazy and incompetent deserve to encounter hardships. I hope Jonson figures things out before someone smug makes a quick judgment, and shoves him off the corporate ladder for a sudden fall.

The Institute didn't take us out for fine dining during Jonson's last visit. It still won't pay for the apricots we bought for the dig. Never losing hope for a free meal, Jonson criticizes my modest oscilloscope display. Since it's almost Christmas, he decks the hall with old logic generators, meters, and monitors that serve no functional purpose. The colorful array should impress bosses and create holiday cheer for employees restricted from using the Machine during its controlled meltdown, our electronic lobotomy. He adds one large, state-of-the-art, flat-screen monitor so coordinators can watch carnage magnified, a hundred-twenty-volt electrical charge attacking a helpless two-volt circuit board. Jonson also insists on wearing lab coats. It might as well be Halloween.

Quite frankly, aside from the costume theme, I'm excited.

Even if my hands shake, there's no problem this time. Jonson insists on doing the honors. "Is it my trembling that bothers you," I ask. "Do you think I get stage fright?"

"That never crossed my mind," he says. "Recent paradigm drift forces a new protocol. Techs of your stature should do less menial labor."

"How can I disagree?"

As a last-minute preparation, Jonson hot-wires a micro-switch to the Machine. As Mia predicted, there's standing room only. Cramped in the hall with the suits, I feel as crowded as a caged lab pigeon packed in a city pound. I retreat to the Machine's space and join Jonson. Even though we don't need a countdown, everyone should witness fair play and teamwork firsthand. I wear a headset just to hear myself count backward. "Ten, nine," coordinators push and crowd each other, hoping to get to the front for a better view. "Zero."

Jonson presses the hot-wired micro-switch; an electric flashfire erupts on the circuit board, magnified many times on the overhead monitor. Mia watches in awe. Penguin Four perched on her shoulder maintains a perfect poker face. "I'm impressed," Mia says. "No surprise, it's always hard to know what the pigeon thinks." I remove my headset, spectators clap. Jonson takes a bow as if he's a director.

The Machine's up and running, we break for lunch. Eating in the cafeteria is no picnic, but we still find the food palatable. Besides, it's nice to have a convenient place to celebrate. On a napkin, Jonson sketches a new capsule design, more efficient than a one-room apartment. "I'm telling you," he says even though I already know he's telling me. "These capsules solve the housing problems of an overcrowded planet."

"Makes sense," Mia says. "If you decrease the numbers of people competing with pigeons for food and space, you prevent, or at least postpone an ecological disaster."

Glad I keep up with news on the way to work. "Public radio news lady claims everyone has to do their part. We need a two-year reproductive moratorium to reduce our numbers. Coincidence or not, there's a conflict. A new tax write-off for large families supposedly promotes capsule sales."

"That's a problem," Jonson says with a smile.

Jonson stays on for a few extra days, making sure we've solved the excess information problem. The machine's meter reads 40.4 million. No new phantoms, just a little excess information now and then, the most recent: ANOTHER DAY, ANOTHER DOLLAR. One harmless glitch remains. Every so often, a printed document catches on the exit guide, somersaulting in the output tray, casting a shadow on the wall. No reflection on me, my numbers increase four-tenths, and climb back up to three-point-two, the same percentage as beer served on the naval base at Gitmo.

"If incoming excess persists," the Tech Coordinator says, "the only way to save the Institute and keep your job is finding a way to make useless information useful."

45

An old rule of hitchhiking: if you don't look like a bum, it's easier to bum a ride. You'll do even better if you make hitchhiking look like fun. If only the Director were watching Jonson as he steps off the sidewalk, turns, and starts walking backward slowly, arm outstretched, thumb extended upward. A black Mercedes picks him up before you can say, "Penguin on a pedestal."

Mia and I take an after-lunch walk to the rotunda and take time out to admire the spectacular Christmas tree that rises to the second level. If Security would allow, you could stand on the balcony, reach out, and pluck plastic Christmas balls for a fruitful, baby-safe harvest. Amidst the festive beauty, two approaching robots emit eerie, warning beeps. With the promise of less excess information, the mail department plans to retire the robots soon.

The weather's mild enough for Penguin Four's first solo flight outdoors; we're nervous, and excited, like proud parents allowing Junior to go solo, riding his tricycle along a four-lane during rush hour. Folk wisdom: "Give them wings, they will fly." I'm not sure if that's true about kids, but the adage certainly applies to pigeons. Even though the weather's balmy for December, the Institute's barometer indicates Penguin Four might fly into stormy weather. When—if he returns, he can peck a pigeon-smart micro-switch to open an automatic door. We've done everything we can to prepare for the pigeon's separation. At a distance, he can only touch our lives with moments of loneliness.

At first, Penguin Four confronts the temptations of escape. He stands sideways on the windowsill, watching us with one eye, looking outside with the other. He might not understand freedom, but he has a sense of style. Time to leave, he shifts his weight, spreads his wings, flies away, circles, and comes back around the dome moments later.

The penthouse seems perfect for a picnic, but without Penguin Four, Mia's not in the mood. She's sitting at the window, a damsel in purple Lycra, knees tucked to her chin as she awaits the pigeon's return. We hope he comes back before our court appearance. His whereabouts will be hard to explain if he doesn't. While the court decides what's best for the pigeon, he might decide on his own. Jonson's belief that pigeons need food, water, sanitation, and adequate ventilation might make good testimony. But everyone forgets that pigeons need to be one with nature. Residing in their universe, they live between the center and outskirts, always in search of comfort, somewhere in between.

We're ready for our next day in court, prepared to expand the judge's knowledge about pigeon care. To keep things simple, Mia decides not to mention "love," a word that might sound foreign in a courtroom. The sophisticated lab pigeon Penguin Four needs Mia, who, in turn, needs him. Can she save him from Institutionalization? Even if we knew the answer, how can she tell a pigeon the truth with love?

In court, the judge's blood-red, road-map eyes bulge, a possible result of high blood pressure, hangover, or pretense of genuine concentration. As if impatient, as if he knows he needs ample time to convince losers they've had their day in court, he glances at his watch. Believe it or not, pigeon custody cases like this are unusual. Why would the judge's demeanor make you think he thinks he's seen one too many?

Legal people argue, "People caged in small office cubicles lead productive lives. Other than isolated cases of depression, anxiety, hyperactivity, diabetes, and obesity, there are no apparent side effects. For humans displaced from woods to the farm to factories to the Institute, these mild afflictions are supposedly rare. Likewise, there's nothing wrong with caging pigeons indoors, provided there's nutrition, hydration, sanitation, and of course, adequate ventilation."

An animal rights expert makes his argument sound like it comes from an Institute echo chamber. "Park pigeon life in the great outdoors should serve as a precedent for letting pigeons loose where there's food, water, sanitation, and ventilation, all organic and natural."

Everyone must have read the same pigeon text and worked on the same pigeon ranch while attending law school. How can people with the same background disagree? Without bragging or lying, Mia embellishes her testimony. "Penguin Four's active enough to survive disc pecking, ping pong, turntable riding, and its dizzying after-effects. He's performed as background blur for one of the world's greatest Reflexive Fusion Artists."

My statement doesn't contradict Mia's. I tell the judge, "Penguin Four's a key player in the creation—frequent flyer from the center to outskirts and back. There's nothing more beautiful than a pigeon defying dizziness, flying the rotunda, leaping upward into the spiral, returning to a creation that's here today, possibly gone tomorrow."

As if I'm wasting time, the judge tells me to define creation. I'm the one who brought it up; now I'm stuck, trying to explain the unexplainable. Reaching for an answer somehow makes it more elusive. Stop thinking; it becomes apparent. Describe the obvious, my river of thought freezes. Thankfully, I stop thinking and start talking. "You need movement to navigate the paradox of thoughtfulness and mindlessness between creation's center and outskirts."

The judge is bewildered, an awkward predicament for an intelligent being. He must be thankful the judicial process requires that he ignore realities central to the conflict. His mind must flash phantom-like ideas that disappear in less time than they take to arrive. No wonder his belief in justice is blind.

Institute and Animal Rights both insist they need proof Penguin Four still exists. The judge wants evidence that the pigeon doesn't. I find myself hoping the pigeon's flying high enough in friendly skies where stray BBs lose their velocity. Maybe he's on a quest, flying the spiral's outskirts, rising to the vortex. How high can you fly, Penguin Four?

46

The Institute pays Mia for Penguin Four's care, a mission unaccomplished if he happens to be missing. In truth, she's just getting paid to await the pigeon's return. Unfair for the Institute, the deal works well for Mia, who has nothing to lose—unless someone proves Penguin Four made a successful transfer to the afterward. Incidentally, if someone happens to trip over a fallen pigeon, Penguin Four's barcoded number on his leg band is P4 8963.

In the big scheme, the cost of caring for a pigeon that might or might not exist is no big deal and has little or no impact on a recession, depression, prosperity, or recovery. As a tech, I know this: the masses fuel the economy. It takes only a spark to ignite it. Rather than underrate the spark's impact, seek its origin. Remember the Machine. Remember its resurrection, a seemingly harmless arc, an electronic flash fire gone wrong.

Nothing is new; the creation waits. Profits are up, productivity down, more money for less work; it's not a bad combination of events. The three consultants, Smith, Jones, and Jonson, long forgotten, I still consider myself a key player. I should update my resume: "High energy team member, responsible for ten-point productivity drop with twelve-point profit increase." Without explanation, the Tech Coordinator passes my performance numbers up to the Director, proof my efforts don't go unnoticed. Fortunately, the financial stats don't reflect my recent performance at three-point-two. As things are, conflicting numbers confuse rather than enlighten. If mail output's down, why do robots remain busy? Since Jonson and I performed the targeted meltdown on the Machine, no one has complained that we're still getting too much information. But if it's printing less excess, some robots should be able to retire, without impacting the mail system. The Tech Coordinator orders me to investigate.

We should have noticed classic signs that all's not well. As mail flow decreases, people accustomed to sending and receiving go through withdrawal. One keyboard jockey, disillusioned beyond the point of self-containment, has already vowed to "go postal," his words a joke for some, a threat for others. Rather than admit mail is scarce, workers employ robots in new dysfunctional ways. It's not that they're lazy or inept. They need to fill the void of Institutional emptiness and need a robotic reason for being.

People clinging to old mailing methods send new kinds of mail. Let's face it. We're all becoming victims. Having mailed a dozen roses to Mia, I'm part of the problem. By the time the robot arrived at her cubicle, only four roses remained. Now that it is Christmas, people buy rounds of drinks, set them on the robot's top platform, and send them to friends. Like rose deliveries, refreshments end up first come first served. The mailing address is critical. As they say in real estate, "Location, location, location." Employees send lunch to themselves. To avoid embarrassing anyone, I won't mention names. At the rate things are going, we'll need another robot on each floor.

Some keyboard jockeys mail plants to their own addresses. Since they're intelligent employees, I can't call them vegetables. Call them "plant people instead." Why send live, inanimate objects? Here's the theory: If talking nurtures plants, changes of scenery might be just as beneficial. For sure, a trip around the Institute's outer halls provides more exposure to sunlight.

Even with good intentions, mail by robot is hazardous, no matter if harm's way originates in robotic movement, or on rock-solid hallway marble floors. An ivy vine snagged under a robot's wheels, pulling the entire plant onto hard marble, the crash, sudden death for even the hardiest. A Christmas amaryllis, tall or too tall, falls over when its stalk strikes an overhead door molding. Its bell-shaped, trumpet-like flowers wilt quickly, no longer harking the holidays as Christmas makes its dreaded advance. The possibilities for exploitation are endless. Robots carry briefcases and tow young, playful associates on skateboards. Clowns steal plants. On the increase, these crimes overload Security with more to investigate.

The Director calls this new affliction "mailitus." He asks Mia and me to join a task force to investigate ways to reduce robot workload and prevent senseless information addiction from overtaking us. It feels good knowing we can be part of the solution rather than part of the problem. After lunch, our group agreed to meet again next week and unanimously voted to adjourn. A robot approaches. The Chairman of our task force is a team player and a true achiever. Vying for his next award, another coveted birch bark plaque, he waves a hand in front of the robot's motion sensor to make it stop. "Don't worry," he says. "You're with me." We stack our lunch trays on the top shelf, already overloaded. "Move on," he says. Voice-activated, the robot beeps, and rolls away, indifferent to the coordinator's status.

47

We thought there would be more picnics to write about. Taken by surprise, HR disappoints Mia and me with a premature publication: ten thousand copies of *Fifty Places to Picnic: Employee Benefits for Today and a New Tomorrow.* We should be happy. For once, at least, we can judge a booklet by its cover, a glamorous portrait of Mia wearing an ankle-length gown, lying on the cobblestone esplanade, resting her chin on one of her delicate hands, toes feeding birdseed to a wild city pigeon. I took the picture a week after our actual picnic. No one suspects it was staged. As far as the booklet goes, rave reviews abound:

> "Yes! This all-in-one guide and travelogue tells a picnic like it is. New dimensions in exquisite taste, quaint picnics in concrete, brick, and mortar jungles. Simplicity, gourmet food's strange secret."

One review seems to come unglued:

> "We need a law that forces bullshitters to picnic in pastures. There's always one in every crowd? Here, we have two."

We autograph five thousand copies. It would take time to inscribe something personal, fresh, and catchy in each one. It takes almost as much time to write the same message over and over: "We'll always cherish the quality time we spent together at the Institute." We sign "Mia and Sid" on half of the copies, and "Sid and Mia" on the rest. Recipients might think we appreciate the time spent with them. Although that's possible, Mia and I value the time she and I spent together. We're thankful for the Institute's rare act of kindness, introducing us to each other, and asking us to coauthor *Fifty Places*, even if they limited the number of sites to a dozen or so. For better or worse, what are the odds that two strangers in a strange institution would become coauthors and surrogate parents of a lost pigeon?

Inscribed copies of *Fifty Places* double in street value. We've heard people whisper, "There they are. There's that lady Mia." It seems as if recognition skills are only worth practicing on famous people.

The funny part, we get much less credit for doing things we do with much more difficulty—running the pigeon lab or caring for the Machine. My most recent achievement, I caught a spider dancing with life on one of the primal inverter's photo sensors, arachnid shadows switching it on and off randomly. Who knows? Maybe the dancing spider confused the Machine, triggering our information invasion. A spider riding a spider plant riding a robot got me to rethink things, and have another look. The problem's solved. Thanks to Mia for saving the dancing spider's life, thanks to the two spiders now riding the spider plant that's still riding the robot. I keep this discovery quiet; no one needs to find out. The truth might revive a troublesome question: did we perform the resurrection and electronic lobotomy all for nothing?

48

We're sitting on the only dropping-free couch in the pent-house, awaiting Penguin Four's return. Taking a break from lethargy, Mia kicks off her shoes, keeps her socks on, curls her toes, and watches them straighten as if she's doing warm-ups. Unoccupied, my mind starts racing. Taskforce duties overwhelm me so much that I think aloud. "If we cure mailitus, which robots retire?"

Mia curls her toes and reflexes. "It's not just about mail addiction. You always say, 'Humans need movement. Regardless of which robots retire, keyboard jockeys need room to move.'"

A new Institute memo implements a wellness policy to discourage mail and robot dependency. The homegrown prescription requires that everyone picnic four times a week. To make the idea sound like fun, Mia and I suggest employees bring a plant along for a fresh breath of carbon dioxide. *Fifty Places* now completed, HR ignores us, as if they know more than we do.

Thinking a hike is more meaningful than an actual picnic, some employees wander as if they have no sense of direction. Ending up where they started, they spread beach towels on the marble floor, often inches away from their workspaces. Some try sites in the order they appear in *Fifty Places*. A few try the outskirts—generator space and ventilation ducts are favorites. No surprise, the outskirts become crowded quickly. Couples no longer looking for love in the wrong places, treat themselves to intimate picnics at the phone training center. More gregarious souls crowd the bank counter as if it's a local coffee shop that provides mental health benefits to employees and customers alike.

Accustomed to creature comforts, some employees buy popcorn and sit in the auditorium. Afraid they might miss a fresh batch of PowerPoint, they focus on the empty stage. You never know. Maybe a few want to see vintage *Gong Show* videos on the Institute's big screen. Since Security controls the rotunda, it's a far more exclusive destination that requires a reservation. It's a waste of time calling. Unless you know someone, you need to be one of the front office suits to picnic there.

It surprises us that the cafeteria remains the most popular place. If you hate making lunch, enjoy crowds, and love Institutional cooking, the cafeteria's perfect. Employees stack tables to create giant pedestals. Secure with the smug feeling they're above eating on the floor, some lounge on high-altitude tables, the more elevated, the better. Crude pyramids rise to the ceiling, creating a paradoxical sense of openness and privacy. My favorite is the easy-to-climb spiral, a stack of round tables with the largest diameter at the base, becoming smaller as they progress toward the top. Small groups spread their towels in private spots. Shaded from fluorescence, they gaze across the vast cafeteria expanse, with no apparent concern about what neighbors might think. Some send texts, looking downward at their handhelds, tapping fingers beak-like as if pecking sunflower seed.

Communication is critical, even on a picnic. Some people arrive at the cafeteria and say, "Sid sent me" or "Mia sent me." They must be joking. They should know better. According to *Fifty Places*, readers should tell servers that Sid or Mia sent them. As authors, we did. Person to person, we never referred anyone. Let history be the judge.

People who picnic on hallway floors obstruct the robots, a minor problem as problems go. Now that robots move less mail, they have more time to beep their persistent warning beeps, waiting for people to move. Choosing which ones to retire will be easy. Three have already skidded on banana peels and hit the wall. Like little engines that supposedly could, they keep running, going nowhere, draining batteries and burning out motors until they die. No personal injuries; so far, so good.

Security posted signs everywhere: "Take nothing but pictures. Leave nothing but footprints." Too bad there aren't any signs for the birds, a detail that sounds trivial until coordinators realize the Institute will require the continued cleanup of pigeon deposits, mindlessly dropped on the esplanade. Sanitation Coordinator hopes and prays for temperatures to remain cold enough to discourage outdoor picnics, and to allow the miraculous power of snow's whiteness to continue blending with pigeon dung. I've suggested we put out a couple of damaged robots beneath the giant tree that subsists on fertilizer injections force-fed into the soil. As bird feeders, robots will attract the pigeons to one place. Instead of covering the entire grounds with random deposits, they can fertilize the tree with concentrated amounts of pigeon dung. In keeping with the Institute's mythical open-door policy, no one responds to my idea.

For many, picnics become too popular, too exciting, too overwhelming. Exuberant keyboard jockeys return to workstations, energized enough to continue creating and processing more information than anyone needs—Director's beginning to question the threat of any increased productivity that won't raise profits. Our only hope is fads often cure themselves by dying out after becoming epidemics. Some proposed solutions are clear. Revise the original prescription; require fewer picnics; deputize volunteer rangers.

Some think it crazy to suggest Reflexive Fusion. How quickly we forgot old times when most of the suits argued against physical fitness and balanced diets. Mia and I encourage HR to think about mental health. At its worst, Reflexive Fusion might discourage the keyboard jockeys from pissing and moaning about soreness from traditional floor picnics. Since lower productivity continues to boost profits, think big, think sacrifice by Lazy Penguin, a fun way for workers to relax in the shadow of pending layoffs. Best of all, everyone gets a few moments in fame's spotlight, just like Mia, just like Penguin Four.

49

The Machine can't do Reflexive Fusion the way Mia does. It has its own way. Every so often, it shoots paper onto the exit tray, leaning one sheet against another, forming a peaked pyramid that's frozen in time until another print knocks it down. "Sometimes, I blame the dancing spider for the software glitch," I've told Mia. "Maybe the main auxiliary transistor survived Jonson's one-twenty-volt barrage of electrons."

"You, Jonson, and the so-called dancing spider," Mia says. "No matter what the cause, you're all innocent bystanders. Just worry about the trumped-up numbers they use to make you look bad."

Almost convinced that Reflexive Fusion might be safer than picnics, the Institute considers risking its professional reputation, by allowing employees to remove their shoes while working. Their only fear, what if some start wiggling their toes? The Institute can escape its embarrassment by promoting more appropriate activities. Even though Research didn't ask, I risk sounding like a know-it-all. "Spinning on a Lazy Penguin allows you to project a more professional image. How many keyboard jockeys have the background necessary to make foot shadows?"

"Spinning sounds like it could have harmful side effects— dizziness, nausea, in rare cases, a false sense of well-being. Insurance costs could skyrocket." The Coordinator turns to the Director. "Should we consider coordinating with Legal to create a standard liability waiver?"

Building a heavy-duty Lazy Penguin creates its challenges.

At least making foot braces for humans is more straightforward than designing ones for pigeons. As luck has it, I found the right parts at an army surplus store, owned and operated online by a full-time civilian who never served in the military. Prices are right. People don't have to but sometimes thank him for his service.

We install the new Lazy Penguin in the commons, away from the cafeteria. Less foot traffic affords privacy for first-timers trying it out. Fearing ridicule and tarnished professional reputations, some keyboard jockeys try wearing paper bags over mandatory helmets, but a few still feel ridiculous. No surprise, low-level workers with the least to lose are the first to take a few test spins. In time, a few low-level coordinators give it a try, not for fun, to prove themselves team players. It's not long before people stand in line, waiting to sacrifice themselves. No surprise, it's disappointing that a few become addicted.

One reason the Lazy Penguin has become popular, employees can spin to attain dance rapture, without wasting physical energy or making meaningless human contact. We move it to the cafeteria, where spin-offs evolve beyond sacrificial. Some spinners get dizzy. Others enjoy clearing their heads. Lacking the necessary attitude and physical training, trying to leap into the spiral the way Penguin Four flew upward in the rotunda, guarantees failure. What about mental health? The stress of signing a waiver is enough to cause side effects.

Mia takes her lunch hour an hour late. Keyboard jockeys are back at their cubicle desks, dancing their fingers on computer keyboards. Few have time to watch her repetitive attempts to leap into the spiral. One of the fortunate few gifted with the persistence needed to learn the art of flying, Mia's a sight, spinning ten or fifteen minutes at a time, rarely getting dizzy, never losing her balance, and falling off accidentally. It's hard to tell if Mia focuses as if she's in the moment or afterward; there's something I can't see. I become mesmerized, watching her purple Lycra blur until she leaps off the spinning pedestal. Taking the highest leap, remaining airborne longer than anyone else at the Institute, Mia will never reach the spiral's apex. At least Mia's more tranquil than she's been since Penguin Four's departure.

As luck has it, Mia is spinning on the Lazy Penguin, when a Musik Channel agent scouting for talent happens to pass by. Imagine loud, industrialized, Institutional, rock and roll, a bass guitar playing deep warm notes, insistent drums beating rapid-fire. Think rolling thunder skipping across the Institute's marble floors. Imagine that while spinning on a Lazy Penguin. It's not a problem if coordinators can't imagine. The agent can. Too late for publication Mia's tacked these above her desk, words that could have served as an epilogue to *Fifty Places*:

"Spin dizzy on a Lazy Penguin, leap for the afterward. Return to earth. Cop an attitude; call it a picnic."

The Machine passes less information now. Robots are less abused by excess mail and by the antics of fun-loving employees. With the luxury of time, is it too dramatic to wonder if Penguin Four flew into the afterward?

Without our picnic assignment, we talk Institute small talk as if it fills the void. "I don't understand numbers," I tell Mia. "I'm just a tech who fixes a machine that prints policies that bet big money against certain deaths at uncertain times."

"Caring for a missing pigeon that's dead or alive might look like child's play," Mia says. "It's not as easy as it looks. I miss Penguin Four. There's no peace unless I'm barefoot, spinning on that Lazy Penguin."

Riding a Lazy Penguin's not easy. On those rare occasions when Mia gets thrown off in a fit of dizziness, her toes wiggle drunkenly, a state more vulgar than graceful. She never gets to reach out far enough to touch the spiral's tip, but she seems more in touch with the afterward. Her tranquility is an example to us all. After a long day working and riding the Lazy Penguin, she returns to the penthouse, and sits at the window, a damsel in shining Lycra, calm but helpless to save a pigeon, possibly in distress.

I should describe my modest experience on the Lazy Penguin. As a designer obligated to test it before others subjected themselves to its centrifugal whims, I chose dizziness over self-control, focus, or spirituality. Is dizziness better than the other choices? Not necessarily. In the spiral, you rise above it all. When you're dizzy, you move from the center to the outskirts, fall, and become part of the creation. My mind catches up with itself as it spins and spins, creating a sense of movement that might or might not be. Too weak to catch the spiral whenever I take the fall, I remain a humble part of the creation. Who knows? I've sometimes wondered if Penguin Four ever made it to the spiral's tip, the only vantage point to see the entire universe.

Christmas Eve is a time for love to rid the cold winter of its demons. For once, the Institute makes us an exception, allowing us to camp out on the rotunda's second level as if that's a likely place to find Penguin Four. No tent, we just brought sleeping bags and the Lazy Penguin Mia insisted on bringing along. Wearing a rare adult-size, holiday princess dress, Mia spins in a trance, her red Saint Santa hat waving outward, her white Lycra and dress a blur. It seems like it takes her forever to leap, she remains suspended two or three feet above the spinning turntable for a few moments until gravity reclaims her. Instead of getting right back on to spin this time, Mia heads downstairs to the lower level. Despite the guard's objections, she spreads birdseed on the front steps. "Who pays for cleanup this time," I wonder aloud. Of course, I'm not afraid to say this in a moment when Mia can't hear me.

Awakened by reflected rays of light from sunlit snow, Mia looks outside and watches pigeons feasting on birdseed. Half-awake, she tiptoes down marble stairs, sneaks past the guard, and opens the rotunda doors. One by one, pigeons fly into the Institute, perch on spruce branches, and spread out evenly as if partridges in a pear tree. What a beautiful sight to behold. A pigeon perched at the tree's apex glides down, and lands on Mia's shoulder. She strokes its feathers, speaking softly as if the bird's a human. She brings the pigeon up to the balcony, our campsite. Both bird and Mia coo a conversation that expresses nothing beyond warm mutual feelings that remain somewhat fuzzy. She looks up. "It's Penguin Four," she says. "I can tell."

"I'm less certain. If it's Penguin Four, he's suffering from weight loss." It's not that I doubt Mia, but in this world, you can't be too careful. I check the leg band. "Sure enough, it reads P4 8963, a perfect match."

Hundreds of whitish pigeon deposits accumulate beneath the tree despite the guard's objections. What a merry Christmas it is.

50

Penguin Four's return brings peace to Mia, who celebrates, with another blurb for the Institute to ignore.

"Santa Claused angel's silent night, Carrier of the Pigeon spins on a Lazy Penguin. Princess-dressed reflections come and go in tree light glow. Prodigal pigeon Penguin Four, a Christmas miracle, rescues us from the perceptual pain of holiday razzle-dazzle."

Desktop computers stream Musik Channel videos to desktop monitors. Mia, in her purple Lycra, performs video magic, dancing toes to music. My blurred shoes remain in the background. A bass guitar's primitive rhythm accompanies our footwork. Nothing looks or sounds offbeat. Without vocals, Mia's feet say it all.

The video cuts to Mia twirling on the Lazy Penguin, leaping off the spinning platter for a lift into the afterward, remaining suspended moments longer than what's possible in real life. Since I insist, Musik Channel pays me a token amount, enough for them to avoid a costly lawsuit. Now that they're paying both of us, I'm sure we're appreciated more.

The deaths of Penguins One, Two, and Three remain controversial. Research directs me to investigate. It's more work, but at least the task is a nod that I have the mind for the job. I need to think beyond court proceedings and start from scratch with what we know. Three pigeons sacrificed without a Lazy Penguin: three drawn-out, sacrificial ceremonies intolerable for a modern company as efficient as the Institute. What would the gods think? Were the deaths of One, Two, and Three caused by dogs dizzied by hunger? Was the cause more natural than that, possibly old age, famine, shortage of birdseed, or too much suet composed of eighty-eight percent fat? The pottery dig was a convenient place for winter disposal. Maybe someone was too lazy or too cheap to pay someone else to dig a hole in frozen ground. My investigation remains open.

Graffiti that depicted a prehistoric pigeon inside the ventilation duct turns out to be a hoax. Having decided that picnics could destroy the Institute's image, HR hoped to discredit us with primitive but forged graffiti. Better luck next time.

Now and then, the Machine still creates paper pyramids and lean-tos. No one notices. Is another lone spider foxtrotting on a photo sensor? Wishful thinking or not, I'm sure that one rebellious transistor survived the lobotomy.

Rumors about the Machine abound. We hear it might win a free trip to the Smithsonian. It might get crushed, chipped, and baled as scrap for recycling. As the resident tech, I'm one of the few who knows the truth. For reasons unknown, the Director wants it moved to the lower rotunda. In this quiet place, it can pass less paper, create more information, and print phantom documents with a new brand of homogenized, less standardized wisdom. Here's one example I found propped on the exit tray. As is, useful or useless, turn on or turn off, it could use a little tweaking. IT TAKES TWO TO TANGO BEFORE THE FAT LADY SINGS. It's not my job to trash or save random information. You never know. It might reflect well on the Institute, it might portend what's to come.

The good news, some things never change. Framed *Sci-Fi American* hangs on Mia's condo wall, headlined *In the Pigeon's Best Interest*, with a picture of Penguin Four playing ping pong on its cover. Often, Mia takes Penguin Four back to the penthouse, to spend quality time. We rarely have a chance to picnic together.

The Machine's meter, by the way, reads nine-point-four billion if I have the number of zeros right. A minor mystery, my performance scores have disappeared from the Institute's database. Miraculously, my name Sid Sidney remains.

The Director buys in, placing his bets for another spin on the corporate wheel of fortune. If there's profit in people who want money when they die, there should be a profit in people preoccupied with the money they want while living. To avoid a buyout, the Institute does the right thing, restructuring, realigning, reaching out, and partnering. It renames itself the Academy of Reality. So far, the Academy people, buildings, and parking lots remain as they were. But the Institute no longer exists, as we knew it. Even if it went nowhere, it's no longer here. How to make sense of it all?

PART II

The Academy

51

"You're right, Sid. The Director dwells in a metric wonderland," the Tech Coordinator leans forward. "Look at how the num bers work. Keyboard micro switches count keyboard jockey keystrokes, one hundred and two keys."

"Standard keyboard has a hundred and four."

"You're the technician, you should know. But stop and think. Backspace and delete keys are counterproductive in the way they undo work already done. One hundred and two keys add to keyboard jockey numbers, two subtract. Always double-check backspace and delete keys. If one happens to stick, that lowers our numbers."

"Sounds like a plan."

"Get over it. It's not a plan; it's a fair metric that tracks re-ality. The Machine keeps score; it monitors performance. Last month, eight million keystrokes to the ninth power, multiplied by four thousand, ten-fingered keyboard jockeys."

"What was it, four thousand workers? You're talking for-gotten majority. It's not about accountability. It's about who to fire and who to keep. Four thousand, afflicted with carpal tunnel, tendonitis. Finger pads worn to bones, barely enough skin remaining for crime-stopping fingerprints."

"Get over it. Institute's now The Academy. Nothing else changed. Funny thing, your sarcasm about numbers pulls your numbers down. You're better off acting more professionally. Remember?"

Blood's pounding in my head, doing its work, mixing in a healthy dose of adrenaline, making me more alive with a rage that fuels what needs to be said, "You're talking Zen moments of nothingness, useless byproducts of production. How many of your keystrokes fill a molecule? Fill a thumb drive, fill a cloud?"

"Loyal service requires unbiased, statistical reflection—always."

"Accountability, who do you fire, who to keep? Your corporate spin's nothing but an art form to soft sell the next layoff: Package early retirement. Discharge, deport, layoff, cutback, thin the herd, put out to pasture."

"This conversation's going nowhere."

52

Custody issues regarding Penguin Four force the Institute to remain as one separate, almost fictitious entity. As we expected, Mia remains the Carrier of the Pigeon. In defiance of recent court orders that keep Penguin Four from participating in future research, the Academy's coordinator subjects him to new experiments. "Probably the only reason the Institute changed its name to Academy," Mia says. "They treat him like an Academy pigeon, make him work a new gig with a nameless pigeon you might as well call Four B."

We're standing in Mia's cubicle, watching pigeons Penguin Four and Four B in their small cubicle, pecking their respective discs, earning one seed every five taps. Mia sounds bitter. "Academy calls this a study. It looks more like a competition."

"It's hard to tell the two pigeons apart the way you can, Mia. Without a barcode reader, those wing tags are useless. Leg band numbers are getting too small to read. My eyesight's almost bad enough to need glasses."

"Director's afraid this kind of research raises suspicions in the outside world," Mia says. "But it's no problem. If this were about corporate greed, Research would be using rats instead of pigeons. Two birds participating in a ground-breaking study on investment and organized crime are better for the Academy's image."

Now and then, a seed bounces down the reward chute like a loose dollar bill in the wind, or better said, blowing in a weak, computerized breeze. If the pigeon eats the seed, he pecks the disc five times to get another. If he deposits it, he gets two seeds right away, a good deal in comparison.

Realize it or not, the pigeon faces a dilemma: Eat or stash? Invest or gamble? Eat the seed or use it as seed money for more seed? Two heroic lab pigeons, investors hard at work, don't have time or energy to appreciate routine puzzlers that puzzle humans. Spend big on organic or survive on fertilizer-fed; "To be or not to be" would be the wrong question.

"Are the lab people organized criminals studying organized crime?" Mia asks. "Whoever came up with this should investigate coordinators instead of the behavior of pigeons."

"You're right. Ideas: there's no fusion without reflection. You can tell their research depends on work with foregone conclusions. Necessity is the mother of invention, hunger the mother of intention. It takes common sense: corporate crime pays."

Still trying to understand Academy rules yet to be written, we need to be careful. Uncertain that casual intimacy is appropriate, I make sure no one's looking before I gently squeeze Mia's hand.

To cut costs, the Academy buys half the usual pigeon pellets. No coincidence, the experiment ends, bursting investment bubbles of birdseed. Sacrificed once already, Penguin Four is protected. With nothing left to lose, he continues pecking as if starvation's imminent; he gets his pigeon pellets, regardless.

There's no formal evaluation for pigeons. Lacking a sixth or seventh sense of a near-future demise, Four B doesn't give up. Not that it matters, he's no longer needed. Mia refuses to put him down. "It's not exactly a sacrifice," she says. "Not when life's taken."

Lab work is not science fiction. Four B has no idea he's condemned to an alternate afterward, a world unimagined. Mia knows; she never watches the Research Coordinator hook electrodes to a pigeon's wings, flippantly flip a switch, activating a one-twenty-volt life erase. For reasons unknown, he always deposits the remains in a once-shattered pottery jug, its fragments repaired with glue.

We leave the lab and head for lunch early. To help Mia forget about Four B, I remind her of other things she can be unhappy about. "New barcoded photo ID almost looks like an expired driver's license. It's only good for accessing that new cyber guru LaserFunk."

"HR says no more Reflexive Fusion," Mia replies. "Forget the picnics. And the Research Coordinator played the organic seed card. From now on, I can only feed the formulated medicated feed for Penguin Four."

"HR can't stop us. As long as we get our work done, we don't have to roll over and play dead like sacrificed pigeons in pottery jugs." My words make Mia cringe; I try to recover. "I wonder how the girl and kitten are doing."

53

Life goes on as the expression goes and sometimes doesn't. Will time fly too quickly if I gloss over details and summarize? Most employees no longer appreciate *Fifty Places to Picnic*. Most think Mia and I are eccentric. The Director calls a meeting. His newest PowerPoint reveals the downside of using torches and arc welding equipment to inspire employees. Rather than waste time and money studying modern pigeons to understand outdated humans, the Academy rolled out LaserFunk, a new computerized therapist that converts the Machine's spurious output into diagnostic questions for lucrative therapeutic cures. "This new treatment might sound sketchy," the Director says. "Not now but after work, think about that instant cure TV expert Dr. Phil Phoster. LaserFunk makes him look like a monkey in need of therapy himself. Trust me. If Phil ever loses his day job, he shouldn't waste time looking for work here at the Academy."

No applause from the audience; a keyboard jockey mumbles, "What the fuck," as if he's on a stricken ship, responding to a political suit praising God, country, and politics. I whisper to Mia, "Some of these people are TV Phil fans already. They probably go home and turn on their TVs to forget life at The Academy."

The Director continues: "LaserFunk, a brand name that adds appeal, builds credibility: 'Laser' for sharp focused, and fast. 'Funk' for offbeat and extra."

I whisper to Mia. "Sarcastic or optimistic, I'm not sure.

They must like the idea that happiness in a box makes the mind go electric. Sophomoric, street kids must love how the name sounds off-beat, electronic as if it's a dance or mood."

PowerPoint shows a sample question ADVERSITY MAKES US STRONGER. (TRUE / FALSE). The Director describes LaserFunk's instant printouts, the tasteful font on expensive old-fashioned resume-grade paper. Psycho-diagnostics are more credible than those from the best of the best, even Dr. Phil. Therapy's electronic style is cost-effective and more profitable. It detects and cures problems with far more sophistication than you'd ever get from the usual homespun remedies.

Back when life was simple, someone with a screw loose needed a doctor; a bat in a belfry an exterminator; or full of the devil, an exorcist. According to the famous TV Phil, making false assumptions calls for reality therapy.

The PowerPoint shows an employee, the former Tasha Yar of the imaginary starship Enterprise, reading digital therapeutic output. Tasha's mental condition, of course, remains confidential. Out of uniform, she wears business casual. She seems happier now than she was during the time a starship could cross the universe more dependably than the Machine could pass paper.

"User-friendly," the Director says. "LaserFunk's affordable for deserving clients who carry Academy health insurance; it costs a little more for everyone else. Pleasant avatar's intelligence should inspire confidence in any cynic pretending to ask intelligent questions."

I nudge Mia. "Pleasant avatar's semi-intelligence would oversell it."

Must be the Director noticed. He pauses an extra moment and continues. "Like I was saying, our user-friendly avatar's intelligent, always a guru, gender of choice depending on which option you choose."

Avatar's wearing a sleeveless rose-red sundress and flip flops; she's slender, someone who works out at a virtual gym. She gazes outward from the monitor, longingly, with a warm, come-hither smile. Too bad LaserFunk's clients only get to answer true or false questions. Her sad expression could ease confession of sin, accept humble confessions of superiority, or bold admissions of inferiority.

The Director raises his voice. "Unaffordable is no excuse. Get the word out. If you know someone uninsured, get them to try it out. Help them tweak their budget or steal a barcode. Hack into someone else's computer, just to try it out. Self-improvement's not selfish; it enriches the lives of everyone around you."

Director continues. "You're already fortunate to work at the Academy. No need to ink your wrist with a barcode. Just use your new ID. Find one of our easy-to-find kiosks. If you're feeling brave, scan in, dance with lady luck, electronified and personified. If impatience is not your virtue, don't worry, you won't have to wait long. A terminal analyzes up to twenty-four people in eight hours, one every twenty minutes."

The next PowerPoint slide shows Tasha Yar touching electrodes, one on either side of her keyboard. Her face glows, Mia thinks the radiance comes from bleaching with diluted lemon juice.

The Director's voice is almost mesmerizing. "Imagine, sensations of mild electroshock pulsing, massaging, touching every part of your being. If it feels good, wear the wristbands for electronic stimulation to achieve Nirvana's sensations of well-being."

I nudge Mia. "Everything but the techno-spoken truth. Electric keystrokes on and off, bastardized ones and twos, the binary logic gets lost in the mire of gray-shaded threes and fours."

The Director becomes more animated. His voice gets louder. His right arm waves horizontally, robotically as if his mind just fried a resistor or transistor. "A Posibyte flashes well-being, a drawback for new business. Shadow of mental affliction, a negabyte numbers bring in revenue."

The Director doesn't tell you what to do if LaserFunk says you're lost. Take it from me. If lost in a forest, stay in the same place so searchers can find you. Lost at the Academy, go to the therapeutic wing. If you're a tech with work to do, keep moving. You'll find yourself sooner or later.

Mia's smile makes it look like she might start laughing. "It all makes people-friendly picnics and Reflexive Fusion sound like junk science. Is this a fad? Or electronic psychobabble; just another promise of quick personality fixes and easy profits for the Academy?"

"I don't trust it. If you're talking funk, you need to know if you're living on the upbeat or downbeat. Good news or bad, how much does LaserFunk know?"

"Electronic therapy for everyone? I'm not so sure," Mia says. "The Academy nurtures abnormality then exploits those who seek balance."

"I've seen most of the diagnostic questions. Some are hard like this one: ON SCHOOL DAYS, DID YOU TAKE YOUR LUNCH OR TAKE THE BUS? I'm not trying to talk this up or down, Mia. We can't let a user-friendly name like LaserFunk fool us. It shows no mercy. I saw a guy leaving a kiosk who seemed more depressed than he was when he arrived. I remember him stepping away, eyes bulging from anger or pain, fist-clenching a printout as if it revealed truth worth knowing. At a loss for words that might comfort, I hoped my old luggage cart might reflect life's humor, an old-fashioned home remedy, a diversion that might help him look inward instead of outward for wisdom misplaced on a printout."

My luggage cart's a weird constant that never changes. I keep it loaded with tools that only techs who work at the Smithsonian use—screwdrivers, wrenches, pliers. I pull it from module to module, listening to its under-size wheels squawk and squeal in concert, loudly enough to reveal my whereabouts. If I feel rushed and walk too fast, my heels hit the frame—not hard enough to trip, just hard enough to make a bored keyboard jockey laugh. I don't use the tools much, and probably don't even need the luggage cart, the Machine doesn't need much maintenance these days. Relocated to the lower rotunda now, it passes less paper than it did at the Institute. Same old electronics, with new software, it's more productive coming up with brainteasers.

I can't compare digital therapy with a live therapist. I've never visited a traditional one. The only printouts I see are partial results, scrambled output the usual mishmash of psychobabble gone wrong. Here's one that LaserFunk should have rejected: "JESUS WEPT." I'm no shrink, but if you ask me, outputs like this make the mind feel bad. Maybe the two words are just products of the single transistor that survived the Machine's one-twenty-volt onslaught. It must have lifted the phrase "Jesus wept" from the King James version of the Bible. So much for miracles.

Yesterday, Module Three's printer got caught in a loop with a purely defensive output:

CLIENT DENIES THAT PATTERNS REOCCUR.

CLIENT DENIES THAT PATTERNS REOCCUR.

CLIENT DENIES THAT PATTERNS REOCCUR.

CLIENT DENIES THAT PATTERNS REOCCUR.

CLIENT DENIES THAT PATTERNS REOCCUR.

CLIENT DENIES THAT PATTERNS REOCCUR.

CLIENT DENIES THAT PATTERNS REOCCUR.

CLIENT DENIES THAT PATTERNS REOCCUR.

The printer consumes more than a ream of paper, repeating itself over and over. Mia intervenes, transferring the client's data to another module. The output is confidential. I'm not allowed to reveal if an anonymous client has life patterns that trigger denial. For sure, it imitates and emulates Dr. Phil's confidence and competence. Then again, since it's networked with the Machine, it might only be burping and farting misaligned electrons in a cruel logic scramble. Hoping it's a software problem, I check for trouble codes and try uploading, downloading, and offloading software. I give up and clear the memory. A kilobyte of software is worth a megabyte of cure.

The bug disappears when I'm troubleshooting, and reappears after I leave. Luckily, Tasha Yar didn't try this module out while posing for PowerPoint slides.

I report the repetitious diagnostic loop to the Tech Coordinator who yawns and asks, "Why fight it? I can't help it if a client has something to deny. Who cares if some random pattern reoccurs? Problems are opportunities. Be happy for a change. We're getting good numbers."

My inability to fix the bug doesn't seem to be a problem. He spins low numbers into opportunities. "Does 'opportunity' somehow rhyme with Performance Improvement Plan," I ask.

"Here's the score," he says. "Twelve million keystrokes to the eleventh times twenty-eight hundred keyboard jockeys, all with ten fingers apiece. Negabyte number forty-eight point nine."

Even though the cold, impersonal nature of laser therapy discourages the usual pissing and moaning we hear when humans involve themselves in conversation, I wonder if there will ever be enough collective contentment to allow old-fashioned therapy again. When I'm moving data from one place to another, from the Machine to the laptop to one of the terminals, for instance, there's time for my mind to wander. Is electronic therapy better than Dr. Phil's? How long will I have a job? In the days when you twisted screwdrivers, there was time to daydream about the creation. Now there's barely time to worry about survival.

Mia's take on all this:

"LaserFunk, paradise lost or found in electric fluorescent paint by number. Now and then, here and now gets distorted by True and Falseness."

"Philosophical tidbits drift off like evaporated truth serum. The Academy might be a den of high-tech iniquity.

LaserFunk says, "YOU CAN TUNE A PIANO BUT CAN'T TUNA FISH."

"The Machine seems too simple to make up the TUNA FISH question. Maybe I sound too negative, Mia. Did the Machine pick it up somewhere, at an online comedy club, or rock concert, or old-fashioned album cover, maybe?"

54

The Machine's most recent question sounds like a quote from that crackpot who invented the World War II pigeon-guided missile: NO ONE GOES TO THE CIRCUS TO SEE THE AVERAGE DOG JUMP THROUGH THE AVERAGE HOOP. This time-worn wisdom inspires the Research Coordinator to learn as much as he can about average pigeons.

Research's plan is a problem. The Academy has sacrificed its pigeons, all but one. Technically, Penguin Four still belongs to the Institute. Mia taught the pigeon to jump rope to keep his neck muscles loose enough so he could relax after playing ping pong. Now, the Academy Coordinator wants Mia to make Penguin Four jump through hoops.

Maybe Mia wants to prove Penguin Four can rise to the challenge; she might want to confuse Research. "Do you know the diameter of an average hoop," she asks.

The Coordinator shakes his head.

"What about experimental height? Are the hoops made of plastic, fiberglass, or carbon fiber?"

"Offhand, I'm not sure," he says. "Let's be positive. I'm sure you can spec a credible hoop setup."

Mia laughs out loud, and says under her breath, "Yeah! Right!" Best guesstimate or pure subversion, she suspends the hoops a few feet above the floor, a perfect setup to disrupt beliefs that science is always scientific. In his bird-like way, Penguin Four understands the challenge. Instead of jumping like a gymnast, he flies and glides through the hoops, super-bird-like.

The Coordinator says nothing. He looks disappointed.

"Was that burst of avian genius a result of premature experimentation? Was that good for you?" Mia asks.

The Coordinator seems embarrassed.

"Not to worry, it's not your fault. To say you get yourself too worked up would be an understatement. Next time, take it slow."

It's Mia's coordinator, not mine. The timing's not right to remind him that a weak anticlimax makes just punishment for failing to think things through. There's not much Mia can do, other than try to help Research understand complicated circus tricks. Since it seems like he doesn't have all the answers, questions might at least help him. "Do average people go to the circus," she asks. "How can you tell if a circus is above or below average? How can a bird that flies ride the bell curve of normality?"

Coordinator glances at Mia and glares at me. "Do you two have work to do," he asks.

Mia monitors all one hundred twenty kiosks. One benefit, obvious but unintended, allows her to gain access to the Corporate Adjustment Test, the CAT. "Just for reassurance that I don't fit in, I answered a whole set of questions," she tells me. "What do I end up with? Without saying why, it thinks I have a criminal mind."

Luckily, I'm here for Mia. "Criminal mind's not about you. It's a symptom of shallow analysis." I touch Mia's forehead. "Anyone who would attend my funeral, anyone who discusses dreams and talks about reality the way you do is too childish to be criminal. Who knows what's wrong with LaserFunk?"

When things are slow, Mia retakes the test, using her thumb drive to answer some questions the same way as always, but changing certain ones to get different outcomes. Last week, she tried so many changes, her avatar, an almost pleasant, handsome man who otherwise shares many of my features, froze as if posing for a movie still. Even without movement, he looked as if he were competing on *Dancing with Stars at Bars*, reality TV for viewers too tired or socially awkward to dance unless they're out drinking. Sensing a problem, LaserFunk alerts Security as well as Research who contact me.

Reboot's not exactly a dance move; it's just a simple, electronic three-volt kick in the butt, a reset that resuscitates the avatar. Even after recovery, the avatar's movement is much slower than it should be, moving from one frozen frame to another. His dance moves are awkward and stilted. Is the network overloaded or compromised? Who cares? It's not my job to find out.

My numbers suffer slightly. It's no disappointment that my coordinator didn't call a meeting. Fourteen million keystrokes to the twelfth, times twenty-two hundred, all with ten fingers: Negabyte number, forty-four-point-six.

Mia doesn't let failure go to her head—changing answers is a logical reaction to LaserFunk's electronic output gone wild. So far, her favorite question is this: WHEN I'M SAD, I COUNT MY BLESSINGS.

Up until recently, LaserFunk's idiosyncratic bugs kept me so busy I never took the time to try it myself. But a dead battery triggered a sudden failure in my fail-safe, state-of-the-art, Fahrenheit Two-Twelve, Diagnostic Scanner, known as the FTDS among techs in the know. Most of the time, it's just costume jewelry hanging from my tool cart. I can't say it inspires clients to have faith in me the way a doctor's stethoscope inspires confidence in patients. The Two-Twelve sports a powerful Two hundred and twelve gigabyte memory. It's even capable of diagnosing self-diagnostics, its own or any device it happens to be testing.

All I can do without a scanner is conduct tests the old-fashioned way. At first, I made sure no one was watching while I answered test questions. But I soon realized that anyone who catches me running tests would probably think I'm putting LaserFunk through its paces. I do one or two items a day, recording my choices on a cheat sheet, an outdated mode of handwritten information storage. No one except Mia knows that I keep it hidden in my shirt pocket, so I can run the answers while testing an actual repair. If the output says I'm OK, I put the module back in service. My wise strategy creates a conflict of interest. Will documenting my mental health lower my stats enough to suggest I'm a professional failure?

The Academy's new code of ethics forbids cheating, in some instances, and allows it in others. It all depends on which test I'm taking, or which test I'm testing. I can't reveal specifics, but I can say this: with diagnostic and therapeutic questions, be honest. With ethics testing intended to protect the Academy from potential lawsuits, cheat if you need to. Even if the rules are clear, it's hard to know which ones the Academy wants us to break. As far as motives go, who could argue during these economic times?

My latest question today: A WATCHED BOIL NEVER POTS. I'll keep my answer to myself so that readers won't have a clue should they try LaserFunk. Always base your answers on your life, not mine or Mia's.

55

At night, Mia and I climb into our new capsule, Mysterious Traveler, put on headsets, and compare notes. "A watched boil never pots?" I ask Mia.

"Never is a long time."

"What if it's a typo? What if it means a watched pot never boils?"

"It depends on how much water."

"Never is not as long as it was a minute ago."

Such is life in our capsule. Time to think makes time fly. Sometimes we feel so close we don't need talking to bring us closer together. We listen to music or watch movies on a monitor above our feet. I can't kiss and tell, but I can say this. Sooner or later, we adjust volume controls to quiet our amplified breathing and moaning. We sleep well in each other's arms at night, consciences clear, minds sedated by after-love.

Our decision to live in capsules goes back to Jonson, always ahead of his time, always promoting higher standards of living. I can still recall our conversations. He told us about the Greek philosopher Diogenes living in a barrel to prove you don't need to live in a castle to survive. "The need for living space is becoming more critical," Jonson said. "Our survival depends on new human storage methods. Already, Japanese businessmen out on the town rent capsules, just to avoid unnecessary trips back to the suburbs."

"Things are already changing in America," I remember saying. "Capsule life could be the beginning of a solid financial plan, a contingency for possible unemployment."

"Look at the way some folks already live the dream in cardboard boxes," Mia said. "Funny how things work sometimes. There was some urban myth about a homeless refugee becoming a little uppity after finding a spacious wooden shipping crate."

"Next logical step for upward mobility, capsules." Jonson pointed at Mia and me. "Not just for box people, for that homeless woman you talked about, the one who built the igloo, and for Academy people like you two."

"This new laser therapy might keep us employed and pay enough to buy into the creature comforts of capsule life."

Jonson was persistent enough to talk us into getting two black, carbon-fiber models, manufactured by a startup called "Cutting Edge Capsule." More room, more freedom. When one of us gets sick or tired, we take care of each other. When we both get sick and tired, one of us retires to our second container, our den. Whenever Mia thinks enough is enough or thinks I'm too much, she goes to watch her toes make toe shadows. Sometimes she takes a nap.

The first time I sought solitude in the capsule I call the den, I planned on enjoying obsolete online videos featuring troubleshooting tips for vintage equipment. Well presented for their time, most of these classics turned out to be boring, at least for my tastes. It is better to close my eyes and daydream, allowing memories of technology past to inspire questions about the future. How can LaserFunk diagnose loneliness in people living on an overcrowded planet? A good bet even Research wouldn't know the answer to that one.

Mia and I escape loneliness in the privacy of our shared space, a place to daydream, and think about the creation. At first glance, our bedroom looks like a new-age dinosaur's medicinal capsule. On second glance, it's more like a space capsule. Score energy bars fill two small shelves inside. Insulated drink jugs hang on the exterior, one filled with an energy drink called Sustaine, the other with pure water. Clear plastic drink tubes snake into the interior, enabling us to be well-hydrated, energized lovers.

Mia stenciled "Mysterious Traveler" in red vintage calligraphy on the black carbon, her choice of colors a symbolic refusal to give up on the American Dream. As far as "Mysterious Traveler" goes, the name is not that much of a mystery. In space emergencies, astronauts eject. On Earth, a suspended capsule that goes nowhere is an escape capsule. When life gets to be too much, we earthlings encapsulate ourselves, in an attempt to escape the planet. Where we think we're going remains a mystery.

It doesn't help when word gets out that Penguin Four lives in another capsule. Some think the idea eccentric. If the Institute's Director hears about it, he'll probably assume Penguin Four's new home violates custodial guidelines. Smaller than ones designed for humans, it's well suited for pigeons. We built it into one of the room's two windows, a modification Mia's condo association objected to until we paid an additional fee. I equipped the pigeon door to the outer world with a sensitive pigeon-friendly micro-switch, part number Eight Six Seven Five Three Oh Nine, the same as the admin password used to upgrade LaserFunk's software. Coincidence or not, the numerical sequence comes from an old, easy-to-remember rock-and-roll title. As a computer password, it's often scorned for being too popular, and too easy for any would-be hacker.

Penguin Four can come and go as he pleases, not that he ever does. It bothers us that he doesn't get out much. Mia would do anything to relieve the devastating effects of Institutionalization on the pigeon.

Capsule interiors are neat and clean, the rest of the room's in disarray with a complex pigeon maze. Mia's trying to design a magnified version of round, clear plastic hamster tunnels that you find in pet stores. She's not crazy, but her plans don't make sense. Supposedly, from the inside looking out, the tunnel creates an illusion that humans are pigeon-like.

We're reclined in Mysterious Traveler, taking small sips of coffee from our auxiliary drink tubes, and pigeon-watching Penguin Four. Wandering inside his maze, he amazes us with the way he acts caged, trying different routes to find a way out. Mia holds her drink tube as if it's the stem of a wine glass. "How do you suppose we could make the pigeon's indoor flying space self-cleaning," she asks.

"I know they make self-cleaning kitty litter boxes. As far as I know, there's no plumbing that makes pigeon droppings odorless and invisible, at any price." I remember a circus huckster who sold self-cleaning birdcage cleaners for a buck. It taught me to question opportunitators who say, "Step right up." The huckster's demonstration video featured a parrot trained to hold a wiper in its beak. Believe it or not, the huckster didn't include the bird in the deal, just the cloth. What a lesson about human nature and ornithology. What about the wasted dollar's value?

Although Mia often looks at things from Penguin Four's point of view, her project doesn't impose on my rights. I'll admit it is fun watching her assemble parts, look things over, and take the maze apart again. I'll bet when she finishes, the maze will look like a distillery.

What about life living in capsules? Mia's not sure.

"Shifty or thrifty? Sid thinks of efficiency. I'm thinking snug escape from shadowed existence. Perfect for dim light's white-washed shadows, room to move, and a place to meditate."

56

The Director thins the herd. So far, most keyboard jockeys survive; few coordinators and opportunitators remain. To dispel rumors that the Academy is going bankrupt, the Director holds a meeting for survivors. Despite a bad economy, he claims the market's trending positive. To reassure investors, he's cut employee incentives and filled the parts room with empty boxes. Everyone claps in unison. Well-timed applause makes him feel good and helps us hide our thinking, a wise career strategy more important than ever. A negative side effect of pretense, my mind starts racing. At least I'm still able to stop clapping at just the right moments.

A day later, just when my mind drifts to things that need doing, the Academy requires everyone to attend an emergency state of the company address. All I need is another interruption. Four LaserFunk sub-connector interface units need replacement, along with routine reprogramming. All I want to do is just encapsulate myself.

In the newest crisis, the Director's forced to admit that Supply had already filled the parts room beyond capacity with more empty boxes. He denies rumors that the empties create collateral for the acquisition of more empties. "What are the boxes for," I ask. "Will you sell them to clients as keepsakes, pleasant reminders of a nagging sense of emptiness?"

"Be positive for a change. Emptiness creates a void to fill."

We're walking out of the meeting, Mia and I. A keyboard jockey pulls us aside. "I didn't want to say anything. If the Supply Coordinator keeps his job long enough, the

Academy makes a profit selling those empties to another failing business."

So far so good, my numbers uninspired, too unremarkable to attract negative attention: sixteen million keystrokes to the eighth power, times sixteen hundred keyboard jockeys, ten fingers apiece, the only exception, one nine-fingered worker. Negabytes, forty-four-point-eight. For reasons unknown, the Tech Coordinator informs me that I now report to the Director.

In a conniving move to evade customary maintenance costs, the Institute exerts legitimate but limited power on Mia and Penguin Four. The legal department demands proof that the pigeon is living in his quarters. Mia replies with a photo of Penguin Four perched in his capsule, its deck spackled white with pigeon droppings, and littered with random bits of birdseed.

Jump rope for Penguin Four was Mia's idea. Now the pigeon does it because he wants to. Spinning the end of a string that we call "rope" gets tiring. It doesn't matter if Mia runs out of energy and loses her enthusiasm. As Carrier of the Pigeon, her responsibilities don't allow giving up. Whenever the string slows down, Penguin Four gets lethargic and trips. We pick up the pace; the pigeon jumps as if he means it again. Gradually we decrease the speed. The pigeon's legs get tangled in the string. Mia keeps saying, "When it comes to jumping rope, we need to go solar. It's on you."

So I build a solar-powered jump rope twirler for Penguin Four. Building a prototype is routine; the challenge is finding a durable white string with the right thickness and texture. I'm glad I've lost touch with most of my Technical Academy friends. What would they say if they found out that I design recreational devices for pigeons?

Another day, another meeting, nothing's new. If I had skipped the meeting to do real work, the Academy could save enough to buy more empty boxes that it doesn't need, without borrowing money. Unaware of this logic lapse, the Director also forgets that inefficiency nurtures a need for more talk, his reason for being.

"Today, there's good news. A depressed economy depresses

the people and creates more demand for LaserFunk, a win-win for winners and losers alike. Employed or jobless, hope is always a dividend. Winners think they should keep winning. With some sense of entitlement, losers think they should stop losing."

The Director concludes, "It's time for less talk and more action." He stops talking long enough to pass out fancy stock certificates worth less than the expensive paper used for printing. Mia folds hers into an elaborate paper plane. Since the Director watched her fold it, it's no longer a fake stock certificate promising false hope. It's a ticket to nowhere.

We meet with the Director right after the meeting. He smiles his robotic smile; I hide mistrust with my best poker face. He shows us one of LaserFunk's many recycled ideas, another upshot of obsolete software: TYPICALITY IS ABNORMAL. If the statement's diagnostic value diminishes, it could hurt his professional reputation. Worse, the Machine might create more awkward phrases and questions. "You're the one who knows what to do," he says. "You've already proved yourself, performing the lobotomy on the Machine."

I'm glad that he forgot that Jonson was the one who performed the lobotomy. "What you say is true," I tell him. "I don't question your appraisal. But an electronic meltdown, even well-controlled, might not work well on a diagnostic tool. You should just add the usual True or False to make the statement a question."

"That sounds typical, coming from you." He shakes his head, making me wonder what's wrong with including another true statement. I should apologize—I'm not supposed to suggest which response would make a better choice.

57

I assure Mia, "The solar jump rope motor's just powerful enough to twirl the rope, not so powerful it would hurt a pigeon or castrate a mosquito."

Mia laughs. "I wonder if mosquitoes are a good food source for pigeons, wild or domestic."

"That's something we never discussed at the Technical Academy," I reply. "We should investigate. Along with the likely nutritional benefit of protein, catching mosquitoes might be an enjoyable sport for domestic pigeons."

"We can't be too careful. Maybe you can dream up a pigeon-friendly way for Penguin Four to control the rope's speed."

"I'm working on it; I'm having trouble concentrating." To calm myself, I head for the freight elevator that we often take to avoid clients and staff. As it rises, passing voices on each floor fade in and out—like a dream, my ascending reality fuses with passing ones. My mind stops racing.

In the third meeting in the same week, the Director says there's an overabundance of empty parts boxes. Trying to sound impressive enough to boost morale without inspiring us to go on a meaningless search for more emptiness, he challenges us to find space for one more. Some people still clap at the right times, but I'd rather not. Without my help, the applause is loud enough to cover my talking in a low voice, "He's blowing more smoke."

Mia leans toward me and whispers back. "Aren't we getting cynical again?"

"Aren't we both? I know someone so perfect she'd never fold another stock certificate into a paper plane?"

"You're always rude. You never applauded that Institute guy with his cutting torch. You'd probably pay to watch a real circus dog-and-pony show. You never appreciate free performances here at the Academy." Mia blows a gentle warm breeze in my ear. The Director stares as if he just caught her wiggling her toes in an open elevator.

Friday, on the way to work for another early meeting, Mia counts twenty-eight abandoned apartment buildings. Plywood covers window openings. Stoves and refrigerators litter lawns and smother grass and weeds enough to lower landscaping costs. A desolate cityscape makes a perfect distraction, I could get arrested for problem-solving while driving. "If people continue to populate the planet at the current rate, we'll have to raze more buildings, reclaim enough space for more farmland, to sustain the masses."

Mia yawns. "Just food for optimistic thought, the polluted soil provides a perfect opportunity for chemists to purify urban wastelands. But then, what do you do with the people left behind?"

"Save a few houses. Pull the plywood, let some light in, and hang a few capsules so squatters can colonize houses that remain. There's nothing to lose. Street crime is more eco-friendly than military operations. It takes less fossil fuel for a quick drive-by or curbside drug deal than it takes to run a war."

"You have to be fair," Mia says. "Does the military reduce our numbers more efficiently than street violence? Either way, you have to admit population control sounds evil."

"We can't be players in the religious realm. We can't deny anyone the joy of procreation. The question's Shakespearean: To be or not to be. To procreate or not to?"

Stuck in a traffic jam, just a block from the Academy, finding a parking place and walking would get us to work faster. We'd probably get to see the homeless girl, take a minute to say hello, and chat about who knows what. Mia must be thinking the same thing. She walks the last block, leaving me to drive back whenever the traffic frees up.

I catch up with her at the security booth. She blows a kiss my way. Even without the warmth of her breath, it feels good. I just hope the guard doesn't jump to the conclusion that she intended her distant kiss for him.

58

Mia crawls through Penguin Four's life-size maze-in-progress and tries a tricky vertical U-turn, more doable for pigeons than humans. She settles for something more horizontal. As if afraid, Penguin Four refuses to run a flight test to see if the maze idea flies. If he trips or falls in such a small space, you wouldn't be able to tell if he's a flapper or screamer. Subject to ornithological laws of gravity, flappers try to fly; screamers scream and die. Though the maze proves useless so far, Mia still dreams of a self-cleaning system. I dread the fallout if we pass inflated water bills along to the Institute.

Mia and I lie together, watching Penguin Four in his adjacent capsule, still jumping rope, faster, higher, for longer time stretches than usual. I hope his solar generator keeps the batteries charged long enough so he can last all night if he wants. His paint-blackened legs interrupt a sensor beam that calculates cadence and adjusts the rope twirler's speed accordingly. Penguin Four's doing more than a hundred and twenty jumps a minute, beak wide open, breathing hard, wings flexed slightly for balance, eyes intense, possibly a little glassier than usual. He never looks our way. An exercise junkie tuned in to a marathon high, does he forget who we are?

Mia shuts off the lights, all except the one shining on Penguin Four. In the darkness, the illuminated pigeon looks eerie, almost dinosaur-like, dancing like a human in a nightclub's strobe light. Instead of perpetual strobe-flashed lightning, the pigeon's repetitive movement paradoxically locks the light making the pigeon's motion almost a blur. Fascinated, we continue watching. I mention one of LaserFunk's questions almost lost, lingering on a frozen monitor abandoned by a client. THIS IS THIS sounded meaningless, but it seemed important to add to my cheat sheet.

"What pointless question was ever important," Mia asks.

"You be the judge. 'This is this' could confuse the brightest and most well-adjusted. It must be a useful diagnostic. Skipping the question implies the client's afraid of choosing the wrong answer. Answering implies overconfidence. Which answer works for you? True, False. It's too bad 'None of the above' is not an option."

Mia removes her sandals, wiggles her toes, and watches slightly exaggerated shadows as if they are signs that she's telling the truth. "It's situational. There's no right answer. 'None of the above' doesn't work. Diagnosis might be worthwhile if it sparks entertaining conversation. But really! If something's wrong, what's the rush to find out? Look at how much work it takes to undo my criminality."

Mia questions LaserFunk; it's no wonder it thinks she's capable of wrongdoing.

One by one, Mia identifies the critical questions that determine criminality, clinchers that profile innocence or guilt: THERE'S ALWAYS WORK FOR THE WICKED. As usual, I can't reveal her newest answer. No secret, she'll try both responses at different times.

We make love without microphones, headphones, or headsets, a romantic step back in time. Penguin Four's undignified, child-like squawking interrupts our orgasmic ecstasy. Must be the rope twirler tripped him. Before he could recover, the rope wrapped his feet, leaving the pigeon hog-tied. In our rush to the rescue, we forget to dress. Despite Mia's fears, Penguin Four seems unaffected. I fumble, awkwardly trying to untangle the string, frustrated by pigeon interruptus, a primitive form of birth control, even for birds. In the sidelight of the pigeon's spotlight, I'm slightly distracted by Mia's beauty, the darkness and lightness blending, shadows harmonizing movement.

59

The Director invites Mia and me to another meeting. Custom usually requires that we accept or decline. Consistent with this unwritten rule, we accept by not declining. The Director wears a black, wrinkle-free suit and the usual red tie, appropriate attire for projecting good character and belief in the American Dream. Everyone looks the same with pigeon crap on their Lycra. I hope he drives that Mercedes with his sunroof open.

He motions for us to sit, and paces back and forth as if movement inspires bland corporate-speak. "I'm concerned," he says. "Clients are refusing to answer LaserFunk's newest questions. Are they too confusing? Are they possible results of a saboteur's nasty virus? Listen to this! BAN THE FIFTIETH PERCENTILE. THE MEDIAN'S OFF CENTER. To make matters worse, I can't wipe out questions I don't like."

His suspicion shouldn't impact our numbers. Before speaking, I try mixing the right thoughts with things that don't need to be said. "LaserFunk's questions don't necessarily prevent an accurate diagnosis. They're harmless if they boost self-esteem, an important leadership trait, proven to work so well here at the Academy."

"You're right," he says. "But here's the real deal. A hacker, some techie on our team, is tampering with LaserFunk. We have a suspect. I still have questions unanswered. We have the technology and metrics to figure this out." He pauses, glances at me briefly, then turns toward Mia. "Considering the number of client inputs, there are too many implausible outputs. Quirks originate in one module at a time. I'm thinking they're coming from an insider, not a client or program bug."

"Thank you for sharing your concern," Mia says, in a voice softer and more polite than usual. "Vigilance is the key to finding solutions. You have our support."

Not that we're competing, it's hard to match Mia's response. "I can check for voltage drains on the logic generator." Taken by surprise, it's the best I can do.

Speechless, as if he just discovered us having an elevator picnic, the Research Coordinator doesn't agree or disagree. Thankfully, he doesn't show us the door.

The Director might be onto us. We should be asking ourselves what next? Some people find a mountaintop to ask themselves questions. We wander behind the Academy to the old river park picnic site now abandoned, and less romantic than it was during Institute times. Yellow from malnutrition and dehydration, overgrown grass isn't quite thick enough to keep resurgent weeds from growing. Amid the neglect, silence reveals the only hint of a peaceful creation.

Mia breaks the desolate peace, and tells me, "Penguin Four's wings have atrophied to the extent he has trouble flying. Jumping rope, the best leg exercise, cripples him with addiction."

There's nothing I can say to help; I say it anyway. "Mia, never give up."

We sit by the river. Paddlers in a carbon canoe glide under a bridge. Pigeons roosting on steel beams flutter majestically, spreading their wings, and flying away. Light gray feathers float downward. White droppings splatter the black canoe, racing hats, and fancy synthetic shirts. Who looks like a coordinator now?

Whenever she thinks she needs time to think, Mia works her pigeon maze. She's afraid to ask the Director who he suspects of corrupting LaserFunk. How can she question his questioning without arousing premature incrimination? The U-turn sends the tubular maze back the way it came. No matter which way Penguin Four flies, he goes nowhere, like a canoe racing up and down the river, ending up in a river park, strapped to the same car roof, exactly where it started. Mia adds another section, steps back, looks for a moment, and crawls in to see how it feels. Ecstatic, she dreams of a simple daydream aloud. "Fly the friendly skies of Plexiglass tubing—forget you have atrophied wings. Believe, achieve."

I recline in our shared capsule and notice a new tablet next to my population counter. The decal centered at the top says *FERTILITY CLOCK,* the readout counting time backward. The numbers are in a larger font than those on the world population tablet. Digits blip downward at one-second intervals, it seems like it takes hours for the minute counter to change. I look outward; Mia's too busy to glance back my way; I understand what LaserFunk means when it says, SO CLOSE, SO FAR AWAY. Must be Mia and I need to have a conversation.

Penguin Four won't take lunch breaks. That's not to say he eats like a bird. He's consuming more than four tablespoons of birdseed daily, forcing Mia to request that the Institute increase the pigeon's dietary allotment. On rare occasions when he sleeps, Mia shuts off the jump rope twirler. She has a feeling something's wrong; she's not sure why.

60

Blinded by the incandescent brilliance of the bathroom light, light-seeking bugs burn to a crisp and die. I'm shaving, my disbelief suspended. Another TV news flash about a resolution for peace on earth, goodwill toward men, women, children, large and small animals, and some plants. The bill also calls on the government to tax labor-saving robots and redistribute the money to the jobless.

The Director, thug and ringmaster of the Academy, continues to run his circus, dreaming up ways to sell contents of empty parts boxes. Like missing parts, problems have a way of disappearing on their own. Even when they won't, it's a comfort thinking they will. My numbers multiply. Eighteen million keystrokes to the seventh times twelve-hundred, ten-fingered keyboard jockeys. No need to subtract the new employee missing a finger. Rumor has it that she resigned in fear of being fired; my Negabyte score, fifty-point-two.

Not wanting to stop paying customers, Mia always chooses an out-of-the-way, vacant kiosk, hoping to evade discovery. She continues testing new answers for old questions, to figure out which ones might clear up LaserFunk's belief in her great potential as a criminal.

The Director's suspicions keep him busy enough to curtail meetings. With less to do, he finds extra time to cultivate his fear of nasty viruses attacking the Machine. He blames saboteurs in our midst, mysterious evil forces for causing its irrational outbursts of false information. He doesn't know or can't admit electrical artifacts might still reside within the Machine, triggering new random questions, and causing clients to leave mid-diagnosis, mystified by the true or falseness of it all.

Here's an old one that sounds like career advice from the Technical Academy. I wonder where LaserFunk found it or how it managed to make it up: FAKE IT UNTIL YOU MAKE IT.

On my way to meet Mia, I pass a space called the EggRoom, a place almost as easy to spell as EEG, a word that takes less effort to pronounce than electroencephalograph, a device that measures brain activity. Some say "EggRoom" comes from an overbooked sign painter's careless lettering. Facilities claimed that a spelling correction would be too costly. The name doesn't matter much; sarcastic employees call the place Robotheatre. All said and done; it converts numerical reality into theatrical truth. I've heard rumors that it works well enough to cure Trivial Pursuit Disorder, a common condition that causes victims to focus on meaningless details. The jury's still out; it might also cure Attention Surplus, an affliction that makes people pay too much attention to all things right or wrong.

To satisfy my curiosity, I once pretended to be a client and tried to sign up for the EggRoom. Without LaserFunk's referral, the tech couldn't allow me that privilege. At first, I was relieved. I've since heard they never let you sit in the back, good enough reason to count me out. Out of heightened curiosity, I now take LaserFunk more seriously. Not that I want to increase negabyte numbers, I just need to know: What is it that makes all this sound so magical?

Robotheatre doesn't impress Mia much.

"EggRoom's a sanctuary, a retreat. Eggman's a real live lab tech. A conveyor serves up repetitive eggs, visions of still life moving nothingness. Why would Sid consider going there to find himself?"

61

RUDDERLESS CRUISE SHIPS ALWAYS DOCK IN DENMARK. More sarcastic and offbeat than usual, LaserFunk seems in a mood, an unusual state for an inanimate being that's powered by artificial intelligence.

Restless, I wander the Academy's main corridor, wondering when I'll arrive and if so, where. I pass old portraits of Institute directors, coordinators, too. Few of them remain at the Academy. How many more faces will change? One picture portrays a portly coordinator who still works here, He poses, shamelessly holding glasses and a book to suggest he's not only literate but smart enough to add and subtract. Even though I question his abilities, there's no need for props. Why press the point that a company officer can read and do math? Pure coincidence: the same man in the portrait shows up in real life, wearing glasses but he's without the book. He walks fast enough to catch up with me. I hold a door to be polite. He thanks me and goes a different way.

Coordinators walk out of the main conference room. One whispers something about "tapioca," a code word I've heard keyboard jockeys use for bankruptcy. It's no wonder Supply won't even sign off on a can of canned air for blowing dust off electronic circuit boards.

Lying in our capsule, Mia lowers the music's volume. "I'm sometimes afraid my trial-and-error testing on LaserFunk might make my identity obvious," she says. "What if I carry an old-fashioned clipboard, a few random pages attached to distract Security from noticing my thumb drive?"

"One thing's for sure. Security will never figure out your access code for hacking in. Who would think? Social security number backward, divided by three, the result an even number? I've got the whole thing memorized, everything but your social security number."

Mia remains devious, responding differently to the same questions—all to prove she's not a criminal. No matter the latest diagnosis, LaserFunk's endless tabulation of normality, typicality, and criminality confuses her. You can't blame her for being concerned.

Mia teaches Penguin Four to loosen up before jumping rope. As usual, I'm more than willing to help: "Don't be a birdbrain, Penguin Four. Remember. Warm-ups prevent leg and wing injuries." Penguin Four ignores me, circles the jump rope apparatus, stops, lifts his head, and spends more energy than he should, watching us watch him. The Plexiglass keeps us from getting too close and keeps familiarity from becoming contempt.

Possibly bored or lonely, not at all sluggish, Penguin Four starts jumping, faster and faster, increasing the rope's speed until things are hopping. He's still jumping like a mad bird when we wake up the following morning. His beak's wide open, chest pumps air like an overworked blacksmith bellows. His refusal to stop for food convinces Mia he should be getting transfusions to sustain his movement and momentum, sustain the pleasant blend of endorphins and adrenaline, bringing peace to the here and now and afterward. "What's the rush, Penguin Four?" I ask. "You'll never get far jumping rope. You'll never arrive."

The following evening, we retire in our capsule, and watch the pigeon jumping, his pace slowed to the point that the twirler's barely twirling. He collapses and lies panting for minutes that seem like hours. He gets up to resume jumping but passes out. Mia puts a tiny pillow under his head. I wonder where she found it.

Mia and I settle in and hold each other, staring out into the darkened room, its dim light only coming from the pigeon's capsule. Passed out, Penguin Four looks as if he lives on a hostile planet that forces him to rest comfortably.

62

Mia spends her income and pigeon support payments from the Academy and remaining charge card credit to buy two hundred feet of large diameter Plexiglass tubing, various shapes—bends, curves, and cross tees. The tubes connect horizontally, vertically, up and down, in and out, round and round, without any dead ends. All turns inward and outward to form a series of perfect loops. Even if he lacks a sense of direction, Penguin Four can't get lost. No matter which way he goes, he'll always get there. To call it a distillery understates this new beginning. Until the pigeon takes advantage of Mia's hard work, it only represents hope.

Penguin Four ignores Mia's maze. Instead, he jumps the twirling rope, maintaining his usual fast rate. Most birds cool themselves efficiently while flying, but things are different for the minority who jump rope. Penguin Four's soaked chest feathers drip sweat, making the slippery floor a skating rink in progress. Mia pleads with the pigeon to explore her new creation. "Get lost in the maze," she says. "Try a little food, the black oil sunflower kind you like."

She teases him with birdseed, an incentive that lacks the power of addiction. Penguin Four's hooked for sure. Even if he understood English, he'd keep jumping rope. The obvious solution: a timer that shuts off the rope twirler gradually decreases his workout time, controlling the pain of withdrawal. He'll also need an IV feed to keep him alive until he's healthy enough to afford time for eating.

Gently, Mia picks up Penguin Four, a desperate attempt

to make their connection human. Reciprocating as any self-respecting lab pigeon would, he pecks her fingers. Mia crawls into the maze to show how it works. Lacking a pigeon's grace, she's more like a child crawling through tall ryegrass. If she loses her sense of direction, will she see more clearly?

A stranger in a black suit wearing a black Victorian mad hatter hat is wearing gas welding goggles usually worn above the brim. He's not cutting or welding at the moment. I don't know how long he's been standing at the door and don't know when Penguin Four stopped jumping rope. Both must see something curious, something of interest, possibly Mia crawling through a brave new world of Plexiglass, transparently razzle-dazzled in a psychedelic way, without the glitz. The stranger stares at us—the pigeon stares at the stranger.

Mia smiles, but the stranger doesn't smile back. He looks startled, like a child spooked by Jack jumping from a Jack-in-the-box. Jack-in-the-box or not, the stranger looks like he just met Jack at the airport, accidentally. One thing's for sure; the stranger didn't stop at an airport to see Jack off. He only stopped here to borrow a screwdriver to fix an obsolete loudspeaker so that he could listen to an old New Age disc, a library antique he bought at a flea market. He can't tell if the speaker's blown or if the distortion's intended. The stranger is on edge, hard to know why. Maybe the edginess comes from tranquil disconcerting sounds of too much old New Age. Or it might come from Mia crawling like a reptile, cooing like a lost pigeon.

The stranger introduces himself as a new neighbor, just relocated here to work at the Academy. Believe it or not, he claims his name's Jonson. He removes his goggles. It turns out he's our friend, the same Jonson who tended the Institute's generator, the same one who performed the Machine's lobotomy. It's quite a pleasant surprise.

63

Maybe Penguin Four's jump rope provides relief from his structured time at the Institute. Is Mia's kindness as much a detriment as the Institute's science? Endorphins, adrenaline, and brain chemicals combined are powerful. A local university lab maintains a large pack of drug-dependent rats for less than it costs Mia to care for one pigeon addicted to jumping rope. His medical requirements exceed those of the typical lab pigeon. He's hooked to an energy drip. Running out of fluid triggers an alarm that signals it's time to replenish his IV bottle. The needle taped to the pigeon's left wing is close to the point where an elbow would be if he were human. Now that he's used to the tube's lopsided weight, it no longer throws him off-balance. Penguin Four's determined, no matter what challenge he faces. Adversity or not, jump rope can only make him stronger.

It's Monday; compared to jump rope, it's a slow day. Mia monitors LaserFunk's monitors to make sure clients don't get stuck on easy-to-answer questions. Not counting me, only seventeen other clients signed on today. If Mia wants, she can even monitor me. Of course, I have nothing to hide. I'm working on my last set of questions, all having something to do with success:

USE LOTS OF ELBOW GREASE. KEEP YOUR NOSE TO THE GRINDSTONE. KEEP ON THE STRAIGHT AND NARROW.

The secrets of success are well-kept. I know people with sore elbow joints, skinned noses, and minds burned out from living the straight and narrow. It doesn't matter. LaserFunk keeps sending well-worn true and falsisms my way:

KEEP YOUR EYE ON THE BALL.

CLEANLINESS IS NEXT TO GODLINESS.

I marked one true and the other false, can't remember which one I marked which. To my surprise, LaserFunk prints out a stark diagnosis, less detailed than most: ARREST RESTLESSNESS, SURRENDER TO CHAOS. ADVANCE TO THE EGGROOM, SAFE ASYLUM, FUNHOUSE FOR BEING.

The referral, if that's what you call it, makes it easier to understand clients who precede me. Those who respond with trueness and falseness have no way to prepare for revelations of a new reality. It's much easier to think nothing's wrong. Supposedly, my brain's networks short circuit, allowing my chaotic thoughts to take scenic routes, off-the-beaten paths that create a bigger bang for the mind's intellectual buck. So far, it works for me. I'm not sure what constellation of artificial ideas works for LaserFunk.

We're home, snug in Mysterious Traveler, its dome lights off. A spotlight shines on Penguin Four, not to make him a star, but to help him avoid tripping on the rope. Mia changed his IV—he'll be able to hop, skip, and jump as much as he wants until morning. Penguin Four makes fast jumping and frantic breathing look easy. He picks up the pace until he's almost a blur. Mia and I hold each other, listen to a slow drumbeat, and mournful electric flute filling our headsets, dreaming our daydreams in nighttime silence.

What's the EggRoom all about? Rather than celebrate, I can't help wondering how LaserFunk selects those chosen.

My mind drifts to a world without capsules, no Institute or Academy. I was a carpenter, always on the move, carrying lumber, cutting boards, and sinking nails one after another. I remember crouching on a roof sheathed in plywood, wind-swaying treetops, and clouds moving across a sunny sky, all creating the illusion that I was floating over an imaginary sea, two stories below. Aside from the cutting table's circular saw and the sounds of a nail gun's rapid fire, there was silence. I felt alive, in sync with a world blowing in the wind, alive enough to forget my fear of heights, fear of falling, fear of failure—no need to talk, no need to apologize for not talking. My mind stopped racing. Life perfect or imperfect, smug or humble, measured or not. Nothing matters when my mind goes nowhere fast, slows down, and gives in to movement, building houses, building muscles—I felt very much alive—maybe that's Penguin Four's reason for jumping rope.

I keep asking myself, how does the EggRoom fit in?

64

A mind that studies itself risks serious addiction to junk psychology. Penguin Four's problem is different. His behavior poisons pure science with answers too simple. As bright and accomplished as he was in the lab, Penguin Four's think tank of happiness is near-empty. No instant cure available, we limit jumping rope to fifteen hours a day. Mia can't bear watching the pigeon's symptoms of withdrawal. The pain pains her so much that an electronic timer turns on the rope before she gets home and shuts it off after she leaves for work. Its intelligence artificial, the timer doesn't know we get to stay home on weekends. In its usual electronic Saturday morning fog, it shuts off the twirling rope while we're having late breakfast at a time we'd be at work on a weekday.

"Turn on the bypass switch," Mia says. "Please."

There's no bypass switch; she wants me to reset the rope twirler's programmable settings. "Out of kindness to you, and kindness to the pigeon, I can't."

"You don't care. If you loved me, you'd turn on the timer, make it pretend this is a weekday."

Penguin Four's in pain, his beady eyes bulge, as if they're faulty pressure relief valves that somehow prevent insanity. Without a jump rope, he's frozen in time. It's so hard to watch, Mia wins. I turn on the jump rope; in turn, it turns on Penguin Four. How much does he know? Is he giving up every ounce of energy in a quest for nirvana, actualized by a neurochemical cocktail swimming in his brain?

Penguin Four's problems make the prospect of EggRoom

life look easy. Tech attaches wristbands just like LaserFunk's. Each electrode pulses relaxation. More electrodes, attached to my forehead, capture brainwave samples and transmit them to the EEG. In turn, minimalist props project a stark but dramatic sense of nothingness. A built-in cubby frames a pigeon-size egg; pointed end down, perched on a golf tee. Room lights dim. A shining spotlight brightens the cathedral-shaped cubby. I breathe deeply and focus on the egg, centered in its sanctuary. Maybe it's a calcium shell containing life that can't be. It might be there to help me relax, react in minimalist ways, and transmit brainwaves piggybacked on radio waves casting themselves out to the EEG.

It might not be an egg. Maybe it's just something that happens to be oval shaped, and white. Whatever, it sits on a golf tee, centered in the cathedral-shaped cubby, projecting life, with or without meaning. It might be for Easter, not to be eaten or hatched. In and out of focus, my mind swims in its neurochemical ocean, scrambling to escape itself. My eyes blink away tears, not from sadness, but from the effort required to focus on something meaningless, an egg too real to lack nothingness, a void too empty to fill.

There's nothing to fear but emptiness itself. My eyes can't blink fast enough.

65

I wake up, afflicted with tunnel vision, a darkened beam as narrow as the EggRoom spotlight. I miss the vast expanse. All I can do is focus on that which excites me. My perception of things was never a problem until now. What does an inanimate pigeon egg on a golf tee mean if nothing's amiss? Maybe I shouldn't ask. According to LaserFunk, IF IT'S NOT BROKE, DON'T FIX IT.

Mia's still asleep, her slight smile a hint she's in a dreamland of toe shadows. Last night, she told me her recent performance evaluation went better than expected, even though the Director had directed the Research Coordinator to address her insubordination. "Folding a worthless stock certificate into a paper plane was certainly rude," her coordinator said. "How do you suppose the Director felt?"

Old-fashioned therapeutic magic of open-ended questions won't work on Mia. She opens her purse, pulls out another plane, and unfolds its wings so her boss can read LONG LIVE THE ACADEMY. Unlike a dollar bill, a paper plane's worth more than the paper on which it's folded.

All is not well for Penguin Four. Barely noticeable, small wisps of acrid smoke rise toward the pigeon's nostrils. As if he senses the twirler's burnout, he jumps as fast and high as any pigeon can jump. The rope stops. He leaps to keep from tripping. To test the theory of cause and effect, he tries a few trial jumps but the string doesn't twirl. Confused and frustrated, he pecks it a couple of times, grabs it with his beak, and drops it. Neck feathers stand upright with rage. He walks in circles, pecks the floor, flaps his wings, and flies straight up, a couple of feet into the air like a whirlybird. He lands and claws the rope. He scratches Plexiglass.

Mia awakens, sits up, and rubs her eyes. Penguin Four's rolling on the platform like a chicken with its clichéd head cut off. There's no pecking, just lots of scratching, getting up, walking in excited circles, all flying and dying movement until fatigue delivers salvation. To hide from a world of pain, the pigeon tucks his head under a wing as if to sleep. Now and then, he peeks out furtively toward the jump rope, as if afraid to give up. It's a comfort he's not crying.

Mia stiffens, covering her eyes. She must be losing positive visions of health and abundance for Penguin Four. Now the pigeon just needs a rope that twirls. Whether he knows it or not, he also needs Mia, who needs him to be happy. While she's probably not thinking about finance, she needs Institute support for the pigeon's intensive care. My well-being depends on the pigeon to keep Mia happy. Somehow, the small world we live in keeps getting smaller.

Mia can't wait for today's workday to end. We rush home. I replace the burned-out motor and turn on the solar-powered twirler. Penguin Four makes a quick beeline toward the rope, trips on the IV tube and falls. Focused and intense, he gets back up on his own two feet and starts jumping. The existence of the sky or world outside his capsule escapes him. Obsessed, his beady eyes register nothing as he skips lazily at a hundred and ten hops a minute. Watching the desperate bird helps me forget problems at the Academy. For Mia, this is not a show; this is about Penguin Four's healing. The pigeon's relief relieves Mia, who, in turn, reduces my anxiety. Why watch reality TV to live the make-believe when you can witness a real-life struggle between pleasure and pain?

Under the capsule's spotlight, jumping more than a hundred and twenty-two times a minute, Penguin Four continues his one-pigeon show. Reassured, Mia's settled enough to work LaserFunk's newest word puzzle: ONE ROTTEN APPLE SPOILS THE WHOLE BARREL. It's a hard question. True if all the apples rot, false if the barrel remains sound enough to contain next year's harvest. If you ever take the test, good luck with that one.

Does solving one problem create another? Does an addiction cure require a new fixation? Jump rope helps Penguin Four relax. The pigeon's nonstop, repetitious, well-executed jumps make him as dull as Shopper Channel, a program more annoying than a circus that sells merchandise no one needs. Most likely, the pigeon's feeling no pain. For sure, he's not inclined to stop and shop.

Penguin Four's obsessions are beginning to obsess us. Our only escape, Mia and I encapsulate ourselves in the capsule, making love like uninhibited monkeys. Our amplified breathing sounds almost as labored as the oxygen-starved Mr. and Mrs. Jones making love during that Institute teleconference. Caught up in love's vibrations, we're too excited to be thankful that we have no magnets to move. Too bad, we should be stressing over a weak suspension link that's ready to snap. Tonight just happens to be the night. Suspended by three remaining support chains, our capsule sways gently. Afraid of a chain reaction, we freeze like horizontal statues too tired to take a stand, but we're too late. Another link breaks, dropping the foot end of the capsule to the floor, suspending us upright. Mia's tie-dyed sheets fall around our feet as if we're posing nude for a sculpture to replace one of the Institute's old pottery jugs. Mia pulls the sheet upward, toga-like. Maybe she's dreaming that we're posing for formal pictures at the Rotunda. The dome light still works. At least we still have electricity. Thankfully, numbers on both tablets keep blipping.

Our fall caught Penguin Four's attention, enough to stop him from jumping. The string still twirling, he must have leaped sideways to avoid the spinning rope. He peers out at us, swinging his head back and forth, from left to right. The pigeon stares for a few more seconds, saunters back to the twirling rope, and deftly jumps back into the rhythm. I embrace Mia, who thinks on her feet, thinking we should repair the damage.

Life goes on, in and out of the EggRoom. If Mia, the pigeon, and I could trade places, we might find our demons to be siblings, if not perfect clones.

66

My recent session in the EggRoom convinced the Director that I take self-improvement seriously. He must think I share his worry that my performance numbers might continue their spiral downward. Keystrokes, twenty-one million to the eighth, times eleven-hundred, ten-fingered keyboard jockeys. Negabyte score, forty-two-point four. Even though the EggRoom is mandatory, my attendance might suggest I'm sincere. For reasons unknown, I'm at my Institutional best, too bored to clown, too cautious about creating the impression that I might be subversive.

Institutional best doesn't impress the Director. Without stopping to think, he recites that old Institute slogan, "Take it to the next level, Sid."

His words would be perfect for an electronic, multiple-choice marathon, but I should ask, "Take what to which level when? Do you dream up these slogans yourself? Or does the Academy pay you to parrot words created by the Machine's misaligned electrons?"

Recently, living life in our capsule impresses the Director more than self-improvement at the Academy does. When I mention we bought thirty-six feet of heavy-duty, lightweight chain to suspend Mysterious Traveler and its satellite capsules, he asks, "Why a stronger chain?"

Should his interest make me suspicious? Regardless, I can't admit we fear another freefall. Instead, I share a pleasant half-truth: "Quieter than the original, the new chain increases our listening pleasure."

I've noticed that LaserFunk never questions my true or false opinion about honesty. It looks like I can at least tell a white lie if I need to. My phone beeps with a text that another terminal crashed, locking up a mass of confused electrons. How can I be productive when there's work to do?

A delivery van remains in the Academy's parking lot for days. Supply has no cash or credit for parts that cost more than the burden of emptiness. Yesterday, only seventy-eight customers signed on for electronic therapy, not enough to cover expenses. I take coffee out to the driver, a retired man who needs money as much as he needs coffee. I'm sorry he's not getting a check, he's sorry I'm not getting parts. The Academy feels nothing. The driver's plastic credit line funds his return trip to Buffalo, loaded with cargo intended to fill the parts room. In the meantime, the Academy keeps its empty boxes, reassurance for investors who dwell in negativity's profitable vortex.

To quote LaserFunk, the Director's A DAY LATE AND A DOLLAR SHORT. He announces a new opportunity for esteemed but replaceable keyboard jockeys. If each employee signs on for a mental fitness program sponsored by LaserFunk, insurance money will cover the delivery van's return, include payment for parts, and somehow save the Academy from bankruptcy.

At first, it sounds like a scam, but the Director's looking ahead. The prospect of unemployment drives workers crazy and makes the future of electronic therapy even more optimistic. "The jobless should have their heads examined for not having their heads examined when health benefits gave them the opportunity," he says. "Disillusioned workers should get their heads checked before losing their jobs."

The Director puts on a show holding up his Mental Fitness Mandate Memo as proof that he signed it. He draws upon LaserFunk for inspiration, MAKE HAY WHILE THE SUN SHINES. Maybe the Machine got the idea from an old *Farmers' Almanac* that lifted it from the Bible's book of Proverbs. Director probably liked the quaint truth that achievement requires industry and good judgment about the weather, a questionable concept when you think about birds. Rain or shine, how many hard-working pigeons tripped and fell for a transfer to the afterward by hungry dogs? Achievement guarantees nothing.

Another day at the Academy with so much going on, it's good to be home. "Penguin Four's still going nonstop, as long as he can," Mia says. "He hates giving up."

"Keep up the good work, Penguin Four. Tomorrow, your workout time decreases. Time available for jump rope is increasingly imaginary."

The pigeon ignores me. My use of the word "ignore" might sound judgmental. If Penguin Four hears me, he doesn't understand. Even if he could, why would he want any bad news? "Here's the deal, Penguin Four. The shorter your workout time, the longer you get to rest. Take it to the next level. We have great plans for you."

Penguin Four jumps rope only four hours a day now. With less to do, he sleeps more. Awake, he looks upward toward our capsule and people watches. Is he waiting for another chain to break? Guaranteed, he's not waiting for Mia's fertility clock to run out.

"We should check out the Cutting Edge online site, and look for a deal on another capsule," Mia says.

I'm no genius. For once, I know what to say. "Does looking for a capsule have anything to do with your clock?"

"To be honest, your uptake seems a little slow on this one."

"I like life as it is. I need time to think. How many more capsules would we need to house an average size family? How do we parent a kid in a condo? What about twins?"

"You're right. You need time to think. Please—time's running out."

67

Getting lost in thought makes a convenient escape from domestic and Academy realities that don't seem that academic. Whenever I try to think, my attempts to find myself usually fail. Mia says getting lost in a maze creates an opportunity to find her way. True or false, trivial or monumental, she makes disorientation sound too good to be true. Her new playscape for pigeons looks more like an apparatus for mixing and molding pharmaceuticals big enough for dinosaurs. Its sharp U-turns are just too much for crawling humans or flying pigeons. The idea's not a failure. It's just a perfect example of something that won't work. She takes it apart again and puts the old design back together.

The Director announced plans to take the CAT, the famous Corporate Adjustment Test, which Mia failed more than once. To prepare, he studies a how-to booklet, *Balancing Personality for Perfection*. His hard work pays off. He earned the highest score ever recorded at the Academy. LaserFunk's congratulatory news includes every would-be musician's memory trick for learning musical notes on the staff: EVERY GOOD BOY DOES FINE.

Corporate Adjustment Test score ranks the Director, ninety-eighth percentile nationwide. One employee asks what's wrong with the Academy if it can't attract people from the top two percent. It doesn't matter. In a recent one-on-one meeting, the Director revealed his secret during a rare moment when he wasn't thinking: "My smartphone makes up for the missing two percent."

"Sounds like you're running at a hundred percent," I said.

To celebrate his CAT scores, the Director offers frequent flier discounts to insurance people who add LaserFunk to preferred provider lists. Where would we be had he taken the test sooner? No surprise, the Machine has already answered my rhetorical question: IF THE DOG HADN'T STOPPED TO POOP, HE WOULD HAVE CAUGHT THE RABBIT.

The Director delivers a spontaneous victory speech that almost sounds rehearsed. "Thank the Lord," he says. "Test results save me from humiliating sessions viewing pigeon eggs in the EggRoom."

"How did I become successful," he asks. "Let me count the ways:

"Fight procrastination with motivation.

"Read *Ten Reasons Your Youngest Child is Likable*.

"Review the military history of Colonel Sanders.

"If you can't fake it till you make it, fake faking until you do.

"Become a life coach so you'll never have to hire one.

"Surround yourself with people who think they're successful.

"Listen to the growls of your gut.

"Be open to new kinds of closed thinking.

"Be book smart and street smart. Sit on a sidewalk and read.

"Recycle positive feedback in an echo chamber."

I shake his hand to congratulate him. "Spontaneous, you came across as almost unrehearsed." My words surprise me, but I can't stop now. "Sharing your path to success reveals your support for the masses."

The Director doesn't miss a beat. "Sometimes, I blend in by accepting your sarcasm as a positive critique."

"Well said," I said.

His near perfection must make it hard to feel compassion for the imperfect. The Academy will only conquer a problem of this magnitude if Research hires another scientist.

68

We cut Penguin Four's jump rope schedule to the point where it's an almost healthy activity. Who knows? With nothing to do while we're at work, time might force him to dream of a cute middle-aged female pigeon, most likely single and agnostic. Pigeons can't access online mating and dating sites that humans use to escape the luxury of loneliness. Online ornithological stud listings only include a fortunate few pigeons. Thinking of the lost, lonely thoughts of the average Institutionalized pigeon, Mia drafted an ad but never sent it.

"Single male pigeon named Penguin loves the outdoors, exercise, and picnics. Open and honest. Expects the same from a voluptuous, mature female."

Leave it to dumb luck for LaserFunk to generate words of wisdom that could save Penguin Four from the ravages of jump rope: BIRDS OF A FEATHER STICK TOGETHER. True or false as the assertion might be, life without a jump rope could be more bearable if we find a suitable mate for Penguin Four.

It's hard to find a pigeon ranch when you need one, but as luck has it, there's one conveniently located, less than an hour away from the Academy. We pass cases and cases filled with fertile pigeon eggs, all ready for incubation. Many more eggs hatch than mother pigeons can hatch by themselves, even if they do all the nesting they can do. There's more good news: If you keep taking fertile eggs away from mothers, they keep making more. No wonder there are thousands of pigeons to choose from. A sobering thought, animal rights people are letting all these pigeons loose to live naturally in a homeless environment, a trick that could tip that ecological balance between humans and pigeons even more.

There are pigeons of all ages. Mia is looking for one that's mature and sophisticated, but not yet Institutionalized. Walking down an aisle between cages of single females, she whispers to herself, "I wonder who Penguin Four would choose."

The salesman overhears her. "Are you talking about that famous pigeon at the Institute?" Mia says that she is.

It turns out ranchers across the country know of this celebrated pigeon, the first involved in a custody case. It's no secret lawyers want to attract a variety of clients for the lucrative pigeon business, including custody rights, researcher rights, and even animal rights, an issue most ranchers have strong feelings about.

The pigeons are all identical—the way Christmas trees look the same, pruned and preened to look beautiful for someone else's holiday. The pigeons' eyes are always the same short distance apart, beaks the same length, bodies the same design, and feathers the same shade of silver. Mia walks up and down the aisles, occasionally stopping to coo seductively. If a pigeon coos back, she makes a note of its cage number. Pigeon salespeople don't usually allow this, but I gather that Mia's reputation and status as Carrier of the Pigeon make her special.

Mia chooses Fifteen Forty-One, a beautiful female. As I've already said, the pigeon looks just like the others. Either research pigeons are expensive, or the salesman knows about the Institute's generous support settlement with Mia. He charges a hundred and ten dollars, a steep price but worth every penny.

We're on our way home. Mia's voice is animated. "Fifteen Forty-One's calm and patient personality should complement Penguin Four's all-or-nothing attitude. She's young; she won't be running short on eggs anytime soon."

"He deserves a tolerant mate, as we all do. You put up with a cramped life in a capsule suspended from a ceiling. I tolerate inefficient use of space every time you expand your pigeon maze."

"Maybe I allow you too much time to overthink."

Supposedly, love between incompatible spouses can last forever, despite a challenge here, there, and now and then. I wonder about Mia. Sometimes I wonder about myself. Am I tolerant enough? Am I worthwhile, even though I'm hard to get along with? I'm guessing this might not be the best time to check these questions with Mia.

Penguin Four is still recovering. If he can't stop jumping rope, it might be difficult to jump into an instant relationship with a female companion anytime soon. Sharing a capsule wouldn't be fair to either pigeon. Separation should make ignoring each other easier for both.

Only planners with strong forebrains can do what Mia has done. She changes her newest maze design into an imitation one that turns out to be just two open-ended cages, side by side, as if on a pigeon ranch or suspended capsules in a condo. Only then can Mia sleep, or at least pretend to. I lie awake, wondering if I am salvageable. The EggRoom still owes me a report.

LaserFunk says: BURN THE MIDNIGHT OIL. EARLY TO BED AND EARLY TO RISE MAKES A MAN HEALTHY, WEALTHY, AND WISE. Who can argue with either motivational strategy? Excited about Fifteen-Forty-One's arrival, Mia stayed up late and woke up early to get her thoughts together.

"Take efficiency to the next level—pigeon ranching: emulation of Institutionalization. Residing side by side, thousands of standardized pigeons perfected to near-perfect perfection. A cute little birdseed conveyor goes one way. An elimination eliminator conveys waste to the other. Lighting's omnidirectional brightness creates a shadowless life of sterility.

Should we report the world's most massive dung heap to the former Director of Environmental Protection? Or celebrate Penguin Four's new life with Fifteen-Forty-One?"

"I liked the pigeon too, Mia. But we're back at the Academy. Stop dreaming."

"Just because I'm reflecting doesn't mean I'm dreaming."

69

The Director thinks conflicting wisdom proves perception is everything. Rather than satisfy existing clients, he repackages LaserFunk to attract new ones.

"He's twisting Academy logic into common sense," Mia says. "If frivolous complaints make clients sound like complainers, feel their pain; treat them like quality control experts."

"Frivolous or not, malpractice lawsuits against the Academy don't scare the Director. He doesn't believe in LaserFunk any more than he believes in TV Phil Phoster. As far as he's concerned, a good kick in the ass is a more cost-effective way to cure most personality problems."

"Sure," Mia replies. "Kicking ass is just a euphemism tough-love advocates use to look tough on crime."

"Besides, no one knows how to convert a swift kick into a metric, a negabyte score that generates revenue, pushes profits."

Yesterday, after work, Mia stopped at a kiosk to key in new answers to tweak its misguided questions. Believe it or not, she finally convinced LaserFunk she is not a criminal. Her vision of trueness and falseness changed its artificial mind and convinced the Research Coordinator and Director she doesn't need her ass kicked. She's convinced there's no need to write "Long Live the Academy" on paper planes anymore.

LaserFunk lists fashion and architectural design as her artistic strengths; pigeon care is her passion. As far as career advice goes, LaserFunk thinks Mia should add new art forms to expand her repertoire beyond Reflexive Fusion.

"I'm glad LaserFunk didn't suggest dog-and-pony trainer

as a strong possibility, Mia. You'd never put on a cheap show the way an opportunitator would."

"I'm Carrier of the Pigeon. I'm a Reflexive Fusion Artist. If I ever take the low road, I'd look like a director. Besides, with my luck, some rigid, computerized therapist might play the criminal card again. If I get promoted, I'd be too busy to straighten things out."

"You'll never have to go to the EggRoom for truth served straight up."

Mia celebrates, changes into her old purple Lycra, puts on a black baseball cap, opens a bottle of wine, wakes Penguin Four, and takes him on a tour through her newest maze. The pigeon seems unimpressed as if he'd rather spectate than become part of the big picture. Penguin Four returns to his capsule. Without missing a move, he watches Mia crawl up, down, over, under, around, and through clear Plexiglass passages. He turns away and stares longingly at his jump rope. Mia gives up and goes shopping for new funeral clothes—turns out that Lycra's no longer the in thing for anyone who's not an athlete.

What about me? I stay at home, watching the two pigeons. It looks like Fifteen-Forty-One arouses Penguin Four, just by being herself, doing nothing. Penguin Four flaunts his athletic prowess by jumping the rope that's not twirling right now

Of course, Penguin Four still jumps two hours, twice daily. This morning, the rope was spinning at a relaxed eighty revolutions a minute. At that rate, I'm afraid the motor bearings will start smoking again, more likely sooner than later.

Fifteen-Forty-One walks the Plexiglass tube's perimeter, as if unaware she's walking in circles. If there's a courtship, it's well hidden. Every time Penguin Four looks away, Fifteen-Forty-One turns toward him. If Penguin Four sneaks a glance, she turns away.

Mia returns wearing a black dress that must be in fashion. Horizontally striped in different knits, it makes Lycra look gaudy. Even though her dress distracts me in the best way, I can't tell her I'm dying for her to wear it again. She might think I'm suicidal, so I just say, "I like it!"

We climb into Mysterious Traveler, put on headsets, turn

off the dome light, kick back, and watch the pigeons. I'm not one to kiss and tell, but I'll say this much: we make love, our amplified breathing feeds back in the headsets, echoing voice over voice, voicing wordless pleasure and encouragement, from earbuds to mics in a continuous sound loop.

The new chain is holding up well.

70

The Director's new, elaborate incentive plan feels almost imaginary. If the Academy keeps losing money, employees lose nothing but their jobs. If there's a profit, employees get a bonus, two and a half percent of laser paper's discount rate, divided by the square root of the Japanese yen's prime interest. Stockholders approve the unlikely but paltry payout. In a meeting, I congratulate the Director, intending to be sarcastic.

"Anyone can do the math without realizing it's a bad deal," he says. "We worked hard with the numbers."

Why would he admit the deal's a bad one? I'm guessing his honest reply is a dishonest attempt to use reverse psychology, an old motivational strategy from an established school of thoughtlessness. It supposedly works like this: if he admits an incentive is a bad deal for employees, I'll think he's lying and spread the word that it's a good deal. Reverse psychology doesn't work on me. I report things as they are—without clouding reality with the Director's thinking.

In addition to my EggRoom visits, the Director wants me to meet with a psychiatrist, Dr. Phillip, not to be confused with the famous TV Phil. This one asks shallow questions about my unusual responses to LaserFunk. While waiting for my replies, the psychiatrist plays tic-tac-toe on his solar-powered notepad. I'm curious about the score but should ask who is playing before asking who is winning. "Are you playing against an avatar smarter than you or playing with yourself?"

"Are you playing games," the obscure Dr. Phillip asks as if his denial might bring about my rehabilitation.

I worry about what happens if my treatment turns out successful. Would I be dumbed down enough to buy into the new incentive plan? Last time I checked, the keystroke count was twenty-two million to the ninth, times nine hundred, ten-fingered keyboard jockeys. Negabyte score drops to thirty-six-point-seven. What would the Tech Coordinator think if he were still employed here?

My funeral plans with Mia surprise Dr. Phillip, enough, so he stops playing games. Despite good health, I look forward to my funeral; I hope Mia feels the same way. Is it unfair that she buys wardrobes that might go out of style long before I die? If Mia dresses up for me, should I reciprocate? I find myself torn between two choices: an earthy but tasteful tie of medium width, splotched with quiet colors that harmonize with earth tones, or a Mickey Mouse portrait on a wide, steel gray tie, a choice more entertaining but risky.

"Why Mickey Mouse," he asks.

"People will be sick and tired of Penguin Four's Walmart-framed portraits by then."

"I've never seen any pigeon portraits at Walmart."

"They have Penguin Four neckties already. The portraits must be in the works."

Believe it or not, the psychiatrist can't tell I'm only joking. He refers me back to the EggRoom.

I tell Mia about the Mickey Mouse tie. She doesn't know I'm joking either. She claims her striped knit would never work with Disney characters. I should choose something that complements her dress and enhances my ego, an issue that would become moot after my transfer to the afterward.

To encourage activity other than jumping rope, to help Penguin Four's atrophied wings regain strength, Mia starts his physical therapy. The pigeon is up to his neck in water, heated within three degrees of his average body temperature. A bird out of air wishing to be a fish out of water, Penguin Four keeps flapping his wings. Despite his rebelliousness, he's almost weak enough to cooperate. Luckily, Mia doesn't get wet from the splashing.

Standing at the stainless-steel wing therapy bowl, Fifteen-

Forty-One dips her beak, stretches her head upward, and swallows the water that's not necessarily clean and probably too warm for drinking. She stands serenely and watches Penguin Four struggle. They might not be partners yet, but at least she's there when he needs her.

Mia dries the pigeon with a hairdryer and mists his feathers with oil of sunflower, a preening oil of discerning pigeons that calms bird nerves, supposedly. After living at a pigeon ranch, competing with thousands of pigeons for favors, special attention and grooming must surprise Fifteen-Forty-One. Then again, who said pigeons want or need attention?

"Wake up, Penguin Four. You too, Fifteen-Forty-One, wake up."

71

LaserFunk contradicts itself with conflicting choices about abundance and poverty. As luck has it, clients can respond with the usual tiresome options, True or False. These two contrary statements happened to appear in the same session.

THERE'S NO SUCH THING AS A FREE LUNCH

A CHICKEN IN EVERY POT.

Mia and I recline in our capsule, drinking in fluorescence through Plexiglass, drinking Sustaine through tubes, watching the two dueling tablets keep blipping incompatible numbers, projecting a struggle between Mia's reproductive hope and my big picture vision of population doom. Penguin Four is jumping the jump rope, looking out his window toward our TV monitor as if he's catching the local news. I can't help but wonder what the pigeon's thinking.

A news reporter wearing a blue blazer and burgundy tie is doing a man-on-the-street interview. A surprise, today's guy on the street is my friend Jonson. Judging by the way he's dressed, he looks like Everyman in his tastefully faded jeans and a new-looking black, long-sleeve shirt, with WaterWorks Water embroidered over its pocket. We knew he was back in town, but didn't wonder why. The "WaterWorks Water" shirt makes it look like he's on a mission far more exciting than doing technological resurrections.

"Forget seven-and-a-half billion earth people," he says. "There's a new sterility drug, ACE4, the fourth version produced by the Academy of Contraceptive Excellence. Added in large quantities to our reservoirs, ACE4 could slow things down. Lower the birthrate, reduce jobless numbers enough to make room for displaced refugees who might or might not be our problem."

Anchorman interrupts with a question. "You said, 'slow things down.' Does that mean some people get to reproduce?"

Jonson sounds like he's given the topic some serious thought. "Anyone who wants kids can pursue happiness, enjoying our inalienable reproductive rights. Unadulterated water's a known fertility fluid that will soon be available at neighborhood liquor stores."

The plan looks like the work of a genius; it makes sense. Liquor stores, convenient sources of alcohol, fertility's silent partner, are ideal places to sell pure water.

"People who drink water from plastic jugs reproduce. People who drink reservoir water won't be able to. You just need to remember which source provides which kind of water. Think about a new economy. Small business sales and distribution will create demand for private well water. The value of the real estate that sits on an aquifer should skyrocket."

Shocked by common sense, the newsman looks bewildered. "Who treats the reservoir with this miracle drug," he asks.

"I don't have all of the answers," Jonson replies.

Nationwide, the overall unemployment rate is twelve percent, for capsule people eighteen. The Director once claimed that retraining helps the jobless become employed again. I questioned the idea. "If the Machine eliminates the need for keyboard jockeys, where do retrained people look for jobs?" I asked. "No one applies for work at the Academy these days."

The Director directed a blank stare in my direction. "I'm tired of all the excuses. Jobless people are just too lazy to dream the American Dream."

It sounded like a convenient answer. The timing wasn't right to ask if the Director plans to eliminate me.

Mia's not opposed to this new sterility drug, ACE4. It

sounds efficient. She still wonders if anyone has a better idea. We brainstorm, but pressure systems are weak. "Abstinence, pills, discount condoms," she asks, even though her question is a suggestion.

"Those methods rarely work well in movies."

"Rhythm method sounds like a music class for beginners."

There's no time to wait for better ideas. Evicted capsule people can join local street gangs for gainful employment, selling pure water to those who believe in the sanctity of pro-creation, as well as those who just want babies.

Fifteen-Forty-One and Penguin Four are eyeing each other, Mia's trying to move a hand shadow on the wall, possibly a rabbit. I'm trying to think. The four of us live together, each in our own small world. If the pigeons produce fertile eggs, we'll have proof the condo's well water supports fertility, the perfect option for anyone who acquires a sudden distaste for reservoir water. When it comes to commerce, timing is everything. The reservoir needs to be treated soon.

Mia's toe shadow stops moving. The population's not just about the evening news. Our two tablets side by side, world population counter pushing numbers up, Mia's fertility clock pulling numbers down.

72

Sometimes it's more painful watching Institutionalized pigeons than watching unemployed coordinators. Together, Penguin Four and Fifteen-Forty-One refine ways to ignore each other. They avoid eye contact, look skyward, and walk away in opposite directions, turning their heads for glances backward; the only exception is feeding time when they stand side by side, eating refined formulated birdseed.

Luckily, watching the evening news distracts us from the sad world of pigeons. Today's retro day, a TV celebration of back when. A cute anchorwoman wearing a princess dress holds a vintage microphone as if she's a medieval flutist turned vocalist. Surprisingly, she interviews our neighbor Jonson, the new voice of reason and common sense. As you'd expect, the anchorwoman's dress is short enough to increase my attention span, and long enough to cover the subject, a rare instance where concealment is not a cover-up.

It's no surprise that a flamed-out meteor and part-time consultant from the Institute wants to rise from the Academy and become a self-employed star. During his moment of fame talking to the pleasant news anchor, Jonson doesn't dwell on the past. Instead, he announces his new business launch, WaterWorks Water.

"Unlike other brands that precede it, my water promises fertility as well as refreshment," Jonson says. "Water works for anyone who's well-fed and fertile. It's proven, after all. Ask around. Every parent drinks water, if not all the time, sooner or later. Water creates opportunity. Look at me. I'll be more useful, even self-reliant again."

"Just think," the pleasant news anchor says. "How proud will you be if some couple buys your water and produces a child who grows up and becomes president?"

"What a story to tell my grandchildren," Jonson says. He must be forgetting that reservoir water spiked with ACE4 could reduce his odds of having grandchildren, let alone a child who becomes president.

The beautiful news anchor wearing the princess dress of adequate length speaks in a soft, pleasant voice. "What would happen if a couple who drink WaterWorks Water happens to parent one of the world's ten most wanted? Would that make you proud?"

"I think not," he says. "But I can't overstress that reproduction is a God-given right."

Who can argue with that?

Anchorwoman forgot to ask who will be responsible for putting ACE4 in the reservoir. But she brought out the best in Jonson. A dropout's dropout, he didn't dwell on his humble background as a jobless generator tender or after-hours custodian who likes to drink beer while a cute middle-aged waitress counts tips. He's a poster child for serendipity. Afraid that the title "consultant" might make it look like he was hiding his unemployment history, he called himself a spiritual advisor to our other two consultants Smith and Jones. His odds of working at the Academy again, one in a million, yet obsolete skills, inexperience, unemployment, and ability to be in the right place at the right time proved the best credentials for an entry-level maintenance job. Even though he makes less than he did as a generator tech, he feels remorse for displacing a tenured maintenance worker who made more doing the same thing. With a real job again, Jonson plans to call Sky Pilot's cute waitress. Since she's smart enough to abstain from alcohol while counting tips, she's probably still there, hopefully waiting to hear from him.

Jonson, Mia, and I meet for lunch frequently. Now that he's working instead of consulting for the Academy, he's more relaxed when we visit. Having graduated from the Technical Academy with different specialties, Jonson and I have

221

uncommon disinterests that complement each other. He studied energy generation, yet he understands how machines waste it. I was into electromechanical contraptions that squander energy. I wish for nothing more than a world with solar panels, windmills, and water wheels that would allow us to waste all the energy we want.

Of course, I have my ambitions: spending the rest of my life with Mia, suspended in Mysterious Traveler, overlooking a river park where carbon canoes race by, and pigeons fly overhead. One other ambition—if the Academy thins the herd again and fires me, I want to find a place of employment without the Institutional chatter. Nothing is impossible; people tell me. Then there's always the hope and fear for a child running in the river park playing with one of Toasty's kittens, both yet to be born.

73

Jonson stands in the driveway looking dazed, as if he's just awakened from a deep sleep, dreaming an American Dream, possibly in living color. When he sees us, he suddenly comes to life; his purposeful walk's faster than a slow jog, energetic enough to make us think there's some kind of emergency. Before I can shut off the car's ignition, he blurts through my open window, "Twenty-four WaterWorks Water orders. I need to know that I can access your kitchen sink."

"Hello?" Mia's questionable greeting must be a subtle reminder for Jonson that he forgot to greet us.

He ignores Mia. Instead, he reminds us that we've already discussed his easy-to-answer question about access. "I just need to bottle water in your kitchen sink," he says. "You know, it's a shorter walk to the parking lot from your place."

"I know, we want to help," I reply "Just curious. . . How can you sell water if ACE4 isn't available yet?"

"It's in the pipeline . . ."

The condo's backyard well supplies the entire complex. Tested twice a year, it turns out to be the best local water available. Mia and I can certify its quality. We drink lots of it ourselves and provide it to the pigeons.

Jonson is always talking about filling condos with capsules and renting them out. I'm not sure how many trailer truckloads of WaterWorks Water he would have to sell to afford such conversions. At least he's excited. In a world where people lose jobs faster than the stock market yields dividends, a portable capsule in a condo can be an old home in a new place, a new home in an old place, or a home away from home, a great feature, as long as it doesn't discourage humans from homing. His excitement's contagious enough for Mia and me to go along with him. After all, it looks like he's following the golden rule of small business and the American Dream. For sure, he would know how to respond to LaserFunk on this one: EFFICIENCY IS KEY. Of course, Jonson should keep in mind the adage, WORK WITH HONESTY AND INTEGRITY AND YOU SHALL BE REWARDED. Even though we rarely use our kitchenette, he should remember to pay us a little money for water and space, both rare commodities.

Rumors that Penguin Four has a pigeon in his life make us wonder. If Institute people discover we're supporting two pigeons on one support check, Fifteen-Forty-One could become a liability; I hate bringing up a difficult topic with Mia.

"Your paper plane lettered 'Long live the Academy' might have projected a cynical attitude of ingratitude that might get back to the Institute."

"Sometimes the plane trick flies, sometimes it doesn't."

Animal Rights people continue to hear rumors that Penguin Four's so-called healthy exercise jumping rope is an addiction. We admit it's too bad the pigeon was vulnerable to a seemingly safe sport. Thankfully, his recovery reveals the success of Mia's competent care and discourages accusations of pigeon abuse. We're still afraid to divulge his ongoing affair with Fifteen-Forty-One. Animal Rights people might celebrate; the pigeon's exuberance might attract publicity.

What if the Director catches on, especially now that diagnosed attention surplus is going to his head? Better we don't find out. Off the record, his overachievement makes him wish he were less human, a goal some believe he attained already. To increase revenue from LaserFunk, he proclaims Monday Mental Health Day. Misinterpreting or taking advantage of his intention, most employees take the day off. For the few who pursue mental health coming to work, there's a downside. Dwelling on mysteries of the mind, they forget they should be working. "Are there risks for minds that study themselves," I ask Mia.

"I can almost guarantee that most introspective people become junk psychology junkies."

Side by side, asleep with their heads tucked under each other's wings, the pigeons are exercising their rights to privacy and intimacy. Keeping their heads hidden, they can do anything they want without revealing their identities. We still undress with the lights on. Ever since the chains broke, Mia hasn't taken chances. She pulls the sheet over us, right away.

74

The EggRoom tech said he's never heard of Diogenes, the long-gone philosopher who lived in a barrel. No matter. Hopeful that capsules will end up mainstream, he predicts savings might impact our lifestyle enough to allow us to afford large suspension capsules designed to fit in small penthouses. I wonder if his vision somehow includes my recurring dream of river parks populated by pigeons and sleek racing canoes.

Of course, the big picture needs another set of eyes. Mia thinks penthouse costs might drop if electricity, heating oil, and lawn irrigation prices rise.

WHAT GOES UP MUST COME DOWN.

I'm not making this up. I'm telling the truth, a common habit of people with my affliction. According to LaserFunk, I will never be a director, coordinator, or even an opportunitator. EggRoom tech made it clear while hooking me up for a session. "You never concentrate on irrelevant trivia," he said. "That's one of the main ingredients that leaders use for making important decisions. You would never survive, confined in a cubicle, keying data on a laptop, trying to keep up with keyboard jockeys. You're free to move around the Academy. Director's directives only confine you when you stop thinking for yourself."

"If the EggRoom cures me, will the Academy still need me?"

"I don't know," the tech says. "I wouldn't get my hopes up."

75

Believing that old ideas can solve new problems, Mia applies for a historical grant to fund the revival of good, old-fashioned therapy. Its resurgence could save the world from crooks who attempt to deceive LaserFunk. It could help white-collar criminals rejected by the underworld get the best diagnosis possible. Good luck to anyone who wins or loses a crapshoot with LaserFunk. After winning the grant, Mia still has trouble accepting that violence, starvation, and plague can spread. Until she adjusts, Mia vows to continue coping, making the world a better place with better mazes for pigeons.

Afraid that mazes satisfy a need to control her surroundings, Mia seeks the advice of a therapist. Somehow, ever-changing designs reflect what she's thinking. Since Mia won't admit to anything beyond that, I should read up on the maze interpretation. Her therapist thinks that our funeral plans are significant. "What's more important," he asks Mia. "Making Sid believe that you'll wear something outrageous to his funeral? Or giving him hope you'll attend?"

"It doesn't matter," Mia says. "Sid and I are in love. Thinking about a funeral that's outrageous sounds like fun."

"Your therapist's questions sound good enough to mix into the Machine's next software upgrade. Mia—I like what you said about love."

"Would you say the same thing?"

"I know, it's easier to think love than say it out loud. I do love you."

"I shouldn't have to ask."

Talking to Mia, my words don't surprise me. Sometimes I'm afraid my words send invisible shadows that intensify darkness. If there's something wrong with my thinking and the EggRoom cures me, will I lose my technical abilities? If something gets better, does something else get worse?

I remember wrestling with a good friend at recess. He'd pin me on the ground, and slap my face. "Don't talk," he'd tell me. "Say you're sorry."

I apologize. He'd slap me again. "Don't talk."

I'd say nothing. The friend would slap me for not apologizing. Then he'd laugh, his words already recycled on LaserFunk: "You're so mixed up you don't know if you should shit or go blind." I still feel that way sometimes. What are the odds? Even LaserFunk burped or farted, word for word: DON'T TALK, SAY YOU'RE SORRY.

Workers spend so much time seeking self-help that the Director has trouble scheduling meetings. Electronic memos assure us that profits are on the rise—it takes patience, a little more time, and a few hundred additional insurance payments to take it all to the next level. Where's a paper plane that says, "Long Live the Academy" when you need one? Fortunately, none of the paper planes reveal my declining numbers. Twenty-four million keystrokes to the tenth times seven hundred, sixty keyboard jockeys, all with the usual ten fingers these days. Negabyte number thirty-two point four.

"Keep up the good work," the Director says. His tone of voice warns that I shouldn't ask if he's being sarcastic.

Mia contacts the Institute to discuss terms for Penguin Four's continued support. She sends a paper airplane, the closest thing she has to an olive branch. She writes on one wing, "Mysterious Traveler," a neutral expression that lacks hostility or intent. There's nothing to deny or reject—especially when the Institute's remaining coordinator reads the other wing that says, "Long live The Academy." We pack it carefully so that they can fly it, should they have a spare moment. Thinking of us should bring warm thoughts of travel and mystery.

76

The pigeons are eating a Saturday breakfast, an exotic blend of cashew-flavored sunflower seed. Their wings almost touch; their heads bob in unison. I'm checking out Mia's newest maze.

"What is it this time, Mia, another distillery, petroleum refinery, pharmaceutical lab?"

"How could anyone object to an interactive zoo? Not that you're objecting—are you?"

"No, I'm in awe. I'm wondering how two new mazes can intertwine without touching. Mazes corkscrewing with gentle spirals and chutes look like a technological wonder compared to your early attempts."

One maze for the pigeons, two capsules for us. We're inches away. With little space between pigeons and humans, they can watch us; we'll watch them. Supposedly, an interactive zoo frees the inhibitions of birds that never trust humans completely, despite our reputation for cleanliness. For us, it's easier to have our own space, knowing we won't be bothered with feathers or droppings.

Mia's ambitious maze designs take up more and more of the living space once wasted on humans, forcing us to stuff more surplus paper airplanes into the surplus Plexiglass tubing stored in the hall.

Mia's first paper plane from her worthless stock certificate was the beginning. We continued to design our experiment with unexpected aerodynamics. We've included a substantial number of copies of the most successful designs, Equalizer, American Dreamer, Coordinator One, and Random Flyer, in a collection that multiplies geometrically. Of course, folded paper planes don't store well; they take up too much space in a multi-capsule setting. While trying to dream up new places to stockpile them, we've launched a few across the room, and flown a few outdoors. If you own a pigeon ranch, don't try this at home: paper planes and pigeons don't operate in harmony with one another, making mid-air collisions likely.

It only takes an expanded ream of five hundred folded paper planes to fill the space of ten reams of flat paper. Throwing them out would require the sacrifice of more innocent saplings to make up for paper wasted. Of course, finding new ways to recycle is the right thing to do. We gently stuff planes into sections of scrap plastic tubing leftover from Mia's latest maze project. We're careful not to bend, fold, or mutilate them in a way that would make them fly less efficiently.

If only Jonson had waited a day to discuss his plans for going condo. He breezes in, taking us by surprise. He needs to show our setup to a capsule holdings coach, a mentor who monitors the best real estate deals to identify promising trends. I'm not sure how Mia and I fit in. Knowing that Jonson is leaning toward converting a warehouse into capsule condos, he probably wants a second opinion. Right now, the capsule coach seems more concerned that the paper planes fill the hall. "Why would anyone create a fire hazard from something so worthless," he wonders aloud. "If that Mysterious Traveler and your other capsule aren't insured, I'm certain the planes aren't covered either."

To reduce the risk of fire, I gave the coach a plane, its wing slightly damaged. Uncertain that he should try it indoors, he hands it to Jonson, who launches it upward. It levels out and glides counterclockwise back to its point of departure. The consequence of an unintended trick makes Jonson laugh. "I should include a free promo plane along with each bottled water purchase," he says. "If we could damage—I mean modify—an entire lot of planes to fly like horizontal boomerangs, I can use them by the case."

Jonson sells water faster than he can bottle it. In a stroke of genius, he limits his sales territory to the Municipal Water District. Even though ACE4 still hasn't been added to the local reservoir as far as we know, he's already sold enough water to start saving funds for rental capsules. I stand at the sink, filling bottles, an incentive for Jonson to take more planes. He adds the filled jars to the van; it sinks toward the ground, tires almost flat from the weight.

As ordered by the court, the Institute pays for Penguin Four's portion of condo space and, unknowingly, for Fifteen-Forty-One's. Together Mia and I pitch in our share, fifty-fifty. Now Jonson is paying us token amounts for the water. It sounds easy, but don't forget I'm the one who ends up mopping a wet kitchen floor. Jonson seems happier now the American Dream delivers larger pieces of the pie his way. In the meantime, residents ask our condo association to explain occasional drops in water pressure.

As luck has it, an anonymous whistleblower contacts local TV news people to disclose details about unauthorized research that examined the effects of sterility drugs on pigeons.

The news anchor who never forgets to wear a suit presents both sides of the water question "Was ACE4 developed by a miracle worker or terrorist?" he asks. "Is overpopulation a real problem?"

Newsman makes a good point. Population increases encourage economic growth in the hardware sector. According to my calculations, capsules might dominate the housing sector in the faraway future, 2078. Millions of new units would require almost fifty-eight thousand miles of suspension chain. The high-quality suspension creates the illusion of security. How many times could we wrap that much chain around the equator?

It looks like Penguin Four and Fifteen-Forty-One rest comfortably, without having to think or dream bad dreams. Right now, at least they're getting as much done as Mia and me. Although each maze provides more than forty feet of travel distance, they're happy to remain at one end, their small corner of the world.

If we get restless, there's always room to move at the Academy. Despite the mysteries of suspended capsules going nowhere fast, life is good, knowing our suspension chains won't break.

77

LaserFunk says PICK YOURSELF UP BY YOUR BOOT-STRAPS. True or false, it makes good advice for the one in six keyboard jockeys most eligible for the next layoff. The Academy uses Jonson as an example of upward mobility, a trajectory from joblessness to visionary to entrepreneur. Well done, Jonson. Don't trip. Remember. Don't try pulling yourself up by the bootstraps while climbing the ladder of success. Never forget: ALL WORK AND NO PLAY MAKES BOY A DULL JACK. What happens to those unemployed with nothing to do but play? Would NO WORK AND ALL PLAY MAKE JACK BRIGHT?

Five hundred paper planes stored in the spare maze segments are long gone, already shipped. For every water bottle Jonson fills up, I fold a new plane. I'm getting tired of the hard work, tired of what little excitement remains. Mia still tests each one. With so much to think about, gliding paper planes through the hallway eases her mind. Jonson's out of earshot; my complaining at least breaks the monotony. "We're always too tired to picnic. My wrists feel numb from folding these planes."

"That's tendonitis, "Mia says. "My wrists are getting the same thing from the endless test launching."

"Life in the fast lane of a highway that's not imaginary makes us too crazy to relax. Enough is enough."

"You're right," Mia says. "Tomorrow night, Jonson can fill his own bottles, fold his planes, and do the test launches himself. We should go on a picnic."

Once Mia decides not to do something, she sticks to it. Believe it or not, I can only do less if I put in some effort.

The Institute's Pigeon Coordinator and Mia negotiate pigeon custody in the shadows of the law, shadows that Mia thinks are off the wall. She has lots on her plate; the Institute people want to buy an Animal Rights-approved radio frequency bracelet for Penguin Four, like those used to monitor criminals but smaller, the size of a pigeon's leg band. They need to know Penguin Four lives at his assigned home address, no matter where his heart is. What the Academy wants makes no difference. He flies no further than a hop, skip, and a jump these days.

"The pigeon's happy," Mia assures the Institute's Coordinator. "He's good, as long as he keeps a comfortable distance from humans. After all we've done, he seems more comfortable with Fifteen-Forty-One than with us. Why would he want to leave her?"

If there's an answer, Mia doesn't want to know. She doesn't mention our plans this evening, an escape to bring Penguin Four, Fifteen-Forty-One, Mia, and I closer together. Few understand why Mia personifies pigeons.

"Lucky, you didn't mention the picnic. That could mean your job."

"There you go with meaning again."

Our first indoor outing since our Institute research for *Fifty Places*, we picnic in the shadow of Mysterious Traveler. It's a perfect spot for an Institute ambush, should the Coordinator decide to prove Penguin Four's hiding in a home not necessarily close to his heart. According to current pigeon theory, Penguin Four's heart still resides in the penthouse.

We bring an easy-to-prepare picnic, five different flavors of Score energy bars, still wrapped. A mixture of gravity-fed Sustaine and seltzer water flows downward through a tube, directly from Mysterious Traveler. Talk about convenience. It doesn't take us long to arrive since we're already here. Mia throws sunflower seed for Penguin Four and Fifteen-Forty-One, too much, too close to our spread blanket. If you're a human never at home enough to find the way to your pigeon's heart, birdseed does the trick. It's one of the few reasons pigeons have for walking, flying, or being. Supposedly, it's not addictive. We lie down together and watch the two birds go for the sunflower seed, their beaks rapidly tapping the floor lightly. Even though there's enough for both, they often go for the same seed, stopping long enough to peck each other. When it's all gone, Fifteen-Forty-One preens Penguin Four's neck feathers. Penguin Four reciprocates. She sits down, tucks her head under her wing, and sleeps. Penguin Four pecks the Plexiglass absent-mindedly, randomly, without purpose—unless he's reliving incubator moments pecking his way out of an eggshell, a miracle most pigeons survive.

I recline on our blanket. Half awake, half asleep, I get another vision of Mia. No longer a ghost-faced goddess in a beam of fluorescence, she's aglow in the brightness of LED overhead lights. I'm feeling very much alive. We climb into our capsule and put on headsets. We lose our minds making love. The sound system fails to amplify our breathing. Blown transistor? Loose connection?

78

I wake up too tired to move. Our panoramic capsule view takes in Penguin Four and Fifteen-Forty-One, both asleep, two feather balls perched on four puny legs and claws, making the scene prehistoric. Penguin Four pulls his head out from under his wing, yawns like a pigeon, looks around, stands, and turns toward us. As if we're both surprised to find semi-intelligent life in a geometric Plexiglass wasteland, the pigeon, and I stare at each other. Penguin Four ambles, around an imaginary out-of-round circle. He stops and stands on one leg, holds the other claw in mid-air, checks out Fifteen-Forty-One, and then stares at us. Without feathers, are we funny-looking? Lab pigeons don't get out much; there's no way we can remind him of monkeys.

Mia drinks coffee from her drink tube and tries to read the paper, a custom more comfortable for those living in places with kitchen tables or so-called living rooms. She finds an article about littering, accompanied by a picture of a slightly tattered paper plane, possibly still functional, sticking into shoreline river mud. One wing's lettered "Mysterious Traveler." The other is "Long Live the Academy." Though paper aircraft is organic enough to decompose in less than two years, the article claims the plane is an ecological threat. Does the reporter forget that careless trash dumping serves as a public service? Do bad examples make the possibility of a greener, cleaner environment more attractive?

Mia notices a small ad on the opposite stock market page, pure coincidence since financials cover her particular area of

disinterest: "Free Paper Plane included with the purchase of
WaterWorks Water, the Modern Hydration & Fertility Method."
"Jonson doesn't know when to stop," I tell Mia. "I get tired
thinking about folding and lettering more planes and turning
the faucet on and off, once for each bottle of water."
"Watch this." Mia squirts water onto a folded plane,
a reject with two broken wings, one of them modified, the
other damaged. Wet, the paper tears more easily. Better said,
wet paper separates without resisting. From dust, it came to
paper mache it returns. Since a paper plane stuck in river
mud decomposes the same way this one does, it never hurts
to pray for more rain. But then, what are the odds that one of
the thousands of newspaper readers might be curious enough
and conscientious enough to trace a plane with "Mysterious
Traveler" lettered on its wing, back to us?

To attract more free publicity, Jonson sends a high-pressure
sales letter to the editor:

"Lacing reservoir water with a scientific dose of ACE4
rescues us from an overabundance of parasitic humans
with the power to deplete vast underground aquifers,
water sources for the WaterWorks Modern Hydration
& Fertility Method. A positive change, fewer babies
mean fewer discarded paper planes. Less demand for
paper planes and more saplings, growing into mature
trees that become fixed and immovable in their ways.

"Power to the people who bring us ACE4. Power to the
people who bring us WaterWorks Water. More power
to fewer people."

79

The Director's mind is the root of his problems; attention surplus continues going to his head. To cut costs, he sends empty boxes from the overcrowded parts room to a storage facility in China. We're not sure if we get the logic, but it doesn't matter. "The Academy's blessed with positive indicators," he tells us. Either he knows something we don't, or attention to detail strengthens his denial that something's wrong.

Better to question when I already know the answer, but I'm curious. "How does the Academy plan to fill the emptiness, once the empty boxes are all shipped to China?"

"Thank you for asking," the Director replies. "Don't forget, you need to leave our meeting early to make the EggRoom appointment on time."

If only we could talk about emptiness, I could avoid going, at least for a few more moments. But the Director has nothing more to say.

"One more visit should prove life fascinates you more than nothingness does," the EggRoom tech tells me.

"I'm somewhat excited already." I try to explain. "It's not the pigeon egg on a golf tee that's remarkable. It's the ambiance of a psychotherapeutic church in a cathedral-shaped cubby that inspires me to bring something of myself."

It must be the lab tech doesn't know what to say. He attaches the electrodes and transmitter that sends the radio waves that carry my brainwaves to the EEG. Of course, a few waves heading outward escape and scatter into space. My mind tells me to breathe, a life skill I usually practice without thinking.

Room lights dim. Pigeon eggs pointed end down as usual, sitting on golf tees, forming a perfect line across the illuminated cathedral cubby. Some kind of hidden conveyor starts moving the eggs from right to left, an unusual direction for mechanized movement. I'm not trying to be critical. In real life, at least in life more real than it is in the EggRoom, things usually move from left to right. One egg departs; another arrives. Counting as they come and go makes a tiresome but better-than-nothing distraction. All white without marks or specks, the eggs are too uniform to count. There's no way to pinpoint a beginning or end, no way to tell if those that pass ever return, no way to know if they recirculate repeatedly. Whatever. The EEG must be trying to measure something important. Conveyer belt quietly moving eggs on tees, my mind hums to accompany silence. Uncertain about what the test is testing, I just want to pass.

If thirty thousand eggs arrive every hour, another thirty thousand depart; no choice, the never-ending procession takes the path most traveled. The eggs come and go, in and out of order, pausing momentarily, moving the other way, left to right always a relief. A strobe light flashes, freezing movement. Eggs take on the ultra-bright shine of Madison Avenue toothpaste teeth.

The conveyor stops momentarily and then restarts. One egg, an escapee from the Academy's mad mechanical dream, went missing. No time for thinking, my thoughts move with the conveyor. Either another egg's gone missing, or the empty tee passes twice as often. How can I tell?

One by one, eggs disappear; golf tees vanish without a trace. Silence masks the conveyor's hidden existence.

I know this: an egg perched on a golf tee can't be any crazier than a pigeon hatching a golf ball.

The strobe stops pulsing. I wait to be disconnected.

$E = mc^2$?

80

Mia and I bask in an after-love glow that's not fluorescent, but otherwise pleasant, possibly contagious. Less than three feet away, two love birds Penguin Four and Fifteen-Forty-One perform their mating ritual. I'm not sure what Mia thinks, but I'm guessing humans are more natural and fun-loving lovers than poker-faced birds.

As usual, the Director gave a motivational Monday morning talk. "People need LaserFunk twice as much when the economy chugs along at half speed. It stands to reason. Even people with solid incomes are afraid the good life might go bad. Concerns that LaserFunk will go out of fashion are baseless. Recent research suggests few people would seek therapy in their cubicles where privacy would allow them to text with live therapists."

I don't need a meeting to listen to his business forecast. I've been watching my stats plummet. Twenty-five million keystrokes to the twelfth, six hundred, seventy-five, ten-fingered keyboard jockeys. Negabyte numbers, twenty-two-point-six.

The Director reports he's repeatedly taken the LEAP, LaserFunk's Evaluation and Appraisal Profile. The appraisal always insists he's addicted to assessments that test for dangerous levels of perfection.

At the end of the meeting, the Director invites Mia and me for coffee, a highly unusual circumstance since we're underlings who don't always clap at the most appropriate times. He didn't ask us to visit because he's lonely or cares about LaserFunk. He wants to talk real estate, a surprise since few invest in housing these days. Leaders, stockholders, and directors know markets better than we do—that's why they're stockholders, why we're the held and directed, prisoners of our creature discomforts. I'm at least thankful WaterWorks Water provides additional employment, even if Jonson doesn't pay well.

The Director asks, "How's that capsule you're living in working out?" Without waiting for an answer, he lowers his voice. "Don't let this get around. I'm thinking about hanging a few from a tree for a new summer home, somewhere in the wild forest land of the Adirondacks."

Talk of a capsule swinging under a tree sounds much too dramatic, but it doesn't sound like a bad idea. It seems harmless to offer a contact name. "I have a business card; the guy's a good guy, I forget his name. He's an English sales rep who works for Cutting Edge Capsule, an American distributor of capsules made in Taiwan. I once considered a franchise for myself."

"Were you thinking about leaving the Academy, spending more time with family, pursuing a new career?" the Director asks.

I look toward Mia. "Family's here at the Academy."

We get home just in time to fill five hundred water jugs, the most tedious part of the job that pays Jonson so well. His ads still promise a free, hand-folded paper plane with each purchase. He doesn't seem worried about the labor required to keep his promise. Mia thinks Jonson should fold the planes himself. If not, his ad could at least stipulate, "Limited offer."

In response to the recent news of a paper plane littering the river shore, I write "WaterWorks Water" on one wing, and "Biodegradable" on the other. These planes could soon become collectible. More likely than not, parents will fly them with children brought to us by the miracle of WaterWorks Water, not to mention the miracle of love, lust, and everything in between, from the center to the outskirts.

I fold more paper planes—one for each water jug filled. Mia still tests two at a time. Who knows why Fifteen-Forty-One is not flying today? With less interference than usual, test flights are uneventful. I miss the fun of watching the mid-flight crashes that provide natural relief from boredom. Collisions cheap entertainment, I shouldn't complain. But all said and done, I am the one folding the planes.

News reports good news. An anonymous source claims that ACE4 the new birth control additive won't increase reservoir water prices. It turns out, ACE4 is organic, algae-like. Taxpayers and water buyers will never bear the burden of paying for its renewal. The paper reminds couples who wish to remain fertile to avoid drinking reservoir water and to seek out natural, unadulterated water instead.

I wonder, "Is Jonson the anonymous source?"

"Let overpopulation solve itself," Mia replies."

"ACE4 could solve the problem more efficiently than army brass, corporate management, or politicians. Who would suspect that a small load of algae can accomplish so much? Will the public condemn the public service if they think it violates the sanctity of life? How many right-minded people would ever think giving half as many babies twice as much love is better than loving twice as many half as much?"

"I'm suddenly more optimistic," Mia says. "Zero population could make room on the planet for another baby—ours."

"You're right. Just because we want a baby doesn't mean we can't promote birth control. We can support two opposing views without having to compromise. It's fair. We deserve at least one baby to replace two of us."

"One? Or maybe two, depending on how well ACE4 works."

81

Ready for a quick flight down the maze's straight-away, Penguin Four and Fifteen-Forty-One line up. Even with the risk of a two-foot free fall, they must feel safer at each other's side. They lift off for a series of fly-bys—I lose count after twenty-four. Short-distance flying requires more quick starts and stops than Mia had imagined during the maze's construction. Fifteen-Forty-One gets impatient, waiting for the feeble Penguin Four to catch up. Worried about so much stop-and-go, Mia opens their door to the outside, to give them a break. No surprise, they remain inside.

Penguin Four goes for the birdseed. Without any apparent invitation, Fifteen-Forty-One joins him. What a miracle. After ignoring each other for days, Penguin Four and Fifteen-Forty-One have finally become inseparable. Penguin Four seems to have forgotten about jumping rope. Is an addicted bird always a marathon bird? Will a new love life replace his dependency?

We arrive at work. Coincidence or not, the Director meets us in the parking lot. An unusual circumstance, he's already dressed down to business casual, long-sleeved shirt and baseball cap, both dark blue, both lettered *Cutting-Edge -Technology.*

"That Cutting-Edge hat looks good on you," Mia says. She sounds sincere. Sometimes I wish she could be more sarcastic.

The Director wastes no time on small talk. "Which suspension model would you recommend for my favorite tree in the Adirondacks?"

I give him an honest answer, not that that's what I'd do

if I had to do it over again. "Any Cutting-Edge model should work well. No surprise, we always recommend a stronger chain than that supplied by the manufacturer." I don't explain that a strong chain absorbs every stress from love's vibrations to an earthquake's shock waves. To be honest, there's no guarantee about a tree's reaction to seismic shock. In its search for trueness or falseness, LaserFunk would say WHEN THE BOUGH BREAKS, THE CAPSULE WILL FALL.

Jonson already knows everything he needs to know about suspension chains. He has already sold enough water to acquire a few capsules. Some of his tenants insist on buying condo space so they can suspend their own. Their lifestyle might not improve, but they'll become members of condo associations, groups that don't require religious or political affiliation, ethnic or racial membership, initiation, or hazing. Capsule tenants only need to become homeowners. Everyone should feel like they belong to something.

Mia still hopes her therapist can help her adjust to the craziness around her. So far, the therapist has offered his insight that guardianship of Penguin Four satisfies an intense need to protect pigeons. Mia also protects me, probably a defense mechanism that makes her less vulnerable should they fly away. I'm beginning to think pigeons and hand-folded, organic paper planes are the foundation of our relationship. I probably need all the help I can get.

Thanks to her live therapy, Mia thinks I'm rebellious in some adolescent way. She recalls her most recent therapeutic conversation. "Do you think wearing an exotic costume at Sid's funeral would be purely artistic," her therapist asked.

"It's possible. Sid likes to dream of my attendance when he's alive, more than he'll want me there when he's dead. It's unlikely he'll know the difference. As long as I live, my promise to attend gives him something to die for."

"What use would Sid be if he lived forever?"

Hard questions without easy answers fail to provide Mia with much insight. Besides, the promise of ACE4 presents problems more immediate than existential. "What would happen to the reservoir fish," Mia asks.

The therapist, an amateur environmentalist, says, "You can rest easy. Acid rain has already killed the fish."

"Is it ethical to sterilize people who can't afford bottled water?"

Mia doesn't believe the therapist when he predicts someone will discover a new underground water supply that could make pure water more affordable. She finds no comfort in his assurance, "It's just a matter of time before acid rain sterilizes people too."

"Does that mean ACE4's only an ice cube in the energy drink of progress?"

"Speaking of progress, what have you and Sid decided about a baby?

82

So far, Fifteen-Forty-One hasn't laid an egg, not even one. Always the self-proclaimed pigeon expert, Jonson wonders how this can be. After all, the pigeon gets food, water, ventilation, and sanitation, above and beyond reasonable expectations. "Why do pigeons bother mating if the mother doesn't lay any eggs?" he asks.

We don't volunteer an answer that would be more obvious if Jonson were less distracted by his water business: Human or pigeon, sterile people usually mate for the same reason fertile people mate. Mating happens to be the best recipe for creating one of Mother Nature's best neurochemical cocktails. Believe it or not, I've heard rumors that having a child might provide a head rush even greater. Childless, it's hard for me to know for sure. There's only one way to find out.

In his own conflicted way, Jonson thinks his thoughts about reproduction. If Fifteen-Forty-One's eggs turn out to be duds that don't grow baby pigeons, Jonson will lose one of the best possible endorsements for WaterWorks Water. He also hopes for nature's seal of approval from Mia and me, should we happen to start a family. No immediate plans to reproduce, we're still talking. Our game of bedtime roulette assures us that we are negotiating in good faith.

Our condo is somewhat crowded. Keeping pigeon ranch guidelines in mind, a baby would require another capsule, along with more food, water sanitation, and ventilation. And we need our jobs. I could tell Jonson the truth, but it's none of his business, even though it is his business, in a way. If we were more ambitious, we'd be selling a unique brand of water to make reproduction more affordable for ourselves.

Just another Monday meeting, I can't help thinking nothing new, something blue. "Good morning," the Director says. "It's a great day with more good news. Recent tax reform, the value of the Japanese yen, and plain common sense, all make it necessary to break down another LaserFunk kiosk. Component salvage increases parts inventory, helps alleviate the overabundance of emptiness."

"A box filled with emptiness sounds like an expensive luxury with limited demand. Are the empties coming back from China?"

The Director smiles; it must be he appreciates that Cutting Edge Capsule card I gave him. But I still don't know how a yen converts to American dollars, or if there's such a thing as tax reform. I know this. Director's achievement score in the ninety-eighth percentile and tenure at the Academy makes it hard to argue. I should quit while I'm ahead. But I have to ask, "This salvaging parts project brings about LaserFunk's demise?

"That's a good question; I'd like to answer. Too bad we're out of time."

"Will you have time to answer during our next meeting?"

According to LaserFunk, A FRIEND IN NEED IS A PEST. In reality, the Director is more pest than a friend. No surprise, he joins Mia and me as we leave the conference room. Now that his meeting's over, he has time to waste being friendly. "I'm looking for standard layout dimensions you'd need for suspending large numbers of capsules. No big deal if I were hanging a few that would serve my family on an Adirondack getaway. But twenty would allow me to invite friends and relatives."

I don't have to be honest, just because he's the Director. Sometimes honesty is the best policy for having fun. "I'd need to know the heights of tree branches and distances between them. Otherwise, I can only provide approximations."

Director's clueless. I promise to look for a hard-to-find hard copy of my only Cutting Edge Capsule owner's manual. Mia threw it out after Penguin Four dropped droppings on it. Fortunately, it caught my eye when I was bagging trash. I stored it in an airtight, acid-free sleeve, dry-caked pigeon dung and all. Mia thinks Penguin Four messed up the manual by accident. But we all know how pigeons are. Like a four-year-old human, Penguin Four was probably showing off to impress Fifteen-Forty-One.

"Don't forget," I tell the Director. "You get a better deal if you increase the size of your capsule order." None of my business, if he were to own all available Adirondack real estate, how many capsules could he suspend? According to LaserFunk, THE SKY'S THE LIMIT.

I'm not sure why Mia tells the Director about a New York artist who raised pigeons in a cage attached to the side of a skyscraper. If pigeon hens fly high enough to reach an upper nest, their eggs roll down a chute that delivers them to an incubator. Achievers from the newest brood fly even higher and lay eggs that make it down another special chute to the same old incubator. The beauty lies in genetic selection. Every new generation flies higher than previous ones, requiring nests at greater heights than ever before.

Mia says, "Science can be fun; art remains an awkward topic. No way would I do the same thing with Penguin Four and Fifteen-Forty-One. Attaching pigeon cages to skyscrapers, and installing the necessary plumbing to deliver eggs to incubators isn't child's play. Besides, I only prefer my art with science on the side."

"Scientific pigeon studies are worthless, especially ones from New York," Director says.

Mia seems to forget the Director is a director. "Research could create a maze of horizontal nesting sites to encourage future generations of pigeons to cooperate. Politicians might learn to accept the poor, tired, and hungry masses seeking refuge in a concrete and asphalt world."

"Like your favorite homeless person, that lady with that

silly little cat?" Despite his cutting sarcasm, the Director promises to grant a grant. I wonder where money from an almost bankrupt Academy comes from.

83

We strip more LaserFunk modules, salvaging more parts that supposedly save the Academy from financial ruin. Upgrading the so-called physical plant should be a top priority. But why bother when the power company threatens to shut the lights off, and the Director continues to destroy it? East Wing's doors remain locked. The maintenance department works around the clock. Judging from the rubble, they're removing cubicles, modules, walls, and ceilings.

Everyone sounds busy as if their job is on a deadline. Should we worry about LaserFunk, our jobs? We can't see what's happening on the other side but hear loud whining, grinding, vibrating, and buzzing of power drills, air wrenches, and screw guns escaping through the walls. If I didn't know better, I'd say it sounds like a capsule assembly plant. Three eight-hour shifts, keep workers going around the clock, suggesting new purpose and urgency.

The big picture remains blurry. When the Director sees the light at the end of the tunnel, it's no longer a curious expression; it sounds like LaserFunk talking true or falseness. At meetings, I feel helpless listening to canned promises, sad mixes of wishful thinking, and blind optimism. The Academy keeps thinning our herd and keeps hiring workers less skilled. Recruiters welcome referrals from employees, soon to lose their jobs to new replacements.

With fewer kiosks, client demand for those that remain trends upward. Academy research suggests mental health doesn't fluctuate with income and the stock market. People in need go crazy. People with too much get lazy and go crazy. Keystroke counts become top secret. Mysteriously, my negabyte numbers disappear.

Penguin Four's condition deteriorates. Mia takes him out of his capsule for wing therapy, a move that often triggers bird-like temper tantrums. He pecks her hands and face, and rolls on the floor, squawking the way obnoxious pigeons do. He doesn't let up until Mia releases Fifteen-Forty-One, allowing her to join him. Fifteen-Forty-One seems more matter-of-fact about their relationship than Penguin Four. She can take it when there's love, leave it when there isn't.

Penguin Four is so domesticated that he takes too much for granted. He avoids exercise as if jump rope's nothing more than a plague that spreads in the name of physical fitness. The rope twirler's solar batteries remain fully charged. Occasionally, I turn it on, just to keep the motor's bearings running freely.

Fifteen-Forty-One needs to get away from her mate and get out for a fly. She tries pecking the micro-switch to get outdoors, but the small trap door hinges are frozen shut, ravaged by rust, a symptom of disuse and neglect. I perform a minor miracle squirting its hinges with penetrating oil, making Fifteen-Forty-One and Mia grateful, even though Mia will never fly, and Penguin Four has given up. His mate out on the town, Penguin Four flaps his wings as if he's stretching, but that's it. Fifteen-Forty-One returns shortly, making me wonder if homing pigeons weakened by Institutionalization get homesick more quickly.

At home, the two pigeons spend most of their time together at the maze's far end, near a window, wings touching intimately by chance or intention, beady eyes watching a small world go by, throats cooing conversation, possibly with deep meaning and obscure innuendo. Oblivious of our efforts on their behalf, both Penguin Four and Fifteen-Forty-One eat sunflower seed sparingly as if it's just a food supplement that provides nutrition they don't need. My guess, the two birds don't stop to appreciate that we dovetail their needs with ours. It's just as well. If pigeons understood English, the word "dovetail" might offend them.

Despite wing therapy and feeble fly-bys, Penguin Four's wings continue to atrophy. Too impatient to be much help, the vet says Penguin Four might be mating more often than he should, at least by contemporary pigeon ranch standards. Problems, problems, too bad there's no LaserFunk for pigeons.

"Penguin Four's background as a lab pigeon is well-documented," Mia says. "The vet forgets the pigeon's an incubator baby. Since the pigeon's parents never knew him as a nestling, neglect was unintentional. Love is so hard to regulate; I refuse to interfere. I wonder if it could help if we give the pigeons less attention."

"I'm more than willing to try."

84

Penguin Four and Fifteen-Forty-One fly an awkward fly-by. Wings flutter weakly, slowly, creating just enough lift to propel them on their toetips for a half-hearted, lame-duck run. Plexiglass muffles the sound of flapping wings and blocks cool but weak sporadic breezes. From the outside looking in, Penguin Four's physical existence and half-hearted movement are all that remains. His decline suggests Mia should consider giving up on his rehab. Maybe the pigeon only flies with Fifteen-Forty-One because he can't invite her to join him for jump rope. He must remember the loneliness while caged in the Institute lab, loneliness when flying the sky dodging BBs. Either way, an ounce of flying is worth more than a pound of therapy.

Maybe a little love is worth much more than flying or therapy. Penguin Four circles Fifteen-Forty-One, cooing. Fifteen-Forty-One coos back, and crouches. Penguin Four hops aboard to copulate the way birds do, flapping his wings enough to maintain balance. The pigeons' coupling is intense, almost passionate as if they're not fooling around. After love, if that's what you call it, Fifteen-Forty-One rests, without tucking her head under her wing.

Under the influence of Fifteen-Forty-One's spell, not to mention the newest euphoric dose of adrenaline and too many other neurotransmitters to mention, Penguin Four seems livelier now, possibly more curious. He stands in front of the Plexiglass, staring at me staring at him. From his expression, I can't tell if his stare is one of contempt or admiration. He remains a stone-faced pigeon that will never win a pigeon show, not with silver tail feathers dulled, wings so atrophied they'll never recover, and legs muscle-bound from skipping rope. All said and done, Penguin Four's a loser with a funny name. He's Institutionalized, can't fly well, and makes an annoying house pet.

I try to outstare the pigeon; my eyes dry faster than usual, forcing me to blink twice as often. The pigeon stares back like a hawk named Eagle Eye.

Mia reaches an artistic plateau, running out of dreams for designing new mazes. A New York real estate entrepreneur website promotes a 3D art seminar, claiming it can stir the imagination the way a gentle breeze prevents stagnation. The message is inspiring enough to get Mia to sign up right away. I hope it works.

She returns from her trip, excited but disillusioned. Profitable for organizers, the seminar provided nothing of value beyond inspiring her anger. The rage is a dividend she can channel into new visions of Reflexive Fusion, tasteful integration of shadows, carbon fiber, and Plexiglass built on a strong foundation of reflection. If she stops planning funeral plans, she'll be able to manage stress until death do us part.

Adjusting for population growth, I revise my estimate of the worldwide need for more residential space. Taking plague and war into account, we will be short two billion capsules in the distant future, 2525. The news is both good and bad. There will undoubtedly be enough people to build them. Unless scientists discover a way to reconstitute the Pacific Ocean's plastic soup into Plexiglass, resources will be scarce. Even without a material shortage, real estate analysts project, we will run out of room to suspend capsules in the following year, 2526.

Jonson stops for another load of water. He fills jugs and folds planes. His maintenance job's only a front. Recently, Jonson slipped a requisition for the Academy's helicopter in with a routine request for tools. Supply signed off, possibly without reading, more likely without thinking. Jonson happened to overhear a phone argument between the Academy's pilot and his wife about having another baby. He enlisted the pilot who was more than happy to drop ACE4 into the reservoir, his family's water source. It sounds like a sound plan that could go bad if the pilot's wife substitutes bottled for reservoir water.

Depending on how you look at it, things could get better or worse if the wife spikes his WaterWorks Water with a little alcohol.

85

My mind swims within itself. In a rush to get things over with, I want to leave the EggRoom before I arrive. The tech offers me the usual chair. He attaches the electrodes to transmit new, hopefully improved brainwaves to the EEG. A suspended screen blocking the cathedral cubby retracts upward. Room lights dim. The only remaining light source is a spotlight's beam, a lonely beacon of hope or hopelessness, depending on who's watching. It shines on the cubby, illuminating a blue spruce tree, a purple cloth draped around its base, center to outskirts. A pigeon egg perches on a golf tee sitting at the tree's apex. It's not Christmas, so you can't call it a Christmas tree. It must be about symmetry, perfection, and truth, ecological or otherwise. Alive, it's the ideal. Dead, it's a consequence, a caution against tree harvest, especially ornamental ones.

Most people buy holiday trees at the same time every year. Someone from the EggRoom must have happened upon this one. It's quite a tree. I want to talk to it; the way people talk to plants. But I'm afraid the tech might be listening, I try telepathy.

The pigeon egg is plain and simple. I wonder how it can sit on a golf tee, how a tee can balance on a tree. The light beam fills the cubby with surrealistic ghost-likeness, blanketing the tree in whiteness. Its base vibrates, shaking the branches until they rain needles, reducing the tree to a barren evergreen, a skeletal ecological tragedy, nothing but a suitable perch for Penguin Four and Fifteen-Forty-One. The pigeon egg remains perched on the golf tee, sitting at the apex. At first, the bare tree and illuminated egg retain their geometric identities. The spotlight brightens gradually, transforming the egg into a star. Its bright intensity lingers like a well-timed, well-placed musical note. It's almost alive with short-lived magic. The spotlight dims. The star fades into a memory—electric, candle-shaped Christmas lights filled with a reddish liquid boil and bubble.

In the EggRoom's darkness, I get a vision of an upraised hand above my face. That voice again, half stern, half-mocking, "Don't talk. Say you're sorry." There's nothing to be sorry about. Room lights gradually brighten.

86

Tonight's the night. We watch the six o'clock weather report on a twenty-four-hour weather channel and check three different internet sites. They all provide the same entertainment—maps, collages, charts, Triple Doppler radar patterns doubled. For once, we're not getting too much information. Each source predicts a light, steady, nine-mile-an-hour breeze. If it blows from the north, big waves will mix and mingle with ACE4, in time to make tomorrow's news.

Jonson insisted that Mia and I come along for the ride. "No problem," he said. "I know the right people."

Mia declined to join us. It's the first time I remember her coming up with so many excuses. "What if we crash and die, or return safely and get arrested, Penguin Four needs me. I'm the guardian, the Carrier of the Pigeon. What if a stray pigeon drinks reservoir water, mistaking it for rainwater? I want no part of it," she says. "You're treating this ACE4 deal like it's a real-world EggRoom. It looks like you're doing the kind of evil we speak out against at the Academy."

We climb out of our capsule and kiss a standing vertical kiss. "Be careful," Mia says. Knowing that I don't pack a lunch in a wicker basket, she hands me a backpack purchased from another outdoor store she found online. "No surprises," she says, "Just wine and cheese."

All said and done I'm a spectator, afraid of losing my job, I want to be part of something bigger than me. I didn't arrange it; I'm not the pilot. I'm along for the ride; playing a small role is better than nothing.

Even without a costume, I know how a Trekkie feels, pissing in the wind, trying to save a planet. To be honest, I'm not sure if there's much of a breeze in outer space.

We meet at the Academy's hanger, the helicopter's heartless home. We take off, and head for the Municipal Airport. We pick up our payload, already loaded into an army surplus helibucket, designed to drop water on forest fires. Thanks to Yankee ingenuity, the favorite element of the American Dream, Jonson modified the release valve. To compensate for the contents of ACE4, he added ballast to help the bucket straighten up and fly right, with a load that would otherwise be too light.

The pilot turns out to be the same one who delivered Smith, Jones, and Jonson to the Institute for the resurrection. A victim of enhanced attention, the pilot rarely misses a detail, a good thing for a human who likes to fly. According to Jonson, the pilot lives in an almost mythical, win-win world that's too good to be true. When he buys life insurance, he's betting he'll crash someday, and win a jackpot posthumously. Flying the helicopter, he's always betting on a safe landing. He doesn't mind if the insurance people keep the money he loses on premiums, as long as he prospers and lives a long life like the famous Captain Quirk. How much would he bet on the Academy's survival? What are the odds of successful realignment and restructuring? Anything can happen. After all, who would have predicted the Institute would give up its helicopter to the Academy, and retain custody of a celebrity lab pigeon that doesn't fly outdoors?

The pilot hooks up to the bucket. On takeoff, the helicopter lifts tightening the cable attached to its load. We fly over the pitch-black reservoir, its gloom darker than the EggRoom when the spotlight's dimmed. The pilot makes a second pass. With the pilot signaling OK, I press the release button, to prove to myself I'm a participant, to prove to Jonson and the pilot, we're in this together. The payload drops, helicopter lifts slightly. My heart sinks under a hint of uncertainty.

We head back to the airport. From the reservoir's east, a blinding searchlight tracks us until we land. The pilot shuts off the ignition. Rotors gradually lose momentum and stop spinning. Spotlights from all directions surround us like a thousand points of light, more sinister than a famous American president of the United States once suggested. A bullhorn voice doesn't sound as friendly as the voice you'd hear on *Candid Camera*, an old, entertaining TV show that ambushed people, catching them in awkward situations with pigeon egg on their faces, so to speak. Believe it or not, I wish I could hide in the EggRoom.

The voice through the bullhorn says, "Come out with your hands up," a command often used by TV cops when catching robbers, less frequent when robbers capture cops.

We sit in the airport conference room under armed guard. We have the right to remain silent; it's a good thing we have nothing to say. The pilot made a dry run; if undetected on the first trip, we would have picked up ACE4 for a second. We're waiting for the environmental police, state police, district attorney, and National Guard to investigate. Since most of the evidence is now in the reservoir, it's going to be a big job. How many gallons of water does the lake hold? Detectives have to sift through evidence but are uncertain how to go about filtering wet birdseed and trout food mix. Can they prosecute us for kindness to fish, birds, and aquatic plants? Press charges for possessing ACE4? Since we break laws in such responsible ways, we ask if there's a better way to drop birdseed; we're open to suggestions.

It rarely pays when you plan. Environmental Police only charge us with littering.

Newspaper editorials correct the common belief that Jonson failed. Equally shocked by the threat of ACE4 and by the promise of WaterWorks Water, people take birth control quite seriously. Merchants report a dramatic rise in condom sales; doctors an uptick in birth control prescriptions. Unsubstantiated reports claim more would-be percussionists are practicing the rhythm method. I almost forgot what LaserFunk expresses so well: GOING FOR IT IS MORE IMPORTANT THAN ARRIVING.

Academy employees and keyboard jockeys treat me as if I'm notorious. The Director approaches me cautiously as if he's afraid to be seen talking with a suspected felon, guilty of a misdemeanor. I don't know why he seems to think it better for workers to see him with me than with Jonson. He's persistent; no surprise, he still wants to learn more about capsules. He asks questions about layout, in case he buys an Adirondack potato field. It's possible. But how many poles, and how much overhead cable would he need for suspending the suspension chains?

Director, Mia and I talk small talk about rumors that claim reservoir trout and pigeons attracted to free food will poop more frequently, polluting the reservoir organically. Even though the water's still safe to drink, many avoid it and buy Jonson's water instead. Sales should remain brisk. Word on the street suggests people who want babies are drinking bottled water just to be fashionable. We marvel at how such a simple substance can make such a complicated business.

87

Prosecutors discover an invoice that documents the sale of ACE4 to Jonson. They're still puzzled about the trout food and birdseed. They continue to investigate, hoping we might react in new ways with new answers to old questions they think they already know the answers to. Unfortunately for them, our eco-friendly payload makes it hard to prove we did anything other than what we did.

The pilot, Jonson, and I appear in court. An expert witness confirms the fish food meets the dietary requirements of reservoir trout. Unfortunately, birdseed is a problem. It's impossible to find an expert who will testify that a grain mill formulated it for ducks. Our defense remains somewhat weak. Why would we drop birdseed in a reservoir, an unlikely place to find anything other than ducks and seagulls? Pigeon feed would make a good alibi, except that pigeons can't swim. It doesn't matter. Our lawyer asks, "What's worse—acid rain or a little birdseed and trout food? If the reservoir contains nothing but acid rainwater, what's the harm if someone tries to help the few remaining trout survive?"

The judge seems moved. Too bad, there's no jury.

The prosecution claims there are better solutions for overpopulation. LaserFunk points to one that's most obvious: FIGHT FIRE WITH FIRE. If a place gets overcrowded, people starve to death, a natural remedy more painful than drinking ACE4. But at least everyone gets a shot at survival that way. Maybe the prosecutor's sarcastic. "Dropping ACE4 on the second trip would have sterilized the very trout these thugs heroically fed," he says. I never looked at it that way. Neither did our lawyer. I didn't dare mention that Mia's therapist said there were no trout left in the reservoir. Admitting I knew there were no trout would have ruined our defense. For the record, we were holding the ACE4 for safe disposal.

Mia and I revisit plans for my funeral. We're beginning to agree I'd look better in business casual than in Lycra or a suit. She has to save the show more than ever. Even though less is sometimes more, she thinks a chic, white robe gives modesty and revelation equal time. What would LaserFunk say? SOME PEOPLE HAVE IT. SOME DON'T.

If we're not supposed to spike reservoir water to help couples with family planning, we can at least plan our afterward. As a dweller of the EggRoom, I'm inclined not to rush things. Mia and I encapsulate ourselves in Mysterious Traveler. We turn on our headsets and share a free bottle of Jonson's WaterWorks Water that we drew from our faucet into one of his bottles. We watch the pigeons watch us as if they're waiting for more action.

88

The creation waits. Too much information blurs the big picture, that vast space between the center and the outskirts. Details overwhelm us less when we picnic at the river park. We always face the river, backs turned to the withered plants, keeping them out of sight and mind—Current's hypnotic. Shallow water keeps flowing over, under, around, and through diminished trashwood still trapped on the riverbed. Pigeons fly overhead. Sleek carbon canoes cruise by, paddlers in synch, their silence only interrupted by an occasional "hut" to switch paddles to opposite sides. We are alone.

The Director still believes EggRoom miracles combat cynicism, promote teamwork, and build trust in the American Dream. His attention to detail always distracts me. That's alright. I guess I have nothing to gain, searching for ideas too vague to define or too apparent to describe.

Mia's stopped doing shadow art but still wiggles her toes, now and then. Recently, a famous daytime TV celebrity appeared on a morning talk show, live at the Academy's dining commons. She was almost middle-aged, quite cute in business casual, red heels, black slacks, burgundy blouse, colors of the American Dream. If she has a suit, it looks like she could be a director. Her eyes sparkle, enough to help forget she delivers more sound bites than in-depth wisdom. But I open my mind when she claims that moving her toes keeps her from crying whenever she gives a eulogy, a unique talent that supplements her income. Next time I get a chance, I'll have to try this to see if wiggling my toes redirects my mind when it races.

The Director thinks that just a little more effort will make me a positive thinker. I'm not so sure. Maybe he wants me to accept Academy life as is. He directs me to visit the EggRoom once more. As usual, it's no fun wearing electrodes and staring into the cathedral cubby. A golf tee balances an egg basket filled with pigeon eggs, a visual that's more exciting than a single egg on a tee, countless eggs on a conveyor, or a tee on a tree. With nothing better going on, I focus and pretend to relax. I feel a dull ache. My eyes blur. Keeping my shoes on, I wiggle my toes, as best as I can.

An amplified voice whispers, "One egg is real."

The golf tee leans back and forth, side to side, rotates, and wobbles slowly as if a gyroscope, its weak spin preventing a fall. As far as I can tell, the unreal eggs look like the real one hidden among them. The basket spins on its tilted axis, with just enough momentum to maintain equilibrium. The amplified voice whispers, "This is it."

The basket tips beyond its point of balance, falling to the floor. Eggs bounce, roll, and scatter. A wooden clatter drowns the sound of a lone egg's shatter, sending traces of egg yolk outward, center to outskirts. My toes stop moving.

A voice out of nowhere, "Don't talk. Say you're sorry." Silence doesn't work; apologizing won't either; I squirm. How do I say sorry without speaking? From the cathedral cubby's base, a digital flatscreen emerges. The last word from LaserFunk that goes beyond trueness and falseness: TRUTH HURTS.

89

Late for an early mandatory meeting at the Academy, we park in the visitors' lot. Forbidden convenience makes our walk more tolerable. For the first time in months, Mia brought Penguin Four along as if today could be more than just another day. But how would she know I wonder. The odds are no better than fifty-fifty that the day could go either way.

Standing at a portable podium, the Director's wearing a Cutting Edge Capsule hat and a WaterWorks Water shirt. His smile somehow makes him look clueless. Morphing from director to opportunitator to dog-and-pony show ringmaster, he raises his voice and stretches his words. "Are we ready?" His sense of drama is too weak for Hollywood, too dramatic for Bollywood, he pauses and waits too long. His yell overloads the microphone and sound system, creating an almost endless echo, "The Emporium of Encapsulation."

A remote-controlled curtain opens, revealing an almost dark, prehistoric sea of carbon capsules. Suspended in fog, they resemble dinosaur eggs defying the laws of gravity. A fog machine shoots an operatic silver mist upward, capturing the overhead light of a stage or movie set. Mia's expression is more pensive than usual, she looks like a ghost-faced goddess sensing the beginning of the end. On her shoulders, Penguin Four remains passive, unimpressed with the prospect of flying through the Academy haze, in another crisis mistaken for an opportunity.

The Director's voice continues in loud echoes. "Population forecasts have driven us to real estate diversification. This new project is subsidized by the same taxpayers who will fill these state-of-the-art capsules that combine apartment comfort and efficiency."

Twice the size of our capsules, they're suspended by a thicker chain, links welded to allow passionate lovemaking without the usual squeaks or rattles that might inspire a fear of falling. Foggers stop simultaneously. Academy clouds lift, revealing theft-proof stairways anchored in concrete, and luxury capsules suspended at high ceiling altitudes. We check out an economy unit, a carbon-fiber module with Plexiglass windows projecting fluorescent red from within. A transparent cabinet reveals Score energy bars stacked neatly, a black refrigerated tank storing Sustaine, its digital display reading full. Refillable from the outside, occupants will remain undisturbed. Imagine. Working and living under the same roof, no more commuting, no more traffic jams. Imagine tenant discounts for Academy employees.

The Director speaks pompous corporate speak. "Now that the Academy partnered with the Emporium of Encapsulation, we can engage in a new age of symbiotic fair trade. Self-help fanatics who spend too much on electronic therapy can still afford capsule rent. Frugal people confined by capsules can afford LaserFunk's soothing relief from cabin fever."

"Scumbag," Mia mutters. "People living in capsules get addicted to the same LaserFunk that supposedly relieves cabin fever. It's a self-devouring snake, commercialized." Mia must be referring to that mythical reptile that curls so it can keep eating its tail, regenerating forever.

"I have to confess," the Director says. "My Adirondack vacation plans were fictitious, a pretense to protect the Academy. Thanks to Mia's sense of style. Thanks go out to Sid Sidney for providing expertise on layout."

If there's a joke, it must be on me. Pleasant, somewhat nervous laughter mixes with light applause. There's not enough sound to fill the vacuum of silence, not enough to replace the emptiness of the Emporium.

There's more. The Director announces the discovery of a giant aquifer located directly beneath us. He commends Jonson for founding WaterWorks Water and says plans to acquire the business will leverage the value of the aquifer. No mention of the promo paper planes. It's hard to know if anyone wants that part of the action. Jonson will probably make more money, owning less than one percent of WaterWorks than he did with the whole thing. Of course, he'll have to quit working at the Academy to avoid a conflict of interest.

There goes Jonson's job again. Are there any conflicts for the Director? Will LaserFunk refer clients to live in the new capsules? Will the Emporium refer residents to LaserFunk? At least the Director won't be heading for upstate New York to destroy the Adirondacks.

Looking out at his captive audience, the Director waves his Cutting Edge Capsule hat. "No matter how often corporate changes, change is a good thing. Teamwork is a good thing. Go, Team!"

I clap and yell, "Right on," an old counterculture expression that only works as sarcasm these days. The Director ignores me. Maybe he's too excited to notice.

90

Jonson's living quarters make it impossible to hitchhike. He departs incognito, wearing his black suit, mad hatter hat, and goggles. He drives off, towing his miniature house with his new wheels, an old faded Chevy blazer. He has two carbon capsules strapped to the roof's peak like scrap missiles, dead-ended ten feet from the ground, incapable of even a doomed takeoff.

"I didn't realize how bad things were, Mia. Academy sold us out completely and screwed Jonson. Proof certain, LaserFunk can't solve every problem. Scientists need to discover ways to treat victims of excess logic, victims of overdeveloped forebrains."

"Please! Even if there's a medication that might help, don't start a shopping list of pharmaceuticals to mix in the reservoir."

All said and done, ACE4's promise led people to spend more than usual on birth control, and more money on WaterWorks Water. With all the publicity for and against reproduction, more babies were born. What if we try to control logic and end up generating more? Is LaserFunk's timing random when it suggests, PATIENCE IS A VIRTUE?

I still wonder. Which came first, the pigeon or egg? Did unusual circumstances at the Institute and Academy inspire this account that's true but admittedly offbeat? Or does my idiosyncratic outlook describe life as it is in the hallowed halls of commerce? Great questions inspire science projects for kids.

The Emporium of Encapsulation is another story, of course.

There's less sunlight now. Some scientists think the sun's burning out. Some say we're looking at smog. Since I don't always keep up with the news, I'm not sure. I know this: Penguin Four rarely uses the jump rope; it takes the sun much longer to recharge its batteries.

There's some hope that crime might make it back to the streets where it belongs. A local civic group plans to run a camp for some of the kids who overpopulate the planet. They've already applied for grants to build Camp Firewood in a yet-to-be-announced, national forest. A dual-purpose facility, parents will see the camp's sign and stop to drop their kids off for summer camp. Tourists will see the same sign and stop to buy firewood. Either way, the name "Camp Firewood" creates warm, nighttime visions of children sitting around campfires, singing pre-electric folk songs. Since they need to sell all the firewood they can, they toast marshmallows on stoves that burn clean, hydro-fracked gas. almost too good to be true.

Things get even better. During the day, campers will gather firewood, stack it neatly, and sell small bundles to tourists. It's all win-win. Instead of adventure, kids learn the value of doing something useful. Some might grow up to become camp rangers. A very few of the more fortunate could become directors of forest management. Tourists do their part, taking small bundles of the seasoned wood home, gathering around winter fireplaces or summer fire pits, to relive primitive times, and tell quaint stories about juvenile wood gatherers. Mia wonders if such an idyllic life will make it hard for kids to grow up to accept life bankrupted by the Academy. She's probably right. How can they adjust? Another diagnostic riff for LaserFunk: camp skills help a helpless camper get an awkward foot in the Academy's door.

Helpless campers already, the homeless girl and kitten, Toasty, now full-grown, couldn't get a foot in The Emporium door when she tried. Mia and I pooled resources and bought another capsule. The girl doesn't say much. She and her kitten earn a few dollars panhandling by day. She prefers the open space beneath her new capsule for sleeping. The cat never bothers the pigeons and seems to appreciate its new litter box.

Mia insisted she couldn't force Penguin Four and Fifteen-Forty-One to live at the Emporium, its roomy capsules too

Institutionalized to be pigeon-friendly. She built a giant, ring-shaped capsule condo within our condo. The pigeons can fly indoors without having to turn around. A bridge over the circular pigeon dwelling provides access to Mysterious Traveler. Mia says the ring-shaped space provides a more condo-friendly place for the pigeons.

Whenever Fifteen-Forty-One flies outdoors, Penguin Four handles separation stoically. Except for a new neck twitch, he's healthy and physically fit. Thanks to the circular design, he recently did a three-minute solo flight, without stopping to rest.

It's Saturday night. We're lying in our capsule, basking under the florescence, holding each other, looking out through Plexiglass at Mia's room-scaped condo. We're looking upward toward the cathedral-shaped cubby that exudes its usual civilized innocence, its spotlight warming and illuminating an egg, abandoned by Fifteen-Forty-One. The pigeon egg's a simple vision, a silent mantra on a golf tee. A hidden microphone has been amplifying the egg's beautiful sound of silence, up until now. A new, almost inaudible noise from the egg comes through our headsets, so slight we're not sure if we hear it. Maybe it stops to listen to its hush. The noise starts again as if someone's tapping the egg gently with a ballpoint pen. "Are we making up the sound to fill the emptiness that surrounds us," I whisper.

With each tap, a slight imperfection in the eggshell pushes outward slightly. I get bored and stop watching. A speck breaks away. Mia spots a tiny chip falling to the cathedral cubby's floor. Rhythmic tapping quickens as if a baby pigeon's trying to text on a smartphone as if the air flowing into the egg gives a baby beak more energy. You might think all the pecking might give the pigeon chick a headache. Then again, maybe it's turned on by the movement's feel-good cocktail of endorphins mixed with adrenaline. Beak, eyes, matted fuzz, its body breaks through and tumbles out. It summersaults, and lands upright, on its feet, legs collapsed as if unprepared for the fall. The pigeon chick looks lost, bewildered, unimpressed by life's endless possibilities. Mia squeezes my hand.

Little does the baby pigeon know. Some college presidents

confer academic degrees, wholesale on masses of graduates. In turn, grads release pigeons hidden under their gowns, to celebrate the idea that knowledge gives us wings. Like mysterious travelers, pigeons fly upward in a confused spiral, regroup, and fly toward the Adirondacks as if seeking asylum from places like the Academy and The Emporium. Adirondack birdseed is organic. Water's slightly acidic but otherwise pure.

Penguin Four and Fifteen-Forty-One keep snacking on their usual organic black oil sunflower seed, taking precious time out to look upward toward the bewildered hatchling, standing in the cubicle, reflecting on its own shadow, taking time out to look down on its parents. No way an immaculate conception, it must have been a miraculous incubation under the spotlight's warmth. If pigeons can fly to the Adirondacks, a pigeon chick can hatch in a condo, what are the limits? Mia and I raise our drink tubes for a WaterWorks Water toast. We each offer our tube to the other. We embrace, forgetting the limited capacity of chains suspending us. No need for Mia's fertility clock anymore, I promise that I'll find a world pigeon counter app. The two tablets harmonize, blipping the hope and doom of humans and pigeons.

ACKNOWLEDGMENTS

My thanks to Lauren Foss Goodman for her critique of an early draft that energized me to keep going. Also, to Steve Kash for his line-by-line comments and encouragement on a later draft. And thanks to Kim Davis and the Madville Publishing crew.

ABOUT THE AUTHOR

Steve Putnam is living the dream: farm kid, Navy E3, small-town GM mechanic, framing carpenter, and an onsite printer tech at a large corporate account. When the printers were all working, he hid out in a chain link cage, his basement shop, and wrote the first draft of *Academy of Reality*. No one at Corporate knew they were funding a novel about the strange ways of big business. For outstanding customer service, Putnam won "Tech of the Year" and a trip to Arizona. (As a novel-in-progress, a version of this novel was shortlisted in the Pirate's Alley Faulkner Society Competition in New Orleans.)

Milton Keynes UK
Ingram Content Group UK Ltd.
UKHW042337081024
449373UK00009B/108